END GAME

THE DAWSON FAMILY SERIES BOOK TWO

EMILY GOODWIN

To my husband. Thanks for bringing me wine and letting me sleep in when I'm on a deadline. I love you.

COPYRIGHT

End Game
A Dawson Family Novel
BOOK TWO

Copyright 2018
Emily Goodwin
Editing by Ellie, Love N Books
Editing by Lindsay, Contagious Edits
Cover Photography by By Braayden Photography
Models: Jade and Jordan Fisher

This is a work of fiction. Names, characters, businesses,

EXTRAS

Newsletter

Reader Group

Playlist

1

QUINN

I don't know what hurts worse: my wrist or my stomach. The pain there is more concerning, and my wrist could be broken in two and my mind would still be on my baby. I know it takes a lot to hurt a baby this early in the pregnancy, but that doesn't stop me from worrying. I flatten my hand over my stomach, looking at the spot where the guy was just standing. I'm shocked, scared, and unable to figure out why he looked so familiar.

Sam takes off after the guy, and I stand there, rooted to the spot for a moment before I shake myself and get my phone from the floor. The screen has blacked out, and I hold it up, unlocking it with facial recognition, and call 911.

"911. What is the location of your emergency?" the dispatcher asks.

"I, uh, I don't know," I breathe, heart still racing. Am I imagining it, or is the pain in my stomach turning into dull cramps? "I'm at my boyfriend's house," I rush out, realizing that's not helping my case. "And I don't know his address. I'm visiting from out of town. Sorry."

"It's all right, we can attempt to track your location. What is your emergency?"

"Some guy was pounding on the door and then burst in," I say and pull the phone away from my ear, putting it on speaker, and go to Maps so I can see where I am. "He hit me with the door and I think he's on drugs."

"Is he there with you now?"

"No. He left." I drop a pin at my location and give the dispatcher the address.

"Keep your door locked. An officer is on his way."

"Thank you."

I hang up, still shaken, and completely ignore the dispatcher's advice. Sam is out there, and I need to make sure he's okay. Almost tripping over the entry rug again, I step over it and into the hall. Sam rounds the corner, jogging back toward me. He's not black and blue or bleeding at least.

"Fucker ran out into the street. I lost him."

Nodding, I step back inside and lock the door as soon as Sam is inside. "I called the cops. Someone will be here soon."

"Good. Are you okay?" He plows a hand through his blonde hair.

I bring my hands to my stomach and look down. Getting hit with the knob hurt, and the base of the door also whacked my feet. I just didn't realize it until now when I see a broken and bleeding toenail. My left wrist aches something terrible, and it's a little hard to move.

"I'm not sure."

"How far along are you?"

"Eight weeks."

Sam lets out a sigh of relief. "Your uterus is still low in your pelvis. You should be okay. But your wrist..." He gently takes my arm and I wince. "It's starting to swell."

"It hurts. I have carpal tunnel in that one."

"It wouldn't make it suddenly swell like this. Can you move your fingers?"

I carefully bend all five fingers in toward my palm.

"What about move your wrist?"

"Oww," I say when I try to bend my wrist up.

"It's either a sprain of a fracture."

"Great," I mumble.

"Sit and try to relax. I'll get you ice."

Moving to the couch, I bring my right hand to the spot where the doorknob hit. It's right below my belly button, and even though I know the baby is nestled deep inside my uterus, it's hard to imagine it not being right there, feeling the shock wave of getting hit so hard I fell over.

"Are you okay in there?" I whisper, tears filling my eyes. This baby wasn't planned. Archer and I weren't even dating at the time of conception. Knowing I'm having a baby has turned my life upside down. But *not* having this baby would catapult my life into darkness.

Sam comes back into the living room carrying an ice pack.

"Archer got called in for surgery," I say as he sits on the couch next to me.

"I know. He called on his way to make sure I'd look out for you. I'm doing a bang-up job."

"It's not your fault. Do you have any idea who that was?"

"Not at all." Sam puts pillows under my arm, elevating my wrist and then carefully arranging the ice pack. "If the swelling gets worse, you should go in for an X-ray. Sometimes scaphoid fractures can be confused for sprains."

My right hand is still on my stomach. "I can't get an X-ray."

"You'll be well protected, and it's just your wrist. Not your abdomen."

I'm still being exposed to unnecessary radiation, which makes me feel guilty even though I didn't do anything wrong. I fell. More than just fell, actually. I got knocked over.

"The guy knew Archer."

"Maybe he was an old patient or something?" Sam gets up and goes to the window, looking down at the street that runs along the building.

"Are there cameras on the traffic lights?" I ask, moving the ice pack a bit. It's getting cold already.

"I'm not sure."

"If there are, I can hack in and see if I can find anything."

Sam turns, eyebrow raised. "Hack in? You can do that?"

"I *can*. But I won't." I sigh. "I just need something to do to calm my nerves."

"And hacking into the city's traffic cams will calm your nerves?"

"Most definitely," I say and then laugh. Sam laughs too, shaking his head. "Archer said you are good with computers."

"It's my thing."

Sam goes to the door and looks through the peephole before moving back to the couch. "Have you really hacked into things?"

"Nothing that could get me arrested. Well, I did once, but I was helping the police catch a guy who'd racked up thousands on stolen credit cards. My brother is a cop in a small town," I explain. "Their tech department isn't the best."

"That's pretty damn cool." He turns away from the door and comes back to the couch. He's on edge, and not being able to catch and beat up this Bobby guy is bothering him.

"Should I try calling Archer?"

Sam checks the time. "He's still in the OR. I'll call the hospital and have him notified as soon as he's out."

"Thanks, Sam."

A minute later, the cops arrive, and we give our statements. As much as I try to root for the law, the two officers who showed up don't seem too concerned. They don't seem to really care at all, actually. The guy just opened the door hard. He didn't break and enter. He didn't actually touch me. They say they'll keep an eye out, and leave.

Locking the door after them, I debate on calling Weston and asking for advice on the subject. The guy creeped me out because of the way he looked at me, and the way he saw me in this shirt and knew it had something to do with Archer. I guess that's not technically illegal, but I still feel like something more should be done.

Walking back to the couch, I bend over to pick my phone up from the coffee table. A sharp, stabbing pain hits me right in the stomach, and I freeze, waiting for it to go away.

But it doesn't, and the sharp pain turns into a deep cramp.

"**Y**ou're needed in the ER."

I give the medical assistant a quizzical look. "The ER? Are you sure?"

She's sitting behind a desk in the PACU and just got off the phone. Her eyes dart to it and she nods. "That's what they said. I asked twice since it's not your area, but you're being requested by Dr. Harris."

Sam is in the ER asking for me? He's off today and he's never in the emergency room. Why would he—oh shit.

Quinn.

My phone battery was low, so I plugged it in and left it with my clothes when I changed into surgical scrubs. I rush through the recovery area to get it and see I have missed texts from both Quinn and Sam. The most recent one is from Sam, and I have to read it twice because my brain refuses to believe what I'm seeing.

Someone tried to break in and Quinn got hurt. We're at the ER. I'll have you paged.

I scroll up, reading as I run down the hall, stopping only to get into an elevator. None of his other texts give me information, and neither do Quinn's. I get into the elevator and call Quinn, but I don't have service in here.

My heart starts to race. Sweat breaks out along my back. Someone tried to break in? Quinn must have been fucking terrified. I curl my fingers into a fist, rage surging through me. Quinn got hurt. Bad enough to come to the ER. If anything happened to the baby...nope. I can't think like that.

The baby is fine. Quinn is fine.

They have to be.

They're my life. My *family.* I knew I wanted the baby from the moment I saw those bold, black words on the pregnancy test, but the thought of having it taken away from me makes my heart ache, making me realize just how bad I want this. The timing might be all wrong, and we might be doing things a bit out of order, but I'm ready.

I want Quinn to have my baby and for us to be together, living happily ever after for the rest of our lives. I want to marry her when the time is right and add another baby or two, hell, maybe even three, to our family. We'll be loud and crazy, and things will be hectic and chaotic, but it'll be perfect.

The elevator stops one floor down and an elderly couple takes their sweet ass time getting in with their walkers. I do my best not to glower at them and repeatedly push the button taking me to the main floor.

My heart beats faster with each passing second. Sometimes you don't realize how much something means to you until it's taken away. Nothing's been taken—not really— but the thoughts of *what if* are bad enough.

I move to the front of the elevator and ask what floor the old folks are going to. Thankfully, it's the same one, and we start the descent down. It only takes thirty seconds, but it feels like an eternity. I run down the hall, and when people see doctors running, they usually get out of the way, assuming I'm responding to an emergency.

I push through the swinging ER doors and look around for a nurse or attendant to tell me which room Quinn is in. They'll be able to tell me faster than I could look it up myself. Then I see Sam standing near the nurses' station, talking with a pretty redhead. He doesn't look overly concerned, which has to be a good sign.

"Where's Quinn?" I ask as soon as he sees me. "Is she okay?"

"She's fine, I'll take you back."

"If she's fine, why is she here?"

We start walking through the hall. "I was able to get an ultrasound faster in the ER."

I stop dead in my tracks. "If she's okay, why does she need an ultrasound?"

"To give her peace of mind," he says and keeps walking.

"That's not giving me peace of mind. What happened?"

He slows when we get to the room Quinn is in and lowers his voice. "Some guy was banging on the door asking for you. Quinn unlocked it to let him in, and the guy shoved the door open. The knob got her right in the stomach, but she's so early in the pregnancy you know she's most likely fine. She's bruised and scared, so I made a call and got her in to get an ultrasound, and Dr. Taylor is coming down from delivery when she gets a moment."

"Thanks, man." I let out a breath.

"Of course. It's the least I could do. Quinn's pretty freaked out. And she hurt her wrist. It's swelling up, and I told her it might be fractured, but she refused an X-ray."

I blink, taking all that in. "Someone was asking for me?"

"Yeah. He looked fucked up on something."

My phone is still in my hand, and I look down to unlock

it. I go to my pictures only to remember I don't have a single photo of Bobby. Logging onto Facebook instead, I madly scroll through my mom's profile until I find a picture of him.

"Is that the guy?"

Sam narrows his eyes, inspecting the photo. Bobby isn't tweaked out in it, and the filter my mom used makes him look almost healthy.

"Yeah. Why do you—oh fuck. Is that your brother?"

"It is." I bring my hand to the back of my neck. Bobby was at the apartment. Looking for me. I haven't even seen him in years, and I didn't know he had my address. "Why the fuck is he—it doesn't matter. She's in here?"

Sam nods and I go in without knocking or seeing if another physician is in there. I need to get to Quinn. As soon as her eyes meet mine, I know she needs me too.

"Archer." She pushes up off the bed, reaching for me. She's wearing pajama shorts and my Duke University shirt. Her hair is messy, and her eyes are watery.

"I'm so sorry, babe." I sit on the bed next to her and take her in my arms. She's shaking.

"The nurse was just in here," she squeaks out, voice tightening. "She tried to find the heartbeat with a doppler and couldn't. I wasn't really worried before. Sam thought it'd be reassuring to come in and see that everything is okay. But now I'm freaking out more."

Her words send a jolt of panic through me. All I hear is there was no heartbeat, and I have to force myself to think about things objectively in order to remember dopplers don't always pick up heartbeats this early.

"That doesn't mean something happened to the baby."

"But what if it did?"

"This early on, the baby is well protected in the womb. It takes a lot of force to cause damage." Keeping my cool and not getting overwhelmed with emotions is part of what makes me a good surgeon. I feel for every one of my patients, I really do. But I don't let it get in the way of taking the best possible care of them. I have to do the same for Quinn.

She nods and lays back. Goosebumps break out over her flesh, and I get up, going to the cabinet above the sink, and pulling out a white sheet. Shaking it out, I drape it over Quinn and sit back down next to her, squeezing in as much as I can on the small hospital bed.

"Sam said you hurt your wrist."

She winces as she lifts it up. The swelling isn't as bad as I anticipated, but she's obviously hurt.

"It twisted when I fell."

I close my eyes, gently taking her wrist in my hand, and feel a seething hatred for Bobby rise from deep inside of me. Over the years, there have been many times I've wanted to beat the shit out of him. I've held back for various reasons: not wanting to upset my mother, risk getting charged with assault, or damage my hands when I need them for surgery.

But now I don't care. The next time I see him, I'm hitting him as hard as I fucking can.

"Do you think it's broken?" she asks. "I really don't want to do an X-ray. The baby is so little and developing major organs right now."

I carefully examine her wrist, hating seeing her in pain. "No. I think it's sprained."

"Thank God. Wait. Sprains take longer to heal, right?"

"Unfortunately, that's the case many times. And you're more likely to have issues with it later on."

"Great," she mumbles. "I already have wrist pain." Her eyes fall shut and her jaw tenses. I move a pillow under her arm, propping up her injured wrist. She rests her other hand on her stomach and lets out a deep sigh.

When she opens her eyes, she reaches over and takes my hand.

"It's going to be okay, isn't it?" she asks, tears filling her green eyes again.

The words die in my throat, but I force a smile and squeeze her hand. As a doctor, I never promise false hope, never give an overly optimistic answer when I don't know what the fate will be. But for Quinn, I know I have to lie.

"Yes."

"Thanks, Arch." She squeezes my hand back. "Did they pull you out of surgery?"

"No. I just haven't changed yet." I smile and playfully nudge her, hoping to make her laugh. "Why, are you getting turned on from my 'doctor clothes' as you call them?"

She doesn't laugh, but her lips do curve up into a smile. "A little. You can play doctor for me tonight."

"I don't have to play, baby." I lean down, putting my lips to hers. Just then, the curtain is pulled back. Thinking it's Sam, I don't move away from Quinn just yet.

"Ms. Dawson?" the nurse says, clearing her throat. I move back and see Elena, the nurse I hooked up with a few times, standing at the foot of the bed. Her eyes widen when she sees me. We ended things on good terms, or at least I thought so. Our relationship was never serious, and we were both clear about keeping things casual from the start.

"Dr. Jones," she stammers, eyes flitting from me to Quinn.

"He's the father," Quinn says quickly as if she's afraid I'll get in trouble for canoodling a patient or something.

Elena smiles. "I assumed so. Congratulations, Dr. Jones. I didn't know you were having a baby."

"Thank you," I say and put my hand over Quinn's belly. Quinn tenses and I know exactly what's she's thinking: congrats might *not* be in order if things...nope. I'm not letting myself finish that thought.

"Do you want him to come with you for the ultrasound?" Elena asks.

"Yes," Quinn says right away and gets up. Holding her left wrist against her body, we follow Elena into another room, and the ultrasound tech is already waiting for us. Quinn gets onto the bed, folds the waist of her shorts down, and raises her shirt a bit, exposing her belly. She has some bruising under her belly button, and I swear to God I'm going to kill Bobby.

"I bruise easily," Quinn tells me when she sees the concern on my face. "I always have."

I can only nod, too upset to open my mouth. Taking Quinn's hand, I move aside, anxiously looking at the screen next to Quinn. Unlike the OB's office, this room isn't set up with a big TV for us to look at. This is the ER, and ultrasounds done in here have an entirely different story most of the time.

The tech goes over Quinn's information with her and then dims the lights. "How far along are you?" she asks and puts the jelly on Quinn's stomach.

"Eight weeks." Quinn's hand shakes. I grip it tighter. Using my free hand, I smooth her hair back, not taking my eyes off the screen.

"And you were hit in the stomach?"

"Yes. By a doorknob."

"Are you having any pain?"

"I felt some really sharp shooting pains and then felt crampy. It went away though."

I didn't know Quinn was feeling any pain at all. Getting

hit in the stomach in the first trimester isn't usually a cause for concern...unless it's followed by pain or bleeding.

A few seconds tick by and black and white shapes come in and out of focus. And then I see it, a second before the tech stops moving the transducer around. The outline of what looks like a tiny gummy bear, with a fast-beating heart.

"Baby looks good and has a strong heartbeat," the tech says, and turns her screen so we can see better. She points to each little body part and lets us watch that beautiful tiny heart beating for another few seconds. Then she turns the sound on, and Quinn finally relaxes.

The tech prints out some pictures and gives Quinn paper towels to wipe the jelly from her skin. She leaves, saying the doctor will be in shortly. Annoyed no one has done anything for Quinn's injured wrist yet, I leave for a few moments and come back with supplies to ice and splint it.

"I never realized how handy it'd be to date a doctor," she says with a small smile as I finish wrapping her wrist. I sit in the bed with her, wrapping my arms around her slender waist.

"The guy who tried to break in," I start, working hard to keep my voice steady. Quinn turns to me, eyes meeting mine. And then Dr. Taylor knocks on the door, coming in a second later. She goes over the ultrasound—everything is normal.

"Are you still feeling pain?" she asks Quinn, looking at her chart on the computer screen.

"Not right now. I felt it most when I was moving."

"Did it feel like period cramps?"

Quinn shakes her head. "Not at first. It was more sharp, like something was being pulled. Then it cramped and went away after a minute. I felt it again when I was getting in the car to come here."

"Are you bleeding or spotting?"

"No."

"The first trimester is full of aches, pains, and cramps. Everything looks good, so I feel confident saying those cramps are normal and you're currently just more aware of them. And the sharp, pulling pain sounds like round ligament pain to me."

"Isn't it early for that?" I interject.

"Textbook-wise, yes," she tells me. "But I've had enough patients experience it I know some unlucky women start feeling the aches and pains from the start." She looks back at Quinn's chart. "Do you normally have high blood pressure?"

I almost get up to peer over Dr. Taylor's shoulder. Quinn doesn't have high blood pressure. If anything, she's on the low side, and I should—I need to stop. I'm not here as Quinn's doctor, but as her boyfriend and the father of her child.

"No," Quinn answers. "I think it's from the stress."

"Me too," Dr. Taylor says and turns to the computer, putting in an order. "I'm going to get you a dose of Benadryl." She flicks her eyes to me. "Sounds weird, I know, but I've been giving this to my pregnant patients for years. It'll lower your blood pressure and will help you sleep when you get home. Rest will help you feel better. Being stressed and tense will make you all the more aware of those aches and pains."

"Thanks," Quinn says with a nod and finally relaxes a bit.

"Take it easy, and follow up with your regular OB at home. And congratulations, both of you."

"Thank you," I say, getting up to shake her hand. Elena comes in right after Dr. Taylor leaves, with water and medication in hand.

"Are you sure this is okay for our baby?" Quinn asks me quietly before she pops the pill in her mouth.

"Yes," I assure her and she takes the Benadryl.

"This makes me loopy," she says after taking a drink of water.

"I remember," I say with a chuckle. "I think you were like sixteen or seventeen when you got poison oak all over your arms. Your mom gave you Benadryl and it was like you were drunk. Dean and I might have used you for our entertainment, and for that, I'm sorry."

"Oh my God! I almost forgot about that." Quinn shakes her head, laughing. "It was terrible. My goat got out hours before I had to load him up to take to the county fair. He was a muddy mess and I was covered in a rash."

Elena looks away from the computer for a second, eyeing us both. "Sounds like you two have known each other a long time?"

She's a good nurse and a decent human being. She's not going to say anything or cause a scene, but I can sense the jealousy. Quinn turns her head to me, eyes sparkling. It makes my heart speed up.

"I've known Archer since I was fourteen," she says. "He was my brother's college roommate."

"Aww, that's so sweet," Elena says with a fake smile. "Okay...you're almost ready for discharge. You can return back to normal activities. If you experience any more abnormal pain or bleeding, come back to the ER."

"Thank you." Quinn lets out a sigh of relief, and when Elena leaves to grab the discharge papers for Quinn to sign, I turn to her.

"I need to tell you something," I rush out.

"What is it?"

"I went out with that nurse a few times."

"Oh. I thought she looked a little too surprised to find out you're having a baby."

"You're not upset?"

"Why would I be? I've dated other people too, Archer. And you met Jacob already, who's my ex."

"Right. She wasn't really my girlfriend, just—"

"Spare me the details." She takes my hand. "You're mine now, Archer Jones."

I smile. She has no idea that I've always been hers.

"So now that I know the baby is okay, I can say how much my wrist fucking hurts." She holds up her arm, wincing. "Are you sure it's not broken? It feels broken."

"You should have said something."

She makes a face. "I didn't want the attention to be taken away from the baby, in case...in case." Tears fill her eyes and her bottom lip quivers. "I don't know why I'm crying," she says, trying hard to stop the tears from falling. "Everything is okay."

I pull her into my arms. "It was a lot to take in. It's overwhelming."

"Oh my God. Work. How am I going to be able to work? I can hardly move my arm." And then she bursts into tears, and I don't think it's possible to feel any more hatred for my brother than I do right now. "I'm sorry I'm crying," she sobs. "I don't usually cry. It's just...it's just the hormones."

"Babe, it's okay." I cradle her against me, being careful not to hurt her wrist. I don't think it's broken. She can move it along with all her fingers and the swelling is minimal.

"I can order you an X-ray still," I tell her.

"No," Quinn mumbles. "I don't want to expose the baby to anything like that. If it gets worse, I'll let you know."

I brush her hair back and kiss her forehead. "You're going to be a good mom."

Quinn's bottom lip quivers and more tears pool in her eyes. Elena comes back in, looking alarmed.

"Are you all right?" she asks.

"Yeah," Quinn sniffles. "Everything caught up to me and I was so scared." She takes my hand and brings it to her stomach. "I really thought we might lose the baby."

"He's safe in there," I assure Quinn.

"*She's* safe in there, you mean," she says with a smile. "I agree with my mom on this one. It's a girl."

———

QUINN LOOKS AT THE ULTRASOUND PICTURES, EYES GLOSSING over. We're headed home, and I steal a glance away from the road to see her beautiful face. Her eyes are brimming with tears.

"What's wrong, babe?" I put my hand on her thigh.

"Nothing." Tears roll down her cheeks.

"Why are you crying?"

"I was thinking about bald eagles."

"Bald eagles?" I raise an eyebrow. "Bald eagles make you cry?"

"They used to be endangered. But they're not anymore. They're so majestic and beautiful and I'm just so happy they're not endangered anymore."

I don't mean to laugh, but dammit, she's so fucking adorable. "Remember how you said it wasn't fair that I didn't get to experience drunk-Quinn?"

"Yeah."

"I am now." I wink and squeeze her thigh.

She sniffles and laughs, wiping her eyes. "Yeah. I guess so." Her eyes squeeze shut, and more tears stream out.

"Stop thinking about eagles, babe," I try to say seriously but end up laughing. Quinn laughs too, shaking her head. She inhales and looks back down at the ultrasound. She mumbles something about taking a picture of the baby to send to her mom and fumbles with her purse until she finds her cell.

When we get back to my apartment, I get out and immediately lock the doors to the Jeep and look around for my pathetic excuse for a brother. Not seeing him, I unlock the door and help Quinn out.

"You were supposed to leave tonight," I remind her when we get through the door. Sam's already here, and I lock the deadbolt behind us.

"I'll stay tonight," she mumbles, eyelids heavy.

"Do you need to call about your flight?"

"No. I never scheduled a return flight. I was going to today. The driver...no, the flyer...the...the..."

"Pilot."

"Yeah. That guy. He was going to pick me up whenever I was ready." She scrunches up her nose. "I sound like a rich asshole, don't I?"

"You're basically Bruce Wayne when he's trying to convince the world he's still a billionaire playboy and not a superhero."

"Damn," she says, not missing a beat. "Hopefully I'm giving more of a Christian Bale performance over Ben Affleck."

"It's Oscar-worthy." I hook my arm around her, seeing the dark circles under her eyes. After all she's been through today, I know she's exhausted. We get settled into bed, and I pull the blankets up around her shoulders. Resting her head on my chest, I run my fingers through her hair.

The words I've been wanting to say bubble up inside me but are quickly squashed down by the memories of my brother. I'll have to face him eventually, and worse, I'll have to explain everything to Quinn. I look down at her beautiful face, eyes closed but still a bit swollen from crying. There is no one else for me but her, and I'll do whatever it takes to make things right.

I pull the blankets up over Quinn's shoulders, tucking her back in after I get out of bed. She fell asleep quickly, thanks to the Benadryl, and right now she looks peaceful and relaxed. I stand there for a moment looking down at her and feeling so much.

I'm in love with her. Head over heels, crazy, stupid love with her. My heart is so full, more so than I ever thought possible. And it's weird because while I'm standing here feeling all this love for Quinn, a deep-rooted hatred for my brother grows stronger and stronger.

Bending over, I give Quinn a kiss, and turn to leave, silently shutting the door behind me. Grabbing the leftovers from lunch, I go into the living room and sit on the couch.

"Everything good?" Sam asks, turning away from the TV.

"Yeah. She's sleeping."

Sam nods, looks back at the TV for half a second, and then at me again. "Your fucking brother?"

"I know. I haven't seen the asshole in years."

"What do you think he wanted?"

"I have no fucking clue. He seemed on something?"

"Isn't he always?" Sam replies. "And yeah. Bloodshot eyes, pale, and angry. Not that it makes it any better, but I don't think he meant to hurt Quinn."

"It doesn't matter. He did hurt her." I set down my fork and pinch the bridge of my nose, appetite pretty much gone.

"Did Quinn know about him?"

"I'm not sure, actually." And I'm really not. I avoided Quinn most of the time when I was at the Dawson's house. I couldn't get over my attraction to her, and being around her made it worse. We hardly ever talked, but I'm assuming some sort of explanation was given to her about why I hung around so many times.

Dean knows everything, and his parents do too. We've talked about it in length, and my own parents have thanked Mr. and Mrs. Dawson over and over for letting me stay with them during the holidays so I didn't have to spend Christmas watching my brother get his stomach pumped.

"I didn't bring it up before, but she'll find out soon enough."

"Wait, you haven't told her the guy who hit her with the door is your brother yet?"

Shaking my head, I pick up my fork again. "I started to and our conversation got interrupted. She's too loopy to talk about anything serious now." I take a few bites of my pasta and then sigh. "I need to call my parents. Have them come down here and deal with Bobby."

"Does he have a sponsor to call too?"

"Probably, but what good would that do?" I grumble. "This has been going on for fifteen fucking years. I don't know how he's not dead yet."

"I have a feeling he will be once you get a hold of him."

"I plan to beat the shit out of him, that's for sure." Anger surges through me again. More family drama is the last thing Quinn needs. Dean and Kara are still being immature over the due date being so close to their wedding as if Quinn did it on purpose to steal the spotlight.

The rest of her family is back to being supportive but still concerned how Quinn and I are going to make this work since we not only don't live together but live four hours apart. The rational part of me says I should be concerned too, but for some reason, I'm not.

We'll make things work.

I've never wanted anything more, and while I've never been one to leave shit to faith and trust it'll all work out, I just have this feeling deep in my gut that it will. I'd be surprised if I'm *not* offered the job at the hospital at Eastwood. It's still a few hours from Chicago, but it's closer than I am now.

Forcing myself to finish my food, I get up, put my dishes away, and pull out my phone, needing to call my mom. Sam says he's going to take a shower since he hasn't yet after the gym, which is true, but I know he's giving me space. He might come off as full of himself at times, but he's a good friend.

Mom answers after one ring. She must be sitting around waiting for the phone to ring with news about Bobby. I doubt she's slept much if at all. Doesn't he care what he's done to our family? What he puts our mother through?

"Hey, Archie," she says and just from those two words I can tell she's tired. "How are you?"

"Bobby was here," I say, cutting to the chase. "A few hours ago."

"What? Here? The hospital?" she stammers.

"He came by my apartment. I wasn't home. Sam was, and my girlfriend was here. Bobby—"

"You have a girlfriend?"

"Yeah, Mom, I do." *And she's pregnant.* "I was hoping we all could get together soon, actually."

"It must be serious!" Mom exclaims. "Tell me all about her!" She's taking the conversation in the opposite direction of where it needs to go, but I know she needs a bit of good news and some cheering up.

"You already know her," I start, a smile growing on my face just by thinking of Quinn.

"I do?"

"Yeah. You've met her once or twice, and you know her family well."

"Don't make me play a guessing game, Archie! Who is she?"

"Quinn."

"Quinn?" Mom echoes.

"Quinn Dawson. Dean's sister."

Mom audibly inhales. "I always liked her. Isn't she, um, a little young?"

"She's twenty-six."

"Oh, four years isn't bad at all. I was thinking she was much younger for some reason. Your father is three years older than me. Is Dean okay with this?"

I laugh. "Not at all." There's more to it, but I'll tell her that in person. "So about Bobby..."

"Right. Tell me what happened."

I reiterate what Quinn and Sam told me, and she has no idea if he'll try to contact me again or if he'll move on. Where to, no one knows. Bobby is unpredictable when he's using. She also has no idea why he showed up or what he wants. Making amends with those he hurt is part of recovery, but he's far from recovering. Showing up makes no sense. Nevertheless, she and my dad are making the drive down here and will arrive around midnight tonight.

After I get off the phone with my mom, I arrange a hotel for them and then go back into my room, stripping down to just my boxers, and get in bed with Quinn.

"Archer?" she mumbles, eyes fluttering open.

"I'm here, babe."

Her eyes fall shut and her lips curve into a smile. "Good."

"ARCH," QUINN WHISPERS, HAND LANDING ON MY SHOULDER. "You're having a bad dream."

I blink and sit up, confused for a brief moment. The room is pitch black, I'm hot and sweaty, and my head hurts. But Quinn is here next to me, and everything is okay.

"Archer?"

"I'm awake." I run my hands over my face and exhale, reaching for my phone to check the time. It's one-thirty in the morning. I don't remember what time I laid down, but I'm surprised I slept for so long. I don't sleep well when I'm stressed, and given everything that happened, I'm pretty fucking stressed.

Quinn makes all the difference.

"What were you dreaming about?"

"I don't remember." The details from my dream at right there at the surface, but I don't want to recall them. "I think it was about something bad happening to you and the baby."

Quinn takes my hand and puts it on her stomach and leans back against the pillows. "We're okay."

"How's your wrist?"

"It hurts but not as bad as before. Sleeping and not moving it helped."

"I'll get you Tylenol. Are you hungry? We slept through dinner."

"I am. That's actually why I woke up," she says with a laugh. "I'm starving."

I turn on the bedside lamp, blinking as my eyes adjust. "Are you craving anything?"

"I really want the pinwheels my mom makes for parties." She stretches out and gets out of bed. "But mac and cheese sounds good too."

"That I can do." I kiss her forehead and get out of bed, putting on pajama pants. Quinn uses the bathroom while I go into the kitchen, pulling out a pot and filling it with water. I flick on the burner and grab a box of macaroni and cheese from the cabinet. Quinn comes into the kitchen with a sour look on her face.

"Feeling sick?" I ask.

"Yeah. I'm debating if I should take a pill or not."

"You should," I encourage. "They're safe, babe, and you need to be able to keep food down."

"I know." She looks at the pot on the stove. "It's so weird to be hungry and nauseous at the same time."

"That would be."

"I'll take a pill." Turning away, she goes into the living room to get her purse, returning with a bottle of Zofran. Putting one under her tongue, she sits at the kitchen table and waits for me.

I add the macaroni to the water and join Quinn at the table. "Babe," I start, reaching across the table and taking her hands. "I need to talk to you about the guy who was at the door."

"Can we talk about it in the morning?" Quinn asks. "I'm

trying not to be freaked out about it. You make me feel safe, but if we talk about it, I'll get scared. The police didn't find him."

Well, shit. I don't want to put it off. Quinn needs to know about Bobby, about the fucked up uncle our child is related to. But I don't want to upset her, and I can't promise she'll be safe if Bobby comes back. He's a dumbass, the most selfish person I know, but he's not violent.

Unless he's using.

Then who the fuck knows what he's capable of.

"In the morning," I repeat. "Yeah."

"So my mom called yesterday and wants to talk about the baby shower already."

"She's so excited for this," I say with a smile.

"Oh, she's going to love it. And since she's the mom of the mom, she'll head everything up and go crazy with party planning."

"When do you have showers?"

"From what I read online, you can have it any time, really, but most people wait until the third trimester." Quinn laces her fingers through mine and leans back. The color is coming back to her cheeks from the medicine kicking in. It'd be awful to feel like you're on the verge of throwing up constantly like that. "I was wondering," she starts, flicking her eyes to mine. "Do you want to find out if it's a boy or a girl?"

"Yes. As soon as possible. The new chromosome testing they do now can determine the sex of the baby as early as ten weeks."

"Chromosome testing?"

I nod. "It's impressive, really. You only give blood, not amniotic fluid, and a slew of chromosomal defects are checked for, and they can look at the DNA and see if you're carrying a male or female."

Her lips part, but Quinn doesn't say anything. I can't tell what she's thinking, but her brows start to furrow. "Sounds expensive," she finally says.

"Some insurance companies cover it. If not, I'll gladly pay for it."

"But what if something is wrong and our baby has a defect?"

"The chances are low, but it'd give us time to prepare if something was wrong," I tell her.

"Would you still want the baby if there was something wrong with it?"

"Yes," I say without hesitation. "Honestly, Quinn, I don't think anything is wrong at all. I'm impatient and want to know what we're having."

She starts to smile and looks back at me. "I'll ask about it when I get home. It would be nice to know that early what we're having." She takes one hand from mine and moves her hair over her shoulder. "We could pick out a name."

Now I smile. It might be silly to let that have such an impact on me, but it does. Picking out names, planning the baby shower...it feels right.

Like we're a family.

4

QUINN

Sunlight streams through the living room windows, directly illuminating the front door. I'm on my way to the kitchen to find something to eat, and I stop, looking at the door. Everything that happened yesterday is fresh in my mind, including the fear. I was afraid for myself, but even more afraid for my child, and now I understand why some women refer to themselves as 'mama bears' when it comes to protecting their babies.

The rug I tripped over has been smoothed out again, and I remember it all so well. The look in the guy's eyes. The desperation and anger in his voice. The way he looked at the shirt, I was wearing and knew it belonged to Archer. I'm certain I've never seen that Bobby guy before, but he looked familiar.

Tearing my eyes away from the door, I continue to the kitchen. It's seven a.m., and after eating mac and cheese last night, Archer and I watched the final *Harry Potter* movie before falling back asleep. He's still sound asleep in bed, and I didn't want to wake him.

Trying to avoid a queasy stomach, I'm on the search for

crackers. I bend down, looking in the cluttered cabinet filled with nonperishables. The floor creaks behind me and thinking it's Archer, I spring up, box of crackers in hand.

But it's not Archer. It's Sam, and he's naked. He freezes, letting out a shriek.

"Oh my God," I exclaim and divert my eyes.

"Quinn, I...I...I thought you were still asleep," he stammers, bringing his hands down to cover his junk.

"I was hungry," I say, trying not to laugh. I fail. I bring my hand to my mouth and turn away.

"Women don't usually laugh when they see me naked, you know."

I grab a dish towel from the counter to toss to him.

"That's not big enough," he says seriously and side steps away.

"Oh, please." I roll my eyes and turn away to open the crackers.

"Quinn?" Archer calls, voice thick with sleep. He comes into the kitchen, probably making sure I'm okay after hearing Sam yell. "Dude," he says to Sam. "We talked about this."

"I thought you were both still sleeping."

"You talked about this?" I ask, looking at Archer. He's just in his boxers, and there are creases from his pillow on his face. His dark hair is a mess, stubble covers his strong jaw, and he looks so damn sexy without even trying. He makes butterflies flit in my stomach, and with everything we went through yesterday, I feel closer to him. "So this is a regular occurrence?"

"Yes," Archer says with a chuckle. "It's so fun living with him."

"Hey," Sam interjects, walking backward down the hall. "I'm confident in my body."

"Trust me, we know." Archer moves in behind me, arms going to my waist. He kisses my neck and I lean back against him. "I can make you something better than crackers for breakfast if you want."

"This is fine for now," I tell him, spinning around in his arms. "I was going to go back to bed. You should too. You look tired."

"I'm all right. Do you want eggs again?"

"You don't have to make me anything, babe." I set the box of crackers down so I can hug him. "Are you working today?"

He shakes his head. "I'm on call again."

"You won't work so much when you get a new job, right?"

"I shouldn't."

Now's a perfect time to ask him about where he's going to apply, to bring up the great hospitals around the Chicago area. If we want to live together, one of us is going to have to move. I guess it could be me, but when he's actively looking for a new hospital, it makes sense that it's him, right?

"It's morning," he says before I can go on. "We need to talk about that guy from yesterday."

He tenses, ever so slightly, and if I weren't holding onto him, I wouldn't have noticed. I do have questions, but I don't know how Archer will answer. He didn't see the guy. How's he going to know anything about him?

"Okay." I slide my hands down his arms and step back, grabbing the crackers. "We can talk while we eat. I'll make you breakfast this morning. I do know how, you know."

"Yeah, I know." His eyes go to my wrist, and he looks guilty, almost as if it's his fault I got hurt. "But I like making you breakfast."

I smile. "I won't object to that."

"What do you want?"

"Eggs."

"You're getting predictable, Quinn," he says with a shake of his head. I laugh and open the box of crackers, too hungry to wait to eat. I take a bite out of one and go get my phone. I have a bunch of texts from my mom that I didn't hear last night since I passed out. She's excited to see another picture of the baby, but then asks why I got another ultrasound done.

My lack of response must have worried her, and her last text is a request to call me in the morning. I go to call her back and then remember there's a time difference between Eastwood and Indy. And they're an hour behind? No. Ahead. I think? I'm smart, yet figuring out time zones will forever confuse me.

Either way, it's early, and Mom's probably still sleeping or at the very least just starting her day. Taking my phone with me, I go back into the kitchen and check my email, responding to a few, while Archer makes breakfast. Mom texts me, and I exit out of my emails to respond.

Mom: Are you awake? You're worrying me, Q

Me: Yeah, I am. And sorry. I fell asleep early last night. Archer was able to get a doctor-buddy to do another ultrasound so we could see the baby.

It's the truth with a few things omitted, but I instantly feel bad for lying. Though I know my mother and know how much she'll panic if she were to know everything that happened. I could be right in front of her and she still wouldn't be convinced I'm okay.

Mom: Oh, that's good! She's growing! I started a Pinterest board for the baby shower. Do you want to do a gender reveal? We can do something small for that, if you'd like. Just us and Archer's family.

Me: I'll talk to Archer about it. We're going to find out what we're having as soon as we can. Arch said there's a newer test I can do in like 2 weeks.

Mom: Two weeks! I'll start planning! Do you want to have it here? Eastwood is in the middle between you and Archer.

My chest tightens and a new wave of panic washes over me, one that hasn't quite made it to the shore yet. In two weeks, we could know what we're having. We'll pick out a name and can start planning the nursery. But where will it be?

"Do you want toast?" Archer asks, sliding a plate of eggs in front of me.

"No, thanks. And thanks for the eggs."

He takes a plate for himself and sits across from me. "They're easy. Someday I'm going to make you a real meal. I'm not the best cook, so don't have high expectations."

I laugh. "I'll save my high expectations for sex."

"You know I aim to please. Multiple times."

I push my eggs around on the plate, helping them cool. "So far, so good. Trust me, I'll let you know if things start to suck in the sack."

"They won't," he promises. "Though some sucking might happen."

Laughing again, I scoop up some eggs and blow on them before putting them in my mouth. Mom sends me another text with pictures of cakes she found on Pinterest for a gender reveal party.

"How do you feel about having a gender reveal party?" I ask.

"What is that?" Archer gets up to make a pot of coffee.

"Basically a party announcing if the baby is a boy or girl.

You don't tell anyone until the end, and you pop a balloon with pink or blue confetti in it or something."

"And it's a thing people do now?"

"Yeah. If you have a halfway decent Instagram following and you *don't* do one, people will wonder what's wrong with you."

Archer chuckles. "I don't really care either way. Any excuse to have a party is good in my book. Do you want to have one?"

"I know they're a little lame, but yeah." I bite my lip, looking at the photos my mom sent. I haven't told anyone besides my family and Marissa about the baby. I'm a modern woman with a successful job, and shouldn't worry about people judging me over having a baby when I'm not married. But I do, just a bit.

"Then let's do it."

Archer's words make me smile. "My mom is going to go crazy over this. She wants to know where to have the party?"

It's a simple question, but I know it raises the same concerns to Archer too. He turns on the coffee maker and comes back to the table. "If you're going to take impressive Instagram pictures, your parents' farm has the perfect setting."

"I'm glad you have your priorities in check."

He nods. "I gotcha, babe. We'll make sure to have everything posed perfectly. I'll even take pictures of all my food before I eat it. Actually, we could invest in some of that realistic-looking fake food. I hear it photographs better."

I look at Archer, a big smile on my face. He makes it so easy to fall.

"Good idea. Anything for the likes."

"Exactly. The number of likes is a direct correlation to how loved this baby is. We really have to step it up."

Laughing, I finish the last of my eggs and get up to put the plate in the sink. "So if we are able to find out the baby's sex in just a few weeks, shouldn't you tell your parents? They still don't know."

The light goes out in Archer's eyes. "Yeah...they don't. Want to have lunch with them soon?"

"Of course. I haven't seen your mom in years. Do you think she remembers me?"

"She does. I talked to her last night and told her you were my girlfriend. I didn't tell her about the baby yet. I'd rather tell her in person."

"Yeah, I agree. You said she'll be excited?"

"She will. My dad too. They'll be surprised, but happily surprised."

"Good." I put my hand over my stomach. "I don't want any more drama."

Archer tenses again, and his hand goes to the back of his neck. I'm about to ask him what's wrong when his phone rings. It's someone from the hospital, and it sounds like a nurse asking for new medications for one of Archer's patients.

I take Archer's empty plate to the sink, rinse the dishes off and then load them into the dishwasher. Archer is still on the phone, so I go into the bathroom to brush my teeth. I really want to kiss him, but not until after my mouth is clean.

One of Archer's lab coats is hanging up in his closet in his room, and I get it out, smiling when I see his name stitched into the fabric. He joked about liking to wear this out in public, so people know he's a doctor. Biting my lip, I look back into the kitchen. I can't see directly into it from Archer's room, but I can hear his voice. He's still on the phone, and after listening for a brief moment, I think a patient is being difficult and not following post-op instructions.

Hoping that doesn't mean he has to go back into the hospital to deal with the issue, I quickly strip out of my clothes and put on the lab coat, pulling it around me just enough to cover my nipples. Then I sit on Archer's bed, perfectly posed. And wait.

And wait.

And wait some more.

I'm starting to get bored, and sitting here with my stomach sucked in—sorry baby—and my tits pushed out is not comfortable. Finally, Archer hangs up and comes into the room.

"Sorry about that. We still need to talk about—" He cuts off when he sees me, jaw dropping just a little.

"You're late for your appointment." I narrow my eyes, biting my lip. "But luckily I'm still able to squeeze you in."

Archer closes the door behind him and jumps on the bed, landing over top of me. "You do have a very *tight* schedule. Are you sure you can fit me in?" He moves between my legs, cupping my face and pushing me back.

"It'll be hard, but I think I can make it work." With hormones still making my sex drive crazy, I'm fighting with myself to stay patient and not rip Archer's boxers off and bring his cock right to me. Not that he'd mind, but if I can keep this going a bit longer, he'll more than appreciate it.

"I'm so sorry, doctor," he says as he kisses my neck. "I'll make it up to you."

"I'm sure you will." I put my hands on his shoulders and push him off me. "Now, we better get your exam started." Moving out from underneath him, I shove him as hard as I can onto the mattress. He's bigger and stronger than me and there's no way I can really push Archer around. He goes along with it, falling back onto the bed.

"According to your chart," I begin, kneeling over him. I slowly peel the coat back, letting the fabric slide down my breasts. Archer watches with wide eyes. "You're well overdue for a thorough examination."

The coat slips off my arms and I move on top of Archer. His cock is already hard and, even through his boxers, feeling it rub against me almost does me in. I lean forward, breasts in Archer's face. He lifts his head off the pillow and takes one in his mouth, tongue swirling around my nipple. Groaning, I force myself to pull away, but Archer has other plans.

He grabs my waist and brings me forward, my pussy in his face. Pushing onto my knees, I grab the headboard, knowing I'll need it to support myself once Archer gets to work. He turns his head to the side, biting my thigh. Goosebumps break out over my flesh when he gently runs his fingers up over my ass, slow and teasing.

He knows how wound up I get, and how easily he can turn me on, especially now. And he uses it to his advantage. It drives me crazy, makes me feel like I'm going to explode, but in the end, I come harder than I ever have before, and each time we have sex it makes me realize more and more how much we were made for each other.

We click. We fit. And I'm not just talking about physically. Though, physically, I don't think I could find anyone more perfect for me than Archer. He knows how to work his hands. And his tongue. Together, at the same time. He can play my body like an instrument made just for him, and I know, without a doubt, no one else will ever make me feel this way.

I am in love with Archer Jones.

The fact that I'm carrying his baby confuses me, I'll admit it. I *want* us to be in love. I want to be a couple. To raise our child together and be a family. Am I forcing something that's not fully there? Archer has been nothing but amazing to me...but is it too soon to say those three words?

He turns his head in and his tongue lashes against my clit. The fact that I'm currently riding his face might have something to do with me suddenly feeling so in love with him as well.

"Archer," I moan, knowing he loves when I say his name during sex. He brings his hands down, squeezing my ass, and eats my pussy with fervor, not stopping until I'm squirming against him. I'm so close to coming, and tingles jolt through my body, bringing every nerve alive. I rock my hips against his face, and his tongue plunges into me. I grip the headboard and arch my back right on the edge of an orgasm.

Archer quickens his movements, alternating between flicking my clit with his tongue as fast as he can and gently sucking it until I come. He holds me against him, not stopping as the orgasm ripples through me. Everything is so sensitive, almost painful, but he's relentless as I try to squirm away, not stopping until I come again.

I fall back onto the bed and I know we were made for each other.

"Did I pass my exam?" Archer groans, moving on top of me.

"The first part," I pant. "This is a...a lengthy process."

"Well, speaking of length..." Archer wiggles his hips against mine and I laugh. Looking into his eyes, I run my fingers through his hair. Yep. I'm a goner. I don't want to come to any conclusions just yet since I'm still naked beneath him and he's yet to fuck me, but if I'm not actually in love with him, I'm pretty damn close.

"We should continue the exam." I bring my mouth to his, kissing him deeply and tasting myself on his lips. "I don't want to miss anything."

"Right. Thank you, doctor." He moves his lips from mine to my neck. "I know I'm in good hands."

I reach down, trying to remove his boxers and he kisses my neck. He moves back just enough to take his boxers off, and once he's naked, I roll him over and climb on top.

"Put the lab coat back on." Archer's hand lands on my hip. "I want you to wear it while you fuck me."

He slaps my ass when I reach over the bed to get it and pull it on, fastening one button.

"You're so hot, Quinn."

Parting my legs, I move over the top of him and take hold of his big cock. My pussy quivers ever so slightly every time I see it. We've had sex many times, and it still amazes me that thing can fit inside me.

"I'm Dr. Jones today," I say, trying to be sexy. And then I realize I'm trying to make Archer call me by his own name. "Unless that's weird. Then I can be Quinn."

His eyes meet mine, and behind the lust, I see something else. His lips curve into a smile and he looks down at my hand wrapped around his cock. "It's not weird to think about you having my last name."

My heart skips a beat, and suddenly I can't get on him fast enough. Archer feels the same and sits up, pushing me back and moving on top. I widen my legs and he enters me, thrusting in hard and fast. His lips find the spot on my neck that always does me in, and it doesn't take long before I'm close to coming again.

Archer pushes in balls deep, burying his cock inside me

as he comes. He kisses me before he pulls out, and reaches down to the foot of his bed for his boxers, handing them to me to use to clean myself up.

"Want to take a shower?" he asks, moving my hair out of my face.

"Yeah," I say back, still a little breathless, both from sex and from what Archer said. I want to believe with all my heart he's thinking about marriage and me having his last name because we're so in love we don't want to go another day without being husband and wife.

But I know that's not true.

We haven't even said the L word yet.

We don't live together.

And we've only been dating a few weeks.

I love you, baby, but damn, these hormones are messing with my heart...and my head.

5

QUINN

"I forgot to pack a hairdryer." I turn to Archer, who's already dressed and ready two minutes after getting out of the shower. "You don't have one, do you?"

"No, but Sam might."

"Sam?" I raise an eyebrow.

"Yeah. He was really into blowouts for a while."

"You're joking."

Archer laughs. "I wish I was. Let me go look." He steps out of the bathroom and I flip my head over, wrapping my towel around my hair. Archer got quiet again while we were in the shower, reminding me of his old hot-and-cold self that used to drive me crazy. Hell, it still drives me crazy.

This whole one-step-forward-and-two-steps-back thing with him makes me question what I was feeling, furthering the proof in my mind that I'm not actually in love with him. He's the father of my child and being together in a perfect relationship is ideal.

I can't rush what's not there.

"Found one," Archer says, coming back into his bathroom.

"This is a really expensive hairdryer," I chuckle. "Sam *was* really into blowouts." I set it on the counter and put on a bit of makeup before drying my hair. When I turn the dryer off and fluff my hair, I hear Archer on the phone.

He's in the living room and looks stressed. The first thing I think is that he has to go into the hospital and our lunch date will be cut short again. I'll be a little disappointed if that's true, and a little scared to be here alone again. Sam is working today, but this time if someone knocks at the door, I won't leave the bedroom.

I go into Archer's room and look through my bag. I either overpack or underpack with no middle ground. Since I wasn't planning on being here today, I'm down to one dress to wear, and it's more of a date-night dress than a casual lunch-date dress. Oh well. Archer seems to like when I show off my boobs.

I get dressed and go into the kitchen to get an anti-nausea pill. I still feel guilty taking them, but being sick constantly is really wearing me out. Archer is still on the phone but smiles when he sees me, and my heart speeds up.

"Okay," he says to whoever he's talking to on the phone. "We'll see you soon." He hangs up and sits on the couch next to me. "You look pretty, babe."

"Thanks." I lean into him, finding the smell of his cologne irresistible, which is kind of funny since my own perfume makes me want to vomit. "Do you have to go into the hospital?"

"Not yet," he says with a smile. He looks away. "You know how you wanted to meet up with my parents?"

"Yeah, I do."

"Want to today?"

"Uh, sure?" I tip my head, not exactly following.

"They're in town. Just got here last night." He still doesn't look at me.

"Oh, that's great!" Isn't it? Archer doesn't seem too thrilled. I know there was a lot of family drama going on while he was in college, but he never seemed to openly hate his parents or anything. "Did they come into town to surprise you or something?"

His hand lands on the back of his neck. "Or something." He turns to me, brows pinched together. "Quinn, that guy who shoved the door into you yesterday is my brother."

I blink. Did I hear Archer right? "Your brother?"

"Yeah. Robert. But we, uh, we still call him Bobby." Archer lets out a breath and closes his eyes in a long blink. "I haven't seen him in years and I have no idea why he was looking for me. My parents are in town because they are trying to find him. He'd been doing all right for a few months and then relapsed."

"Your brother is an addict?"

"You don't know?" Archer asks, and I shake my head. "That's why I stayed with you so much during college."

"Because of your brother?" I'm repeating myself, but I'm having a hard time comprehending this.

"Yes. No one told you why I was there?"

"My mom said it was because of family drama and never went into it more than that. I just assumed it was about your parents fighting or getting a divorce or something."

He leans back, sighing heavily. "My brother caused drama between my parents. But it's always been him at the root of our issues. Do you remember that first Christmas I spent with you guys?"

"I do. Jamie and I thought you were so cute and got into a fight over who could try to get you to stand under mistletoe with us."

Archer softly laughs. "I actually remember that. Dean was so annoyed with you two."

"You knew? We thought we were being very discreet."

"Not at all." He meets my eyes, smiling. "My brother was in Vegas and overdosed. Before he OD'd, though, he stole money from a Salvation Army bucket set up outside a store. My parents had to fly out and deal with him."

"Oh my God. I remember Logan and Owen saying something about your brother being in Vegas, and how he was a crazy partier."

"He's been 'partying' for the last fifteen years."

I move closer to Archer. "I'm so sorry, Archer."

"No," he says, jaw tensing. "I'm sorry." He gently touches my wrist, which he rewrapped for me once we got out of the shower. "My asshole brother hurt you. He almost hurt our baby. This isn't fair to you, and I should have been there and—"

I cut him off with a kiss.

"Archer, I don't blame you, and you shouldn't either."

Archer pulls me into his lap, hand resting over my stomach. My skin is a little tender from being bruised, and I felt that weird, tight pulling sensation again after sex. But it went away fast, didn't come back, and I'm not bleeding or spotting. I guess I'm one of the lucky ones who's going to feel every growing pain, but hey—I'll take it as long as the baby is okay.

"I do blame myself. I had no idea he was coming, but I still feel like I should have warned you. He hurt you, Quinn. That's not okay."

"No, it's not," I agree. "But it still isn't your fault."

"Bobby is a selfish asshole who will use and cheat anyone to get money for drugs. You don't need that in your life. You said you don't want any more family drama, and that's all he is. He's been missing for days and causes nothing but stress for my parents."

"Days?"

"Yeah. He relapsed and left."

"Why didn't you tell me?" I ask Archer.

"It's not an easy thing to bring up."

I turn my head down, carefully considering my words. "We're having a baby together, Archer. There's going to be a lot of things that aren't easy." Watching his face, I debate on whether to go on or not. The words are there, wanting to come out and be confessed. I bring my hand to his chest, rubbing the hem of his collar between my fingers. "Do you remember when I said it felt like you were playing a game with me?"

"Yeah. Do you still?"

I shake my head. "No, but I still feel like you don't really let me in. I don't know what you're thinking, and it makes me feel like I'm on the outside. Maybe I'm being dramatic and hormonal or whatever, but I want to feel like you let me in."

Brow furrowed, Archer runs his hand through my hair. Then his eyes fall shut and he pulls me into an embrace. "Right now," he starts. "I'm thinking you're too good for me."

"I am pretty good," I say with a smile, hugging him back. "But you are too." Hugging him back, I want him to let the walls down. I'm falling for him and know his hesitation to let me in is holding me back.

It makes me feel like he doesn't trust me with his heart.

"I don't want you to feel like I'm shutting you out," he says. "I've never had anyone close enough to share this shit with. Besides Dean, I guess."

Archer told me he'd rather be with me than be friends

with Dean, but it didn't really hit me until right now just what he was giving up.

"So junior year, you spent most of the summer with us," I start. "Your parents were in Florida."

He nods. "At a rehab center with Bobby. He lasted a month and a half." His brows furrow and he looks away. I can see the anger on his face, and I wish I could take it away. I can only imagine what it'd feel like to have one of my brothers go through something like that. I'd be sick with worry and so angry and frustrated.

"My parents are good people," Archer says quietly. "They tried, and I still don't know how Bobby ended up the way he did."

"They raised you," I say. "And I think they did a pretty good job there."

He smiles and relaxes just a bit. "Yeah. Is it horrible to admit I wish I could just forget about him? I think part of why I never mentioned him was because I'd rather pretend he wasn't there."

"No, it's not horrible. It's easier to forget and not deal."

He nods. "I'm done dealing with his shit. He's never going to get better."

"Maybe he—"

"No. It's been fifteen years. He's been to court-ordered rehab more than once. My parents nearly went broke trying to get him into other private rehab centers. He has a disease where the cure has yet to be found."

I run my nails up and down Archer's arm. I'm sure I'd be just as angry and unwilling to forgive if I grew up with Bobby. I've only met him for a total of two minutes and I already don't like the guy. But he's Archer's brother, and I'd never give up on my brothers.

Fuck, this is complicated.

"I'm sorry to throw this all on you," Archer says.

"You're not. You're my boyfriend, and this little gal's daddy." I point to my stomach. "Your baggage is my baggage. And mine is yours."

Archer runs his hand over my hair. "You don't have any baggage."

"I do," I insist. "And I'd feel better if I confessed."

Archer purses his lips, trying not to laugh. "Should I prepare myself for the skeletons in your closet?"

"Just don't judge me."

"I'll do my best."

"I used to be really into competitive robot fighting. Like *really* into it."

Archer looks at me, blinks, and raises an eyebrow. "That's a real thing?"

"It is. I'm not a competitive person, but it brought it out in me and I used my personal money to sponsor the team."

Archer laughs. "There are teams in robot fighting?"

"Yeah. It takes a team to build. That's, uh, how I met Jacob."

"Your ex?"

Wrinkling my nose, I nod.

"You are such a nerd, Quinn," he laughs. "Is that your biggest confession?"

"Yeah, pretty much. Do you think of me differently now?"

"Oh, definitely. This changes everything, and I don't know if I can go on dating you."

"Fine," I say with a laugh. "My life might be a little dull."

"There is nothing wrong with dull, babe." He kisses me again, and that push-and-pull feeling is gone. Maybe it's not too soon to fall for him.

Someone knocks on the door and I immediately jump. Archer holds me, and I instantly feel safe.

"I think it's my parents," he says. "They were on their way over."

"I'm meeting them now?" I whisper-yell, feeling like I'm not ready. I madly try to smooth out my hair.

"You look fine, babe."

"Fine? Just fine?"

"Pretty. Sexy. Hot. Beautiful."

I playfully push him away and climb off his lap. "Listing off adjectives isn't helping. You're sure they'll be excited about the baby?"

"Yes. They need some good news right now considering everything else going on. And my mom's one of those people who loves babies. *All* babies." He makes a face and I laugh.

"That makes me feel better."

He goes to the door, looking out the peephole before opening it. I'm not sure why I'm nervous to meet Archer's parents all of the sudden. I've met them before, but it's different now. Meeting your boyfriend's parents is always a big deal, but meeting them and then telling them they're going to be grandparents is even bigger.

Archer's mom hugs him as soon as she's in the door. By the way she's gushing over him, I assume it's been a while since she's seen him in person. She gives him another hug and then sees me.

"Quinn!" she exclaims. "Look at you! You've grown up."

"Hi, Mrs. Jones," I say with a smile. "It's nice to see you again."

"Call me Sheila," she says and comes in for a hug. So Mrs. Jones is a hugger, and she smells overwhelmingly like the perfume my grandmother wears.

"Dad, do you remember Quinn?" Archer steps back, slipping his arm around me.

"I do, and it's nice to see you again. I always thought Archer had a thing for you," he says with a wink. Archer got his dark hair and brown eyes from his father but is a few inches taller and many pounds lighter than his dad.

"It's a little early," Archer starts. "But is anyone hungry? We can do brunch instead of lunch."

"That's fine with me," I say.

"I'll gladly go out." Mr. Jones pats his stomach. "The breakfast at the hotel was terrible."

"There's a cute little Mexican restaurant down on the corner." Mrs. Jones motions behind her. "I could really use a margarita right now." She nudges me. "Maybe we could split a pitcher."

"Uh...yeah." I look at Archer, who grabs his phone and wallet from the coffee table. I pull my purse up over my shoulder and go to the door, waiting for Archer.

"Oh, honey," Mrs. Jones—Sheila—says, looking at my wrist. "Archer told me what happened. I'm so sorry."

"It's, uh, okay." I force a smile. This isn't awkward at all. Archer takes my hand and leads me out, locking the door behind him. The four of us head down the hall and get into the elevator. No one says anything, and the silence makes the already awkwardness even worse.

"That's a pretty purse." Sheila breaks the silence, looking at my bag. "Is that Gucci?"

"Yeah, and thanks."

The elevator comes to a stop at the lobby, and we get out. Archer holds my hand and we continue our awkward-as-fuck walk down the block. My family is loud. Between the seven of us, someone is always talking. I wonder how things are with the Joneses, and if the lack of conversation has to do with the fact Bobby showed up, obviously high on something, hurt me, and is MIA.

Yeah, that adds a bit of tension to my first sit-down meal with my boyfriend's parents. Since it's not quite eleven a.m., the lunch crowd hasn't yet moved in and we get a table right away. Normally, I love tacos. I considered them one of the basic food groups while in college. And nothing tested my self-control more than a bowl of chips and salsa in front of me.

But right now the smell of taco seasoning in the air is making me gag. Archer notices and rubs my thigh, and I order a Sprite to try to help.

"So, what do you do, Quinn?" Mr. Jones asks. "I think you were still a college student the last time we saw you."

"I design and program software," I say, keeping things simple. Usually, there's no point in explaining further than that. Most people don't understand what I do.

"Sounds interesting. And complicated."

"She's being modest." Archer gives my thigh a squeeze. "She invented and sold an app to Apple and now she manages one of the most up-and-coming software companies in the country."

"Wow," Sheila says, eyes widening. "That's amazing. What's the app called? I might have it."

Mr. Jones winks. "If it's one of those candy smashing games, she does."

The waiter brings our drinks and I sip at my Sprite. "It's not an app like that. It's more like an app for apps that helps with the way they process and store data, making them more efficient while taking up less space."

"You lost me." Mr. Jones shakes his head and laughs.

"I don't even get it," Archer says, turning to look at me. "But it's impressive."

The waiter comes back to take our orders, and I go with a taco and a burrito, hoping I can stomach at least a few bites of each. I glare at the bowl of salsa. It looks so good but smells so bad right now.

Being pregnant is weird.

Archer talks to his parents about work for a while, and when our food comes, I can't ignore how sick I feel anymore. I take one bite of my taco and feel betrayed. I set it back down on my plate and grab a napkin, needing to cover my nose and block out the smell before I puke.

"Feeling sick again, babe?" Archer asks quietly, and I nod. "Did you bring the Zofran?"

"No. I can't take another yet." I reach for my Sprite. "I'll be okay."

Sheila's eyes dart from me to Archer and back again. "Are you all right dear? Do you think it's food poisoning?"

"Mom. Dad," Archer starts and scoots his chair a little closer to mine. His hand lands on top of mine. "Quinn's pregnant."

"We're going to be grandparents?" his dad asks after a few seconds of silence, almost as if he's afraid Archer is going to tell him it's all a joke.

"Yes." Archer gives my hand a squeeze. "In March. The official due date is the eighteenth."

"The day after your birthday!" his mom exclaims. "Oh, what a wonderful present!" She brings her hands to her face, tears in her eyes. If only my family reacted this way...

"I have ultrasound pictures, if you want to see them," I offer, reaching into my purse with my left hand. The small movement hurts my wrist, and I try hard not to let anyone see. This is a nice moment. I don't want to mess it up by reminding everyone of Bobby.

"Of course! Of course! How far along are you? You said the due date, but I can't think right now."

"She's around eight weeks," Archer says. "We wanted to tell you in person, and with all that was going on…"

"Oh, it's fine." Sheila takes the ultrasound pictures from me and ohhs and awws over them, and then asks about how the pregnancy has been going and what we have planned, which is nothing.

Unlike my parents, however, they don't seem too concerned. I guess next to Bobby, Archer having an unplanned baby is smooth sailing. He's smart. Responsible. He'll figure it out one way or another, and I know without a doubt he'll be an amazing father…even if we're not together.

Unable to finish my food, I get it boxed up to take back to Archer's. Maybe I'll eat it later.

"You should rest," Sheila says as the waiter clears the last of the dishes from the table. "I know what it's like having morning sickness. I had it bad with both my pregnancies. And we should start our search for Bobby."

"Can I help?" Archer asks.

"No," his dad says right away. "Take care of Quinn and that baby. We'll start looking at the usual places and will call you if we find him."

Archer nods, grabbing the check the waiter just dropped off before anyone has a chance to object. "You're still coming over for dinner?"

"Yes." Shelia smiles. "We'll see you tonight. Have a safe flight, Quinn. And I'm sure we'll be seeing you again soon."

We go our separate ways, and I hold Archer's hand, slowly walking back to his apartment.

"What are the usual places?" I ask as we cross the street.

Archer glances down at me. "To look for Bobby?"

"Yeah."

"Jail." He shakes his head, trying not to get angry. "Homeless shelters and free clinics. He tries to go and get pain pills. He never gets any, but he keeps trying. And if he's not there, then he's either at a bar somewhere or passed out in a motel bathroom."

"I'm so sorry, Archer."

"Don't feel sorry for me." He sighs. "I don't want you to waste any time or energy on him."

I have no idea what to say back. So I just squeeze Archer's hand tighter and nod. I wish I could talk to Dean about this, to get his advice on how to handle this situation. He's been through it before, many times I'm guessing, and will know the best way to go about this. I don't want to push Archer, but Bobby is his brother. He's family and will always be in Archer's life...and now mine.

"I'll call you when I get home." Quinn slides her hands up my back. She's already pressed up against my chest, but I pull her in even tighter. I knew her leaving would be hard, but I didn't expect it to be as hard as it is. This long distance thing fucking sucks, and is made worse with her being pregnant.

Not only do I miss her so much it hurts, I hate leaving her alone to deal with the symptoms brought on by our baby. I want to be there for her, bringing her water after she gets sick in the morning, running out to get whatever food she's craving, and helping her with just everyday living since I know she's exhausted.

Having her here with me the last few days felt so natural. We're supposed to be together, and it's crazy to think I was right all those years ago when I first saw her. I wanted her then solely based on her appearance, but the more I got to know her, the more she worked her way into my heart.

I spent years denying it. If I had said something back then, after she turned eighteen of course, would something have happened? Would we be married with children already? Or is it presumptuous to assume Quinn would even have wanted me back then?

Pressing my forehead against hers, I close my eyes for a beat, wishing we were back in my bed. "Hopefully you can sleep on the plane."

"I've never been able to sleep on planes. Or in cars. I'm jealous of anyone who can," she says with a laugh. "At least it's a short flight."

"True." We're at the airport, and she has to get on the plane in fifteen minutes.

"I don't want to go," she says softly, turning her head up to kiss me.

"I wish you didn't have to." There's so much unsaid right now, and bringing it up might sour our otherwise passionate departure. She *shouldn't* have to leave. We kiss again, and I walk her farther into the airport. We're at a smaller one, full of private jets owned by rich businessmen. Quinn, wearing pink leggings, an oversized t-shirt, and pulling a Chewbacca suitcase, looks out of place, but she's every bit as smart, successful, and well-off as anyone in here.

"And I'll let you know as soon as I find out about that blood work from my OB," she says, slowing her gait. We're nearing the hangar, and her departure is nearing. "Hopefully I can get it as soon as possible. I really want to know what we're having."

"Me too."

"And then we can start talking about names. It's not too early to get some lists going."

I smile. The more we talk about the baby like this, the more I feel like we're a family. "I'd like that."

We're by the plane now, and the pilot is waiting. We kiss again, and I have to practically peel myself off Quinn so she can get in the plane and head home. I wave and go back to my car, feeling like a part of me left along with her.

And I think it actually did. Quinn has had part of my heart for years.

SOMEONE KNOCKS ON THE DOOR, BRINGING ME OUT OF THE dream I was having. About Quinn, not surprisingly. I run my hand over my face and sit up. I dozed off on the couch after getting back from the airport. My parents are coming over for dinner, but they shouldn't be here for another hour and a half.

If they found Bobby, they'd call. Unless they found him at the morgue and are coming to tell me he finally overdosed, that his abused body couldn't take it any longer. My stomach knots up and my chest tightens. I can't fucking stand Bobby, but he's my brother. I want him to get better. I want him to be an uncle to my child and be in our lives again.

I'm a doctor. A realist. People like Bobby don't recover just because their loved ones want them to. Getting up, I go to the door. Thinking it's my parents, I open it without looking. It's not my parents.

It's Bobby.

My fingers curl into fists. Anger surges through me, and I grab Bobby by the collar and yank him inside.

"What the fuck are you doing here?" I demand as Bobby staggers, trying to catch his balance. All I can think about is my fist hitting his face. He holds up his hands, and I notice the scratches on his knuckles.

And the bruises on his face.

Someone already beat the shit out of him, and as angry

as I am for him hurting Quinn, a small voice in the back of my mind reminds me he's sick. Addiction is a disease. I lower my fist, still pissed as fuck.

"What are you doing here?" I repeat through gritted teeth.

"I wanted to say I'm sorry."

I let out a snort of laughter. Bobby has apologized a hundred times. Half of those times he doesn't remember saying he's sorry, and the other half were meaningless words said in hopes we'd be stupid enough to think he was better so he could get more booze or drugs.

"I didn't know she was pregnant."

I close the door and round on Bobby. "How do you know she's pregnant?"

Bobby twitches. "She put her hands over her stomach." He brings his hands in, fingers trembling. He's coming down from whatever he took. I need to take him to the hospital and get him checked out. Withdrawal can be dangerous.

"It's yours, isn't it?"

"Of course it's mine," I snap, then realize all Bobby knows is some girl answered the door wearing a Duke University shirt. Putting two and two together leads you to the conclusion Quinn is my pregnant girlfriend, but I'll give him the benefit of the doubt.

"Did you tell Mom?"

"Yeah. I did this morning. They're here in Indy looking for you, you know."

Bobby smiles. His teeth are decaying, which is a fucking shame. We used to look a lot alike. Now he looks like a cleaned-up model on a 'many faces of meth' poster. "Was she excited? Mom's always loved babies."

"Yeah. She was pretty excited."

Bobby swallows hard, still not sure if I'm going to clock

him in the jaw or not. "You didn't get hitched, did you? I've been clean long enough I think I'd remember." He's trying to be funny, and while he almost is, his words just make me sad.

"No, we didn't. So yes, before you ask, this baby wasn't planned."

Bobby shrugs. "The good things in life never are."

"I suppose so."

"Who's the chick? She's pretty, but you always did have good-looking girls on your arm."

I ignore the subtle insult. "Her name is Quinn."

"You two been together long?"

"We've known each other a long time but didn't start dating until recently."

Bobby cocks an eyebrow. "Until you got her pregnant, you mean?"

"Pretty much." Other than Sam, no one knows the nature of Quinn's and my relationship.

Bobby laughs. "And I thought you were the smart one. How long have you known her?"

"Do you remember Dean Dawson?"

He blinks, face twitching as he tries to think. I wonder what a scan of his brain would look like. He's done considerable damage, I'm sure.

"Your roommate in college?"

"Yeah."

Bobby nods. "You spent a lot of time there. Mom and Dad talk about the Dawsons like they're the fucking Kardashians."

I laugh. "They're much better."

"They sound like good people."

"They are. All of them." I can't find fault in any of the Dawsons, not even Logan and Owen, whose main reason for opening a bar was to have one-night stands with female patrons.

"Dean's okay with you dating his sister?" His eyes widen, and he holds up his hand. "Fucking fuck. You knocked up your best friend's little sister," he says with a laugh.

I bring my hand to the back of my neck, laughing. "No, he's not okay with it at all." And in that moment, it hits me hard right in the chest how much I miss my brother. We were close once. I looked up to Bobby. He was everything an older brother should have been. And then he wasn't, and suddenly I didn't matter anymore.

Fuck, I wish things were different. It's weird to think about, actually. Sitting down with a beer, talking to my brother about how dramatic and stupid Dean is being. Confessing how I'm upset over losing a friend but even angrier about how Dean's childish behavior is upsetting Quinn.

I'd tell him how I've had the hots for Quinn since the first time I saw her when she was only fourteen but looked much older in that tight black dress she was wearing. Fifteen years of friendship and brotherhood is gone, and we'll never get it back. And I wish with all my heart Bobby could recover. That he could go to rehab and stick with it.

But he hasn't, and he won't.

There's a good chance he won't even remember this conversation in the morning.

"Dean's pissed at me for hooking up with his sister and pissed at Quinn for hooking up with me. He's getting married two days before Quinn is due."

Bobby's eyes widen. "Man, that's fucked up," he says and bursts into laughter. I look at him hard for a few seconds, and then the knot in my chest loosens. "What about the rest of them? They think they're better than everyone, don't they?"

And the knot tightens back up. "No. They don't. They—" I stop. I don't owe Bobby an explanation. He's not going to change. I'm never going to get my big brother back, and I've already accepted it. Sighing, I turn away to get my phone.

"What are you doing?"

"Mom and Dad are looking for you."

"I'm not a baby," he rushes out and I work hard to bite my tongue. "Can't we hang out? Catch up? Look at you, little bro! You're a motherfucking doctor with a baby on the way." He looks around, almost as if he's realizing where he is for the first time. "Where is your baby mama?"

"Don't call her that. And she's at home."

"Fuck. You weren't kidding when you said you just started dating, huh?"

I get my phone from the coffee table and sit on the couch. Bobby starts to walk forward, but I hold out my hand. "Take off your shoes. And your socks. Actually, hang on."

I hurry down the hall and grab a pair of socks from my drawer and a sheet from the closet. Call me paranoid, but the time Bobby brought home bed bugs is still seared into my memory. He's still standing in the small foyer when I get back, looking around the apartment like he's trying to figure out where he is.

"Bobby?" I extend the socks. Still not sure of his surroundings, Bobby takes the socks from me and puts them on. Our roles have reversed, and he's not the older brother looking out for me anymore.

I spread the sheet on the couch and motion to it. "You should sit. Get something to eat. I need to call Mom and let her know you're okay." 'Okay' is a relative term here.

"You always were a buzz kill, *doctor*," he spits as an insult.

"I'm always looking out for you."

"Are you, Arch? Are you looking out for me?" He wobbles his way to the couch and plops down. I text Mom, letting her know Bobby showed up and is alive.

"I shouldn't have to." I sit on the armchair across from him. I don't trust my brother at all. He might mean well but will end up leaving with anything he deems valuable, desperate to sell whatever he can for drug money. "What the hell happened to you, Bobby?"

"You," he sneers.

"Me?" I huff, leaning back.

"Yeah. Do you know what it's like living in your shadow? Mom's always bragging to anyone who'll listen about her son *the surgeon*. It's fucking sickening."

"You started using before I even graduated high school, so don't even try to put this on me."

"You've always tried to one-up me," he goes on. "And now all I hear about is *my son the surgeon*," he says in a high-pitched voice, imitating Mom.

I think of Quinn's pretty face. Of the sound of our baby's rapid heartbeat. *Stay calm...stay calm...stay calm...*He's sick. It's not right to take it out on him. But, fuck, it'd feel so good to let loose. To tell him how I really feel while throwing a few punches.

I missed senior prom.

Mom and Dad almost didn't make it to my pre-med graduation.

They were out of town and out of touch when I started my residency.

I didn't tell them about *my* child because they were busy dealing with his shit.

He. Hurt. Quinn.

"It's not my fault you pissed away your future. I worked my ass off and went to med school."

"You think I wouldn't like to be a doctor? I could do it, you know. If I really wanted to I could," he rants. "But I'm not a sell-out like you. I stand up for what I think is right, and the healthcare system in our country is bullshit. I refuse to be part of it."

"Okay," I say with a nod. I can't disagree about our healthcare system needing work, but I'm not even going to get into it with him. Bobby becomes the world's greatest debater when he's drunk or high.

Mom replies to my text, saying she and Dad are on their way.

"You think I'm a loser, don't you?"

I look at Bobby and the anger turns into pity. "No, Bobby, I don't. I think you're sick and need help."

"I don't fucking need help!" He stands up, eyes getting more and more bloodshot. I let out my breath, wishing I were back in Chicago with Quinn. Hell, I'd even take Eastwood over this. Dealing with Dean and his petty drama would be a welcome change.

"Okay," I say again, knowing there's no reason to go round and round with Bobby. He's under the influence of something and he's losing whatever small touch with reality he has. "Sit down." I motion to the couch. When it comes to Bobby, I can either be angry and pissed or disconnected. It's how I deal, and I know it's not healthy.

I just don't see the point in investing more.

"Are you hungry?" I continue. "I have leftover tacos in the fridge."

"Yeah. Sure." He sinks back down, shoulders twitching up and down. Hurrying into the kitchen, I take Quinn's leftovers that she couldn't finish and pop them in the

microwave. I move back, needing to keep Bobby in my line
of sight.

He leans back on the couch, and I can't tell if he's
twitching or shivering. The microwave beeps, and I grab the
tacos and go back to the living room. Bobby looks at the
plastic take-out container and narrows his eyes.

"What's wrong with this?"

"What do you mean?" I ask, still holding out the tacos.

"Who the fuck doesn't eat their tacos from a restaurant?"

I wish I could laugh. "Quinn." Saying her name is like
taking a pill, and I instantly relax. "She's been having a lot of
morning sickness."

"Oh yeah. You fucked her and got her pregnant."

"Don't talk like that. She's the mother of my child and I
love her." The words escape me before I have a chance to
think about them.

But they're true.

I love Quinn.

"Sorry, dude." Bobby holds up his hands, shaking his
head, and then goes back to the taco, eating as if it's his first
meal in days. It probably is. "Didn't realize this shit was
serious."

"It is. She's having my baby."

"But she's not here."

Leave it to my junkie brother to get under my skin. I run
my hand over my face and stand, wondering if I should hide
all the booze in this place before Bobby finds it. Watching
the minutes crawl by, I sit back, waiting for Mom and Dad to
get here and deal with their firstborn.

"What are you doing here?" I ask.

"I came to apologize," Bobby says with his mouth full,
looking at me as if I asked what color the sky is.

"Before then. When you threw the door open, hurt Quinn, and almost hurt my baby."

"You're never going to let that go, are you?" He licks taco grease from his fingers.

"No."

Picking up Quinn's half-eaten burrito, he meets my gaze. "I haven't seen you in a while."

I keep my eyes on him, waiting for him to go on. He's lying, and it's painfully obvious. He twitches again, and sweat breaks out along his forehead. Something isn't right.

"Hey," I say and sit up. "Stop eating."

"Fuck you." He stuffs the food in his mouth. Dammit. It's frustrating enough to deal with patients who eat before surgery. The last thing I need is for him to start seizing with a mouthful of Mexican food.

"No, really. Stop."

He shoves the rest of the food in his mouth just to prove a point. I stiffen, trying not to let myself think of the dangers of throwing up while unconscious. Mom and Dad aren't far, but time is crawling. I wait for what feels like an hour and check the time on my phone again. It's been two minutes.

Bobby finishes the food and sets the empty container on the coffee table. He leans back, brows furrowing, and looks at me.

"I am sorry, Arch. I've been a shitty brother."

"Yeah," I agree. "You have."

"It's just...it's so hard, you know?"

"No," I say honestly. "I don't."

He rubs his forehead, becoming agitated. "I can't explain it. It's just there. Inside. Deep inside."

Shaking my head, I exhale. I wish I could understand what he means. Maybe I could help him.

"Forget it," he says and leans back, hands twitching even more. Then he brings his hand to his chest, pressing hard.

"You need to go to the hospital." I stand, phone in hand.

"I'm fine."

"You're going through withdrawal."

"Stop acting like you know everything because you're a fucking doctor."

"I don't know everything," I say. "But I do know what withdrawal looks like." I didn't learn that in med school though. I've seen it enough times firsthand. "Come on. I'll take you." I extend a hand to help him up.

"No." He stands and swats my hand away. "I'm fine," he repeats.

But he's not fine. The color drains from his face and he staggers back, falling to the floor.

7

QUINN

"Fine. Be mad at me. But you're being overdramatic." I take off my shoes and shake my head. "I wasn't gone that long."

My words do nothing, and Lily continues to glare at me. Luna jumps up on the counter, meowing for food, and the others come running. Neville rubs against my legs, and I reach down to scoop him up.

"I think you got fatter since I left." He starts purring, and I carry him with me to the pantry. After I feed the cats, I change into pajamas and sit on the couch to call Archer. He doesn't answer, so I leave him a message letting him know I got home safe and sound. He must have gotten called in for surgery, and my heart aches for him. He's such a hard worker and needs a break, especially with everything that happened this weekend.

I drag my suitcase into my room, pull out my essentials and push the suitcase to the side, saying I'll empty it later. Really, it'll sit there for at least a week before I get to it. Bringing my phone into the bathroom with me so I can answer if Archer calls back, I take a shower.

My phone rings as I'm getting out, but it's not Archer. I wrap my towel around myself and answer.

"Hello?"

"Hey, sis," Logan says. "I haven't talked to you in a while. How are things?"

"Good. I just got back from Indy. I spent the weekend with Archer."

"And he's still treating you well? We don't need to go over and threaten to break his knuckles or anything, do we?"

I laugh. "No, you definitely don't. Archer treats me better than anyone has."

"That's good to hear. I really don't want to have to hurt him. I like the guy."

"That makes two of us." I put my phone on speaker and go into my room to start getting dressed for the night. "Have you talked to Dean recently?"

"Yeah, we all went over for dinner Sunday night."

"And?"

"He's still being an immature ass. All Mom talked about was planning for the baby shower and Dean didn't say anything, but you could tell he was pissed."

"He's such a baby."

"He's always been one. Don't worry about it. He'll get over it eventually and then will realize what an ass he's been."

"They can move their wedding date if it bothers them that much. I can't change my due date."

"I think he's more mad about Archer liking you more than him now."

"Well, I can offer things to Archer that he can't."

"Gross, Quinn."

"Hey, I am pregnant."

"Are you still getting sick every morning?"

"Yeah, and it lasts all day. I caved and started taking medication to help with it. How are you guys? Is Owen around?"

"He's always around. We're good. Nothing has changed much on our front."

"You both need to find nice girls and settle down. Have some babies too so we can have playdates."

Logan laughs. "If I find a nice girl, I'll gladly settle down. Owen, on the other hand...we both know how that'll go."

"Right," I say with a snort of laughter. The day Owen settles down is the day hell freezes over. Though as a believer in true love, I think he'll find someone to come into his life and change all that. "I miss you guys," I admit with a sigh, struggling to get my pajama pants on one-handed. My wrist is aching again, and I know I won't be able to splint it as well as Archer did for me this morning.

"Then move back here."

"But I like my job and the city."

"Then stop complaining."

I sink down onto my mattress. "I'll complain all I want. And I'm not above pulling the pregnancy card."

"You're stooping low, sis," he says with a chuckle. We talk for a few more minutes before hanging up. I go into the kitchen to find something to eat, and the only thing that sounds good right now are Sour Patch Kids. So healthy, I know. I'm down to one box, I take them into my room, sitting in bed while I catch up on emails and the work I'm able to do from home.

An hour later I'm all caught up, and I exit out of my emails and open Pinterest, browsing nursery ideas. My apartment is really nice, with a great view, but isn't family friendly. I only have one spare bedroom, and I use it as an office. I suppose I could combine the office with the master and turn that room into the nursery, but if Archer moves in, we'll be tight on space.

Knowing I'm getting ahead of myself, I log onto the building's website to see if there's anything else available. They offer bigger arrangements, and I can definitely afford it. I took the smaller space when I moved in since it was just me, and this has worked perfectly.

There's another apartment available two floors up with double the square footage of what I have now. I'll have my same view plus another wall of windows on another side of the building. I click through the pictures, thinking it's perfect. There's plenty of space for the baby and me, and of course Archer if things keep going as well as they are.

And then I think about my childhood and how much I loved being in the country. I grew up riding horses and being an active member in our local 4H group. The crime rate is drastically lower in Eastwood, and the pace of life is just slower.

I put my hand over my stomach, unable to ignore the anxiety building inside me. I love my job. I really like the city. But I always assumed I'd end up back at Eastwood. It was part of the big picture in my mind, though I didn't often let myself get that far ahead. I probably imagine raising my kids in a big, old farmhouse just because that's how I was raised.

Lots of people live in the city. They have kids and they turn out just fine. There's nothing wrong with staying here. So why am I starting to feel guilty about it?

Getting even further ahead of myself, I check out houses for sale in Eastwood. There's only five, and none are houses I'd buy, though with Dad being a contractor, it makes sense to build something new anyway.

My phone rings again, and this time it is Archer. Closing my computer, I smile as I answer, missing Archer already.

"Hey, babe," I say.

"Hey. How was your flight?"

"Fine. We got in faster than I thought. Did you get called in for surgery again?"

"No." He lets out a sigh. "Bobby showed up again. He went through his usual bullshit apologies and then passed out."

"Like, passed out drunk?"

"No. His blood pressure dropped when he stood up and he fainted."

"Oh my God. Is he okay?"

"For now. He's at the hospital with my parents. I just got home."

My chest tightens, and I hate that I'm not there with Archer. "I'm so sorry. Do you want me to come back?"

"No," he says quickly. "You need to take care of yourself and I meant it when I said you shouldn't waste any time on Bobby."

I bite my lip, not sure what to say. Worrying about Bobby isn't a waste of time, and it's something I'm going to do because I care about Archer. He might not get along with his brother, but losing Bobby would still hurt.

"What's going to happen?"

"He'll probably be here for a few days, and then my parents will take him home and try to get him into rehab again. This is another reason why I didn't bring him up, Quinn," Archer says, and the emotion in his voice kills me. "This happens over and over, and this won't be the last time." The microwave beeps in the background. "Anyway, I looked up robot fights while I was waiting and I have to say it's pretty fucking cool."

"It is! Careful you don't get sucked in. You'll start watching a fight or two here and there and then it becomes your life and you're under-the-table funding lasers to go on your team's robot."

Archer laughs. "Only you'll go down that rabbit hole. But if you want to go see a competition, I'd go with you. I mean, if you're still interested in that stuff."

"Are you serious?" I exclaim.

"So I take that as a yes," he chuckles. "Then it's set. Our next date is to a robot fight. That's something I never thought I'd say."

"Embrace it, Archer. You're going to love it and become one of us."

"I can't be a nerd. I'm a doctor, remember?"

"Oh my God! I almost forgot. Thank you for reminding me."

"I will start reminding you every hour on the hour."

"Only if you send photos along with it." I get under the covers.

"For some reason, I think the naked and just wearing the lab coat looks much hotter on you. I'm getting a boner thinking about you in it now."

"I'm glad you liked it. I've never done that before."

"I'd hope so. Because I'd question whose lab coat you were naked under."

I laugh. "I mean dress up like that. I own lingerie no one has ever seen."

"I will gladly be the first one to see you in it."

"You need to come visit me soon."

"I want to," Archer groans. "I miss you already."

"I miss you, too." I close my eyes, wishing his arms were around me right now. Maybe some distance between us will help me figure things out. I know you can't rush love, but this baby puts a time limit on things, and I want to know one way or another before I give birth.

"I'm going to get carpal tunnel now," Archer jokes. "Especially if I keep thinking about you in that lab coat."

"I have toys to help me with that."

Archer groans. "And now I'm thinking about you touching yourself. You're not helping me, Quinn."

"You should invest in some toys," I say with a giggle. "I can get you a mold of my vagina."

Archer laughs. "I honestly don't know if I should turn down your offer or not. Nothing will be as good as the real thing."

"We can do a two-for-one special and you can make a cast of your dick. I'm thinking I'll get it made in pink with sparkles."

"Can I do the same for your vagina?"

"I'd expect nothing less." I roll over with a big smile on my face. Archer gets me and my weird sense of humor. He makes me laugh. Makes me feel safe.

I am so falling for him.

"What are you doing the rest of the day?" he asks, and I hear him turn the TV on in the background.

"Nothing really. I caught up on work already so now I plan to watch TV and try to win back the affection of my cats."

"You lost it?"

"They get mad when I'm gone for too long. I have a neighbor come over and feed them and clean their litter boxes, but I got the evil eye from everyone but Neville when I got home today."

Archer chuckles. "Are you going to officially adopt him yet?"

"I should. I've had him for months. All I have to do is email the rescue group too, and I haven't. How lazy is that?"

"You're anything but lazy, Quinn."

I brush Sour Patch Kids crumbs off my sheets and roll my eyes at myself. "Thanks for lying to me, babe."

"My mom is calling me," Archer says after his phone beeps.

"Let me know if anything happens. I'll call you in the morning."

"Okay. Good night, Quinn. I...I...I'll talk to you later." He hangs up and I'm left a little stunned. Was he going to tell me he loves me?

"Whoa," Marissa says, pouring herself a cup of coffee. It's Tuesday morning and I'm at the office. I just got done telling her about this past weekend's events. "Not gonna lie, that's a little fucked up."

"I know." I go for the pot of decaf and fill my cup halfway up. I read online that it's okay to drink caffeine in moderation, but now I'm starting to feel guilty about it. But dammit, I'm tired and it's been a routine for years to get up and drink at least one cup of coffee.

Adding a splash of regular coffee to my cup, I flick my gaze to Marissa. "I know. I feel so bad for Archer. And I feel bad that I've known him for years but didn't really know him."

"That's not your fault," Marissa counters. "From what you told me, you two never really sat down and talked or anything."

"True." I tear open a package of sugar and dump it in my coffee. "And it's not like I'm chummy with Weston's friends. I hardly even know Logan and Owen's friends and they're closer to my age."

"I listened to a great podcast last night about how women feel guilty over pretty much everything. You need to accept that things aren't your fault and stop putting blame on yourself."

I go to pick up my coffee with my left hand and almost drop it. My wrist is too weak to even hold a cup of coffee. Great.

"Yeah. I know. And the guilt game is strong with me. I can only imagine how much worse it'll be once I'm a mom."

Marissa laughs, and we head out of the breakroom. "So when are you going to tell people?" she asks quietly.

"When I'm out of the first trimester. We want to find out what we're having as soon as possible, and once I know, I'll make an announcement." Which reminds me to call the OB office and ask about that blood work.

"And Dean is still being a dick?"

"Yep. I talked to Logan yesterday about it. He thinks Dean still feels like I stole his best friend. Which I kinda did, I guess, but it's not like that."

"It's not like the three of you were some tight-knit friend group before. Dean's getting married too. And he and Archer don't hang out that often anymore, do they?"

"Nope. Archer barely gets away from work. If anything, Dean and Archer will see each other more now that we're dating."

"Exactly. And his best friend is the father of his niece or nephew. He'll come around eventually."

"Yeah, I know. It's just irritating. And given everything going on with Archer's brother, it makes Dean seem all the more childish." I take a sip of my coffee. If only there was a way to prove to Dean that he and Archer are still friends and nothing has changed...

"You look like you're plotting." Marissa lifts her eyebrows and stares at me. "Don't do it, Quinn."

"It's nothing big."

"But?"

"If I can get Dean and Archer together this weekend and they hang out like normal, then maybe my brother will stop acting like an idiot. I know Archer could really use his friend right now. Dean knows about Bobby and has been through this with Archer before."

"I agree with your scheming for once."

"It's not scheming. I'm simply arranging for my boyfriend to hang out with my brother." I take another sip of coffee and smile. "It's foolproof. I mean, what's the worst that could happen?"

8

I take my earbuds out and wipe sweat from my brow, having just finished stretching after a workout. There's a gym not even a block away from my apartment, and though I work crazy hours I try to make it a point to get in some exercise a few times a week. Though I haven't lately. Quinn's been too much of a distraction, in a good way of course.

It's early Tuesday morning, and I don't think Quinn is awake yet. I'm not actually sure what time she gets up and heads out for work, and I don't want to call or text and risk waking her up in case she's still asleep. I stretch my arms out once more, knowing I'm going to be sore for going back into my workout routine hard instead of easing in after a few weeks away. I'll probably stick with it this week and fall off the wagon again, but that's more than fine with me if it means I get to be with Quinn.

Sam worked late last night and is still sleeping. I quietly move throughout the apartment and get something quick to eat and then take a shower. Quinn texted me while I was in the shower, asking if I was up yet. I text her back and she calls a few seconds later.

"You're up early," I say as soon as I answer.

"I'm going out for breakfast with Marissa. She's a friend from work. You met her, actually. That day you came to the office with my bitchy secretary."

"Oh yeah," I say with a laugh. "Funny how that all worked out."

"It really is," she says and the sound of silverware clanking together floats through the phone. And then her cats meow, and I assume she's feeding them before heading out. "When you think about it, it's weird, actually. If you hadn't gone out to lunch with someone from that convention, you wouldn't have run into my secretaries. They wouldn't have brought you back to the office party and I wouldn't have seen you."

And I wouldn't have taken her out and she wouldn't be pregnant. For years she's been right in front of me, in sight but out of reach. It took a crazy push from the universe to finally get us together. "Shit, that is weird to think about."

"Rene is jealous we went out," she tells me. "She doesn't realize all the emails she sends are on the company server."

"That's kind of funny. You know I never intended on hooking up with her, right?"

"Yes, Archer," she says with a laugh. "You told me. And I told you, don't feel bad for the past. I've had boyfriends, you've had girlfriends. I might have even had a girlfriend or two. It's nothing to—"

"What? You had a girlfriend."

"Not in that sense."

"Darn. But thanks, Quinn." She's the most understanding person on the planet, and I'm hit again with a sense of wonder of how lucky I am that she's with me.

"Though if you did hook up with her, I'd totally judge you. Hard."

"I'd judge me too." I hear the beeping of her alarm system as she arms the house and closes the door behind her. "How's your wrist?"

"It hurts," she says honestly. "And I'm not able to wrap it as well as you did."

"You can switch to a brace if that's easier. The most important thing is to rest it as much as possible so it can heal."

"I'm trying, though I never realized how much I used it until I couldn't. I'm right-handed, but I sure do use my left hand a lot."

"Playing with your sex toys, right?"

"It is my masturbating hand."

"God, I miss you, Quinn."

"You're working this weekend, aren't you?"

"I am."

"I have to go over a week before I can see you again?" she blurts, and I can tell she immediately feels bad. "It's fine. I'll send you naughty pictures. We can FaceTime, and I found a website that does the casting to make your penis into a sparkly dildo."

"Well, now I know what to get you for your birthday."

"My birthday is too far away. I want your sparkly peen now. Oh shit. I just walked past a neighbor in the hall and she totally heard me," Quinn adds quietly. I start laughing, imagining her pretty face and the blush coming over her cheeks. "That lady is an uptight bitch too and has this nasty little Pomeranian that tries to bite anyone walking by. The thing is so old. I don't know how it's still alive."

"Living in an apartment is fun, isn't it?" I joke. "Though I can't really complain. No one here is too bad. Sam is probably the one they can't stand."

"I heard that!" Sam calls from the kitchen and I laugh.

"I lose service in the elevator," Quinn says. "Call me later?"

"Yeah. I will around lunchtime. I have back-to-back procedures until then."

"Save lives, Dr. Jones."

"Bye, babe. Have a good day." *I love you.*

MY BROTHER IS TWO FLOORS DOWN FROM ME, AND I HAVE NO desire to see him. I should have brought him to a different hospital. Fuck, I'm a terrible person, aren't I? My parents are here as well, and we're meeting for lunch. Before I go to the hospital cafeteria, which has decent food, I go outside in a staff-only courtyard and call Quinn. She doesn't answer, and I'm leaving her a message when she calls back.

"Hey, Arch," she says and my heart lurches at the sound of her voice. "Sorry. I had my music up too loud to hear my phone ring."

"Aren't you at work?"

"Yeah. I listen to music in my office and sometimes play it through the speakers so everyone else has to suffer and listen to it."

"What are you listening to today?"

"The Descendants Two soundtrack. It's a made-for-TV Disney movie that I'm a little obsessed with. And I'll just say it's because of Jackson if anyone asks."

"He doesn't like it, does he?"

"He hasn't even seen it," she laughs. "How's everything going today? Did you save any lives?"

"If it turns you on, then yes. Though everything I've done today was prescheduled, so no one was in danger. And Bobby...he's back to his old self. Bugging nurses and begging for pain pills. What about you? Did you finish the Batmobile yet?"

"You can't rush art. But I did find a flaw in the system for another part of the project that has to pair with what I'm working on, and I'll just say the people we're making this for were really impressed. It was their guys who messed up."

"That's amazing," I tell her, wishing she was at liberty to discuss her project. She hinted it was for the government and that she had to sign NDAs in order to work on it. Though even if she did explain it, I doubt I'd understand.

"You know how you like to tell everyone you're a doctor?"

"Yeah."

"Well, in my line of work, women are still in the minority for holding positions like I do, and I love when I get to show off how smart I am to a room full of arrogant men who think I'm not as good as them just because I have a vagina."

"I didn't realize you face adversity."

"Oh yeah, we women still do. It's getting better, and it could be worse. Women of color have an even harder time, and it's such bullshit."

Quinn's always been one to stand up for equal rights, and I think having four older brothers just proved to her how she can do anything they can do, and most of the time do it better.

"Anyway, the head of that team is taking me out to dinner tomorrow and wants to introduce me to a professor friend. I kind of feel like Harry Potter going to a Slug Club dinner party, but I'm also at prime laziness right now and am already dreading being out past my bedtime."

I didn't think it was possible to be any more attracted to Quinn than I already am, but she wins me over more and more every time we talk. "If you're trying to get a memory from this guy so you can defeat a dark wizard, don't be so obvious."

"I'll do my best. Oh, tell your parents I said hi. My mom is even more excited knowing your mom is excited and wants to know if it's okay if I pass along her number."

"Yeah, my mom would love that actually. I'll text you her contact info. They can plan parties to their hearts' content."

"My mom sent me at least a dozen pictures today. It's kind of annoying, but I'm kind of having fun too."

"You should have fun. Don't feel like you can't enjoy this or shouldn't celebrate because of the way things came about."

"I do feel that way," she says, and I can hear relief in her voice. "I didn't even want to admit it to myself, but I do."

"I could tell. This wasn't planned, but I know for sure we're going to have an awesome kid."

"Yeah. I think so too." I can tell she's smiling as she talks. "Oh, I almost forgot to tell you. I'm going in for that blood work next Friday, and we should get the results back within a week. And my insurance covers it completely."

"That's great. The time is going to go by slow now," I say, not realizing just how anxious I am to find out what we're having.

"I know. It is. But I did narrow down my names. Can I run them by you?"

"Of course."

"Emma and Aiden."

I consider each one, mentally pairing it with my last

name. Emma Jones sounds nice, but I'm not a fan of Aiden. I open my mouth to tell Quinn that only to snap my jaw shut. We haven't talked about last names. I want the baby to have mine, and I hope and pray one day Quinn does too.

But I'm not proposing now, and suggesting that I think we might someday maybe get married isn't a strong enough argument. Besides, Quinn wants to take things slow and I know she's worried about dating just because we're having a baby.

"I like Emma," I finally say. "Aiden...I don't dislike it, but I don't like it."

"Do you have any names picked out yet?"

"Not yet. I'll narrow it down. Or if you want to keep giving me names, I'll veto until we come to an agreement," I joke. Though that's not a bad idea. Naming a kid is a lot of pressure.

"Dammit. I have to go. A client just called."

"Okay, take care, babe."

"You too. I'll call you later." I hang up, wishing I didn't have to work this weekend. It's going to be a long week without Quinn. Turning my face up to the sun, I close my eyes and sit still for a moment. I don't get outside as much as I should. I'm also most likely dehydrated from standing in the hot OR most of the day, overtired, and I don't eat as healthy as I should. For someone who makes a living taking care of others, I take shitty care of myself.

"Dr. Jones?" someone calls, and I open my eyes to see Elena coming out of the hospital with her lunch in hand.

"Hey, Elena."

"How's your girlfriend doing?" she asks and takes her food and sits at the opposite side of the picnic table than me.

"She's good."

Elena pulls out her salad. "That's good. Congrats again, and sorry if I seemed surprised. It doesn't seem like that long ago you were telling me you didn't want anything serious."

I didn't want anything serious with her. I didn't want anything serious with anyone I dated prior to Quinn. But I can't tell her that. "Things changed."

Elena nods. "Yeah, they do. She's really pretty. Your girlfriend, I mean."

"Thanks. And she is." I want to soak up another few seconds of sun but sitting here with Elena is awkward. Now I get why dating people from work is frowned upon.

"Congrats again."

I nod and get up. "Thanks, and thanks for taking good care of Quinn." Faking a smile, I go back inside. I can hear Sam's voice in my head telling me it's my fault for shitting where I eat. For once I think he's right.

I'm stopped again, but this time it's by Dr. Miller, one of the attending surgeons I worked under.

"Fancy seeing you here." She raises her eyebrows and smiles.

"It's a shock, right?"

She laughs. "I've been meaning to find you all week. I went to a conference over the weekend. Dr. Crawford was there, and he asked about you."

"He did?" I ask, unable to hide my shock. Dr. Crawford is a renowned surgeon offering a highly competitive trauma fellowship. I hardly got a few words in with the guy. I'm honestly surprised he remembered me at all, let alone got an impression.

"Yes. And I told him you are one of the most promising resident surgeons I've seen in a long time. He was quite impressed to know you were performing Whipples indistinguishable from your attending."

We start moving down the hall.

"Don't tell him that mine were better," I joke, though it's true.

"I'm happy to write you a letter of recommendation," she goes on. "If you do apply for the fellowship—and I think you should—let me know. I hate to see you leave my hospital, but you're a damn good surgeon. This is the right path for you."

"Thank you, Dr. Miller."

She gives a curt nod. "Of course."

We go in opposite directions, and as I get into the elevator to go to the cafeteria, my head starts to hurt. My very first thought was to call Quinn and tell her the good news. Only...is this news good? Following my career goals has been everything to me. Surgery has been my life for the last several years, and I've been dedicated to being a doctor since I got into college.

It was my life.

Do I really want to work long, crazy hours for two or three more years? I'll have to start a job search after that, and who knows where I could end up. Though with the more schooling I get, the more I'll earn and the easier it'll be to find a place that'll want me.

Yes, all that was my life before. But now my life has something greater in it, and for the first time ever, I'm completely torn on which way to go.

9

QUINN

I take off my heels and reach inside my dress, unclasping my bra. It's Wednesday night and I just got back from dinner. I'm dying to call Archer and let him know how things went, but he went in for surgery an hour before I left and said he'd call once he was out, and I still haven't heard from him. I never realized how much surgeons work until I started dating Archer. No wonder they make so much money.

I slip my bra off, breathing in relief as soon as it hits the ground. I turn on the TV and feed the cats, then sink down on the couch with my phone in hand. Dad texted me during dinner, asking how I was feeling. I reply to him and search through Netflix for something to watch.

I'm dozing off when my phone rings. It's still on silent from dinner, and it takes me a minute to locate it under the blanket I'm snuggled up in. It doesn't help that Neville's fat butt is laying on top of it.

"Wes?" I mumble when I see his name. It's late. Why is he calling me? Panic instantly sets in and I answer quickly, bringing the phone to my ear.

"Hi, Aunt Winnie," Jackson's little voice comes through the phone. Oh, thank God. Nothing is wrong. He just took Wes's phone and called me. He does this from time to time.

"Hey, buddy. What are you still doing up?"

"Daddy had to catch bad guys. I was at Grammy's house."

"I bet you had fun. Are you supposed to be asleep?"

"I don't know."

"Where's your dad?" I ask with a laugh. Jackson doesn't answer me, and I hear him shuffling around. Then the phone beeps as he FaceTimes me. Seeing his face makes me instantly smile.

"You look pretty, Aunt Winnie."

"Awww, thanks, Jackson. And you look cute."

He scowls. "I'm not cute. I'm handsome like Daddy."

"Oh, you are for sure. You're growing up too fast, mister."

He starts showing me his new toys and a minute later Wes comes in, asking who he's talking to.

"Oh, hey, Quinn," he says, taking the phone.

"Glad it's just me?"

Wes widens his eyes and nods. "Yeah. It could have been you-know-who. Though I don't know if that's even her number anymore."

He's talking about his wife, who ran out on them two years ago and hasn't been seen or heard from since. I'm not one to hate people, but I fucking hate that bitch Daisy.

"You're dressed up," Wes comments. "Did Archer take you out?"

"No, I went out with a rich old guy and his boyfriend," I say seriously.

"That's interesting. Did they at least buy you an expensive dinner?"

"My meal alone was over a hundred bucks. If I could

drink wine, I would have ordered the three-hundred-dollar glass."

Wes laughs. "Sounds nice. I'm guessing it was for work?"

"Yeah. And the boyfriend is actually a professor at MIT. Not one I had, but he remembers me and wants me to come speak at graduation next year."

"Wow, that's awesome, sis!"

"Thanks. I'm not sure if I'll do it. You know how I hate people and public speaking, and graduation will have both." I shift my weight, getting comfy on the couch. I need to get up and shower, but I'm too tired to move. And Neville is snuggled up with me. It's basically a crime to move him. "But, I know how encouraging it can be to hear my tale or whatever."

"So you agreed to it?"

I wrinkle my nose and nod. "I have a year to fret over this. Maybe I'll get Archer to prescribe me Xanax or something."

Wes laughs. "Logan said things are going good between you and Archer."

"Yeah. Very good." I'm unable to keep the smile off my face when I think of Archer. Jackson tries to take the phone back, jibber-jabbering away about how he likes playing cars with Archer. Wes tells him he can't have the phone, and a crying fit breaks out. Hardly able to hear anything over the fuss, I tell Wes and Jackson goodnight and hang up.

It takes me another twenty minutes to muster up the energy to get up and get into the shower. My thoughts are on Archer and I bring my hand down, sweeping it over my clit. It sends a jolt through me, and I rinse off quickly, wrap a towel around myself, and get into bed. Reaching over to my nightstand, I open the top drawer to find my vibrator that I keep stashed under a folded pile of old t-shirts I never wear.

And then Archer calls. I pull the covers up over me just enough to stay warm and answer.

"Perfect timing," I say, closing my eyes and thinking of Archer's body on mine.

"For what?" he asks, and his deep voice turns me on even more.

"I just got out of the shower and am really horny. I was going to pleasure myself."

"Fuck, Quinn." Archer lets out his breath. "I'm still at work."

"That's not my problem. I'm at home. In my bed. Naked and wet from the shower."

"You're killing me, you know that, right? I can't go back into the OR with a hard-on."

I giggle. "I'll wait until you're off the phone to start then. I don't want you to get in trouble for rubbing one out in the break room or something."

"I might not even get that far. Fuck, I want your pussy."

"Keep talking like that, Dr. Jones, and I won't be able to wait. Actually, are you done with work yet? You were in surgery for a really long time."

"Six and a half hours," he sighs. "Perforated bowel from a bike accident. It was a mess."

"Is the patient okay?"

"He will be. I fixed him up."

"You're not done for the day though?"

"Not yet. I have to do rounds on my patients. I had to take a break and get something to eat. And talk to you."

"I could totally make a joke about me and eating, but I want you to be able to concentrate on work."

"Thanks, though the visual is there now and it makes me miss you even more."

"That was my mission. To make you miss me and give you blue balls."

"Mission accomplished," he says and puts something in the microwave. "You know a good thing about having my parents in town? My mom brought me dinner."

"That is nice. I miss my mom's cooking."

"Speaking of dinner," Archer says. "How was dinner?"

"Good!" I cuddle down under my covers and tell him about it. Then he's paged and has to hurry back inside to the OR. I trade my phone for my vibrator and think of Archer.

I SIT AT MY DESK, DRUMMING MY FINGERS ON THE SURFACE AS I scan through a file that was just sent to me. It's nearing lunchtime, and I'm both starving and nauseous. Again. Supposedly this feeling will go away, but right now, I'm convinced it's my new normal and I'll always feel like I'm going to throw up, even after this kid is born.

Archer is off today and is hopefully still sleeping. He texted me on his way home, which wasn't until two a.m. I didn't see his text until I got up in the morning. I forgot the Zofran at home this morning, and I don't think I can win this battle against my sour stomach. Leaning back in my chair, I debate on getting up and barfing in the bathroom or staying here and hope no one sees me leaning over the trashcan next to my desk.

Closing my eyes, I rest a hand over my stomach and pray neither has to happen. My office phone beeps. Feebly, I reach up and hit the button to put it on speaker.

"Ms. Dawson?" Charlene's overly sweet voice rings out. She uses what Marissa and I call her 'office-fake' voice when she calls me.

"Yes?" My eyes are still closed, and I don't move.

"There's a delivery for you."

"Can you bring them back?" Normally, I'll go up and get any sort of delivery myself, but barfing in the lobby wasn't on my list of options.

"I'll be right there."

I take a deep breath, grab my water and take a few small sips and feel a bit better. I expect the delivery to be a computer part I ordered yesterday, not a big bouquet of yellow and white flowers. I don't need to read the card to know they're from Archer.

"You must have a secret admirer," Charlene says as she sets the vase down.

"He's not secret." I'm smiling as I stand, reaching for the card. "He's my boyfriend."

"I didn't realize you were dating anyone." Her fake voice reaches a new level of pitch. "Is it Jacob again?"

I open the little envelope and pull out the card. If I were dating anyone else, it wouldn't seem weird to mention him. Though given the fact Rene is Charlene's best friend and she tried to hook up with Archer, it feels like I'm name dropping in a way. "No." I look up and smile. "It's Archer."

She blinks, trying to put things together. Archer isn't the most common name, but it's not unheard of either.

"The guy we introduced you to?"

It was obvious Archer and I knew each other before then, but that's the kind of subtle bitch Charlene is.

"I've known Archer for years. He's my brother's friend and we recently started going out."

"Oh. Nice." She waits for me to continue, but there's nothing more to say to her. She's never cared about my personal life and the same with me about hers.

"Thanks for bringing the flowers back here."

She fakes another smile before leaving, and I sit back down, feeling slightly less nauseous with the distraction of the flowers, and read Archer's card.

Quinn-

Ten years ago I overheard you say roses are cliché. I hope you still think so.

-Archer

I read the card three times, smiling harder each time. I center them on the accent table that sits in front of a large window and call Archer.

He answers after three rings and sounds like he just woke up.

"I got the flowers. Thank you."

"You're welcome. Don't go crying on me now."

I blink back tears. "I can't help it. It's all the hormones."

Archer laughs softly. "As long as we don't talk about eagles you should be fine, right?"

"Don't get me started on that," I laugh. "When did you have time to send me flowers? You've been working nonstop."

"Yesterday."

My heart swells in my chest and the doubts I had about my feelings start to go out the window. "Thank you again. It made my day and now I can't stop smiling."

"That's what I hoped for."

"Did I wake you? I'm sorry if I did."

"You didn't. My mom called about half an hour ago and woke me up."

"Is everything okay?"

"Yeah," he says, and I can hear the annoyance in his voice just from one little word. "Bobby is being released. They're taking him back home and getting him into rehab again."

"Well, that's good, isn't it?"

"It's pointless," he sighs, and a few seconds of silence tick by. "How are you feeling today?"

"Like I'm going to throw up at any second," I confess. "I forgot the Zofran at home too."

"I'm sorry, babe. What about your wrist?"

I look down at the messily wrapped ACE bandage. "Still the same." It's actually a little worse, but I don't want to tell Archer that and make him feel bad. It's my fault anyway. I unwrapped it and tried to type. I'm a fast typer and only using one hand is annoyingly slow. We talk for a while longer until I have to get back to work.

When I do, I have a hard time concentrating. Time goes by slowly, and when the end of the day arrives, I'm so ready to go home. I'm debating on taking the flowers home or leaving them here when someone knocks on my office door. Turning around, I see Jacob. He waves and steps in.

"Hey. I didn't expect to see you here," I say.

"I was passing by and was hoping to talk to you." He leans against the wall, eyeing the flowers behind me.

"Sure. What about?"

He flashes a smile, looking a little nervous. "Do you have plans tonight? I hoped we could talk about it over dinner."

"She has plans with me," Marissa says, peering into my office from the hall. "Sorry. I mean, if you want to crash our girls' night, you can. But be prepared to talk about periods and how awful men can be."

Jacob turns and I mouth *thank you* to Marissa. "Oh, I don't want to infringe."

"Another time," I say and then realize that might be leading him on. Though I don't know why going to dinner, paying for my own food, and talking and having a nice time as friends is leading him on. Men can be friends with women. Not all men look at women as sexual objects put here to tempt them into eternal damnation.

"Okay," Jacob says with a smile. "I'll be out of town for the next few weeks, so I'll get ahold of you when I get back."

"If you're taking a long vacation I'm totally jealous."

"One of those few weeks is vacation. I'm leading a training group in California."

"Fun."

He makes a face. "I know, right? Now, if this were January and I got to go away somewhere warm, that would be a different story."

I trade my shoes for a more comfortable pair to walk in and grab my purse. Jacob takes a step back and walks along with me to the lobby. Marissa is waiting, and the three of us get in the elevator together, along with a handful of others. I get slight anxiety when so many people cram in. Just wait for the next one. It's not like it's that long of a wait. If we got stuck all crammed in here like sardines, I'd probably have a panic attack.

Jacob goes the opposite direction, and I thank Marissa again.

"No problem. But I really do think we should do something tonight."

"Want to come over? I have a lot of wine I can't drink and I kind of want to order a pizza."

"You had me at wine."

I PUT MY HAND OVER MY STOMACH, FEELING THAT DULL ACHE come back. It's not sharp or shooting like it was before, which matched the description of round ligament pain that I read about on the internet. It's more like an impending period cramp mixed with an I-have-to-poop kind of cramp. Having a crampy stomach when I need to go isn't anything new for me, but right now, I'm having a hard time distinguishing which part of me is actually hurting.

Marissa just left, and I'm doing laundry while talking to Mom on the phone. She's checking in like she always does, and only mentions the gender reveal party fifty times. I fold the last of my towels and set the stack on top of my coffee table. Luna jumps up and sits on them, knocking the stack over. I purse my lips and look at her, shaking my head.

"So," I interject the moment there's a lull in the conversation. "I met Archer's brother."

"Robert? How's he doing? I feel bad to say I haven't asked about him in years."

"Not too well. I didn't know how bad off he was. Why didn't you ever tell me?"

"I wouldn't say we deliberately didn't tell you, but it didn't directly concern you and you were rather young when Archer first started staying with us."

I look at Neville and roll my eyes. My parents and my brothers have always been overprotective. Though I'm being biased right now because Archer is my boyfriend.

"And Archer never wanted to talk about it. I never knew the full details, honey."

"Oh, I thought you did."

"He let us know what was going on the first time he stayed with us, and we could tell how uncomfortable it made him to talk about it. We told him he didn't need to explain. He knew he was welcome whenever, and Dean would simply text me and tell me if he was bringing Archer back with him when he left home. We knew Robert struggled and didn't want Archer to feel like he owed us an explanation."

And now I'm suddenly emotional by my mother welcoming Archer with no questions asked. I hope I'm at least half as good a mother as she is.

"Boots!" Mom yells at one of her dogs. "Drop it. Drop it. I said *drop it*." Dog tags jingle and one of the other dogs bark. "He's been terrible with getting things out of the garbage lately."

That's why I like cats. They're much easier.

"I'm going to have to call you back." Mom sighs heavily. "I need to pick up this trash before your father gets in the house. Love you, honey."

"Love you too."

I hang up, thinking about what Mom said, and it hits me hard again just what Archer gave up for me. And I swear, I'll do whatever I can to make things right between Dean and Archer again.

10

ARCHER

I haven't seen Quinn in over a week, and when we met a week ago, it was brief. She was finishing a project and I was doing back-to-back call shifts. We've talked and texted every day, and FaceTimed as often as we could. I miss her like crazy, and now I agree that absence makes the heart grow fonder.

I just got done working a long shift, and I'm hot and sweaty from standing in the OR for the last surgery I performed. It took twice as long as we expected; once I opened the guy up, I realized the damage was much, much worse than anticipated. It was a tense process, and I'm so fucking grateful I had my preferred team working with me.

"You ready to go get some pussy now?" Sam asks, pulling his scrub top over his head. We're in the locker room, changing out of our surgery scrubs.

"I've been ready since the last time we said goodbye."

Sam shakes his head. "I couldn't do long-distance."

"You don't do long-term."

"That is true. Maybe someday I'll knock up a chick and be forced to settle down."

He's joking, but his words hit a nerve. Sam has a special way of doing that to pretty much everyone. He knows I've liked Quinn for years. He encouraged me to 'fuck her out of my system' weeks ago. *I'm* not being forced, but the worry that Quinn is becomes salient in my mind again. "We're not being forced."

"I'm just giving you shit," he says, able to see the question in my eyes. "She's crazy about you."

I toss my surgical scrubs in the laundry and tuck in my shirt. I have to do rounds with patients and meet with another for a consultation before I can leave. I've been here all night and I'm tired, my shoulders are sore, and I want off my fucking feet.

"And she's good for you, man," Sam says, checking his hair in the mirror. I hang my stethoscope around my neck. "She's hot, smart, and rich. All things I love about a woman."

"Glad you have your priorities in check." Quinn is so much more than that, and I'm feeling even more anxious to see her now. She knows I worked a long-ass shift and thinks I'm going home to sleep for a decent six hours before heading out. We're meeting in Eastwood and are staying at her parents' house for the weekend. We haven't seen her family since we told them about the baby, and Quinn has some sort of grand plan to get Dean to stop being an asshole.

Sam and I stop in the breakroom for water, the whole surgical team makes it a point to stay hydrated between operations, and then I go out to the PACU to check on my patients.

Doing patient rounds, reviewing nurses' notes, and writing in new orders takes a long time, but hey, at least I'm sitting down at a desk for a while. Then I meet with another patient, a nineteen-year-old girl who needs her gallbladder removed and finally do one last check-in with the guy I sliced open hours ago. I'm a bit concerned about his vitals, and probably annoy the on-call surgeon by going over things twice.

Finally, I go home, shower, pack my shit for the weekend, and take a power nap. Quinn was leaving for Eastwood this afternoon, only having to work a half day at the office. She thinks I'll be sleeping the whole afternoon, but I have a different idea.

———

I PUT MY JEEP IN PARK AND GET OUT, FEELING THE HOT summer sun beat down on me already. Dogs run along the fence of the Dawsons' yard, barking and wagging their tails. I go around and grab my bag from the passenger side. Quinn left Chicago not that long ago and should be here in an hour or less.

I've never been this excited to see someone before.

The gate creaks open, and I look up, seeing Mrs. Dawson trying to sneak out of the fenced-in yard without the dogs escaping. There's four of them, and Carlos, the smallest, slips right past and runs full speed at me, jumping up with excitement. I set my bag down and pick him up, hoping he doesn't get too excited and piss all over me.

"Archer!" Mrs. Dawson exclaims, tying a sheer wrap around her waist. She's wearing a big floppy hat and a swimsuit. Country music softly floats through the yard, and the smell of sunscreen and chlorine permeate the air. It instantly takes me back to the summers I spent here, stealing glances of Quinn in her bikini. I wouldn't dare let anyone know I was thinking of spreading her legs and burying my head in between. I hated that I was so attracted to her, and tried to shake it. Really, I did. She's four years younger than me, and while the age difference is nothing now, it was back then.

"I didn't think you'd be here yet." Mrs. Dawson pulls me in for a hug and takes Carlos, tucking him under her arm. "Quinn said you wouldn't make it until this evening."

"That was the plan, but I wanted to surprise her."

A big smile spreads over Mrs. Dawson's face. "She's going to love that. I happen to know she misses you quite a bit."

"I miss her too."

"Come in." She turns and motions for me to follow her back through the gate. The Dawsons have the perfect set-up, looking like something straight from a movie about the all-American family. Their house is a century-old farm house that Quinn's dad restored himself. Well, with the help of his construction crews that is. The in-ground pool and the covered patio are new additions of course. Dean and I spent a lot of time out here in the summer, and it didn't take long to realize how easy it was to get the small-town girls to come back to the pool with us when I dropped the 'I'm going to med school' line on them.

But with the fun aspect aside, something else always struck me. This house is the heart of the Dawson clan, the place where everyone still gathers as a family. If I hadn't seen it firsthand, I don't know if I'd think it's possible. As loving and caring as my own parents are, things didn't work out this well for us.

How the fuck did the Dawsons raise five kids who turned out better than okay?

"Are you hungry?" Mrs. Dawson asks, going to the radio on the patio table. She turns down the volume and grabs a towel, calling Chrissy over. The dog is in the pool again, splashing around as she plays with a floating rubber ball. She comes running, shaking off before she gets to us.

"I'm always hungry," I answer.

"I'll make you something. What do you want?"

"You don't have to make anything."

"Nonsense." She towels Chrissy off only to have the dog take off running and jumping back in the pool. "You can stay out then," she says to the dog and hangs the towel up in the sun to dry.

"Did you come straight from work?"

I'm wearing blue scrubs that have *Archer Jones, M.D.* embroidered above the right pocket. "Kind of. I went in to check on a patient before I left." I technically didn't need to wear the scrubs just to go in—and I'm glad I did. My patient's vitals weren't where I want them to be, so I had him moved to the ICU for closer monitoring. But scrubs are comfortable and wearing my 'doctor clothes' is a bit of an inside joke with Quinn.

We move inside, and I put my bag down and join Mrs. Dawson in the kitchen. She pulls out leftovers, and she asks me about work as I eat. Then she calls Quinn to find out where she is, and she's only twenty minutes away.

"I actually need to run some errands," Mrs. Dawson says, letting the dogs in again. Chrissy is more or less dry this time. "It's up to you, but if I took your car, Quinn wouldn't know you were here until she walked in the house. And then you two can have some time to catch up before the house fills with people." She smiles, and I'm vaguely aware that she's leaving us alone so we can have sex.

"That's a great idea."

"Quinn likes surprises. And I think it's so sweet you came here early in the first place."

"I really care about her. I'd do anything to make her happy."

Mrs. Dawson smiles, eyes glistening. "I know you would." She pats my shoulder and goes to change. I finish eating and put my dishes away. I'm wiping down the counter when the dogs all run to the sliding glass doors barking.

"Knock it off," Mrs. Dawson scolds, coming back into the kitchen. "It's a bunny. Leave the poor thing alone." She picks up Boots, who's the leader of the barking, and puts him down on the couch. "They've been doing this all day. I swear that rabbit is teasing them on purpose."

I laugh and give Mrs. Dawson my keys. Once she leaves, I carry my stuff upstairs into Quinn's old bedroom, and brush my teeth. It's been fifteen minutes, and I'm literally watching the time tick by on my phone.

The dogs are at the back door, barking again. I go downstairs and see a little brown rabbit on the patio. It's staring in at the dogs, and I think it's teasing the dogs too. Yawning, I go to the couch and lay down, closing my eyes until Quinn gets here.

My heart speeds up when the garage door opens and closes. I stay on the couch, out of her direct line of sight.

"Hello?" Quinn calls and the dogs go crazy with excitement. "Mom?" Slowly sitting up, I watch her greet the dogs, going for Rufus first. Her long, brunette hair is in a messy braid that falls over her shoulder, and she's not wearing makeup. Little freckles dot her face, only visible in the summer from being out in the sun.

God, she's beautiful.

I get up, and the dogs take off, coming back over to me and giving me away. Quinn's eyes widen, and she gasps.

"Arch!" Her hands fly to her mouth. She's still wearing the brace on her left arm.

"Surprise."

And now I can't get to her fast enough. She throws her arms around me and I pick her up, spinning her in a circle.

"What are you doing here? Wait. Kiss me now. Talk later." She puts her mouth to mine, and once I start kissing her, I can't stop. I pick her up and put her on the counter, hands running all over her body. "Archer," she moans, and I suck at her neck. "Mmmm...Archer."

Her hands land on my shoulders. I bite the flesh on her neck. She squeezes her legs around me and arches her back, pressing her breasts against me.

"Archer."

Blinking, I lean back. "Is something wrong?"

"No. Not at all. But I really have to pee."

"Oh." I step back and help her off the counter. "I got carried away."

She runs her eyes over me. "Me too. Especially in those doctor clothes."

I laugh. "That's why I wore them. Though I have to say, you look much better in doctor clothes than I do."

"I think it was the lack of clothes." She wiggles her eyebrows and hurries to the bathroom. Letting out a breath, I step back, petting Rufus. Boots is at the window again, growling, which gets the other dogs going.

"What is going on?" Quinn asks once she comes out of the bathroom.

"There's a bunny outside."

Quinn rolls her eyes and laughs. "Such a threat."

"Your mom said they've been doing it all day."

Quinn comes back over to me and hooks her arms around my neck. "Speaking of, where is she? And where is your car?"

I clasp my hands on her waist. "She went out to run errands and took my car so you wouldn't know I was here."

"So you're saying we have some time alone?"

I bend my head down. "I'd fuck you even if we weren't alone."

Quinn moans, tipping her head up and looking me in the eyes. Her tongue darts out, wetting her lips. Slowly. Deliberately. And I can't wait anymore.

I scoop Quinn up and carry her upstairs. She grips me tight and doesn't let go. I fall onto the bed with her, my body moving over hers. I can't stay away. There's something magnetic about her, and no matter how hard I try, I can't resist.

Not that I want to.

Quinn widens her legs, welcoming me between. She rakes her fingers up my back and smiles deviously.

"I've dreamed about this, Dr. Jones."

"You dream about me?"

"Pretty much every night." She lets out a breath and bucks her hips. "And the whole *Grey's Anatomy* sex fantasy is something I want. Don't laugh."

"I definitely won't laugh. And feel free to call me Dr. McDreamy."

I don't laugh, but Quinn does, and I raise my eyebrows, trying to be serious. How is it possible to be so turned on, to have my cock begging to be balls deep inside of her at the same time as we're joking and laughing?

It's because I'm in love with this woman.

I brush loose strands of Quinn's hair out of her face and move back down to kiss her. She bunches up my shirt and I sit up so she can pull it over my head. Her lips part as she looks me over and seeing her getting hot and bothered by looking at me gets me going even more than I was before.

Dragging a hand over my chest, Quinn brings it down and cups my balls through my pants.

"I missed this," she whispers.

"It missed you too." I kiss her again, and feeling her body against mine is the best homecoming I could ever ask for. I knew I missed her but damn, having her here with me now makes me realize all over again how much it fucking sucks to be apart.

I pull down the short athletic shorts she's wearing and sweep my fingers over her clit. I can feel the heat through her panties, and she moans as soon as I touch her. My cock is so fucking hard, begging for a release. Normally, I like to tease Quinn. Draw things out. Make her quiver and beg for me to fuck her.

But I don't think I can hold out right now.

She lifts her ass off the mattress, letting me strip her bare. Kissing her lips once more before moving down, I pull her close and roll over, bringing her on top so I can unhook her bra.

"It clasps in the front," she breathes, taking her shirt off, revealing her breasts, which are held back by a white bra. She undoes it and tosses it on the floor. I take her breasts in each hand, remembering that she mentioned being overly sensitive thanks to pregnancy hormones.

"I think your tits got bigger, babe."

"They did." She looks down, putting her hands over mine. "All my bras are tight." She flashes a smile. "I like it."

"I do too."

Quinn does a little shimmy, wiggling her eyebrows at me. "You do? You like this?"

I flip her over and move down, flicking my tongue over her nipple as I make my way down to her sweet cunt. She settles back against the bed, preparing herself for what's coming.

Precum wets my boxers, and my balls are so tight it almost hurts. With more self-control than I knew was possible, I lick the inside of her thigh, moving my mouth closer and closer to her pussy. I flick my eyes to her face before diving in, eating her out. Quinn moans and moves her hips against my face, wanting it rougher than I usually give it to her.

I slide my hands under her ass and lift her off the mattress, lashing my tongue against her clit. Her breathing quickens and her hand lands on top of my head, fingers tangling in my hair. She pulls it hard, and nearly at the same time I feel her pussy spasm. I lower her back onto the mattress just so I can slip a finger inside her, going to her g-spot.

"Ohhh fuck," she mumbles, pulling my hair again. She's moments away from coming. I speed up my movements, feeling close to blowing a load even though she's not touching me. Being with Quinn is like all my fantasies come to life—but better.

"Ohhh, Archer," she squeals, pussy contracting wildly. Wetness spills from her and I lick up every last drop, getting drunk on her. I set her back down and scramble on top of her. She's still reeling, eyes closed and breaths coming out in huffs. Her pert nipples rub against my chest, and she tries and fails to pull my pants down. Impatient, I pull them off and her hands land on my ass, pressing me against her core.

My cock rubs against her, and I swear I could come right here and now before I even push my big dick into her. Her eyes flutter open and she brings one hand up, running it through my hair.

The dogs start barking at the bunny again, but it's just

background noise to us. I align my cock with Quinn's entrance and kiss her as I push inside. She's so fucking tight, and feeling my cock rub against her inner walls makes me groan.

"Did you miss this, Dr. Jones?" she whispers, curling her fingers and pulling my hair again. "Did you miss my pussy?"

"I missed it so fucking much." I pull out slowly until only the tip of my cock is inside her. Bending my head down, I put my lips to hers again and thrust in deep and hard. Quinn's mouth falls open and she brings her legs up, wrapping them around my body. I pull back again and circle my hips as I push back in. Quinn rakes her nails up over my back hard enough to leave marks.

Her pussy tightens around my cock, and I know she's about to come. I let loose, pushing in and out as hard as I can. I held back and now that I want to come, it's going to take a minute again.

Quinn grips my hips and moves along with me. We're both close, and coming at the same time would be so fucking hot. I'm almost there and feel my balls tighten and the tip of my cock aches from pleasure. We're so wrapped up in each other everything else fades.

And I mean everything. Because neither of us heard anyone come in the house. Or up the stairs. I push in deep, seconds away from coming when the floorboards creak behind us.

"What the fuck?" someone yells, and I don't have to turn around to know who that voice belongs to.

It's Dean.

11

QUINN

"Get out of here!" I shriek and madly reach for the blankets. Archer is on top of me, with his bare ass right in my brother's line of sight. Archer freezes, and I pull his body down on mine once I realize we're on the blankets and I can't cover us up. I'm hidden underneath him but still too exposed.

Dean just walked in on us having sex.

It'd be bad enough to have any of my brothers catch me in the act, but it's a million times worse right now with Dean. This weekend was supposed to make him realize he and Archer can be friends again. That nothing has changed.

But seeing Archer balls deep inside his sister...yeah. Dean's not going to come around any time soon.

"Close your fucking door," Dean yells and slams my bedroom door shut. Archer's cock is still buried inside of me. My legs are still wrapped tightly around his body. I'm shocked. Stunned. Horrified and embarrassed.

Yet I'm not pushing Archer off me.

"Did that really just happen?" Archer whispers, still too stunned to move.

"It did." Fuck. It really did.

"Is it bad I want to finish?" Archer gives me a cheeky grin.

My head spins and my body is reacting to physical sensations. I *was* about ready to come for the second time, and while I'm still amped up and ready to go, my mind isn't. Not at all.

"I don't know," I tell him. He relaxes a bit, and his cock rubs in the right spot. "No, it's not bad at all."

Archer nods but doesn't start thrusting again. We're at a standstill, so to speak, with his cock inside me but not doing anything.

"Should I go talk to him?" Archer asks, and a line of worry forms between his eyes.

I tighten my legs around him, wanting to ease Archer's tension. "Give him a minute or two to cool down."

"Okay."

"You can finish."

Archer lets out a snort of laughter. "So romantic."

"Sorry. I'm trying not to let it ruin the mood."

"It kind of did." Archer starts to pull out. I grab his ass and push him back down.

"We haven't had sex in over a week. You're finishing."

He blinks. "No pressure or anything."

"I'll waive my multiple orgasm rule."

He slowly circles his hips. "It's a rule?"

"Mmm-hmm." I close my eyes, trying hard not to think about the look of horror on Dean's face. The door is closed but not locked. Though it's not like he's going to come back in.

Archer nuzzles his face against my neck. He thrusts in hard and fast, and it only takes a minute to forget about

Dean. Well, until Archer tells me to keep it quiet because we're not alone in the house anymore.

I nod, eyes falling shut. I angle my hips up, and Archer's cock rubs against my G-spot. I'm close to coming again, but also starting to get a little sore, thanks to pregnancy hormones no doubt. I move against Archer, helping myself out, and clamp a hand over my mouth as I come.

Archer pushes in deep, turning his head down and biting my neck as he finishes. My inner walls contract around his cock, and he lets out a groan, muffled by my hair.

"I didn't think I'd be able to come," Archer confesses, moving off me. "You're distracting." He grabs his boxers, quickly puts them on, and goes into the attached bathroom to get me a tissue. I clean myself up and dash to the bathroom to pee. When I come out, Archer is dressed again and sitting on the foot of the bed.

"Should we talk to him now?" Archer asks. "Hey," he says suddenly when I turn to pick up my clothes.

"Yeah?"

He strides over and puts his hand on my stomach. "You're starting to show."

"Can you tell it's a baby?" I put my hand over his and look down. "Marissa says I look like I ate a big meal."

Archer cradles me against him, splaying his fingers over my stomach. "I can tell it's a baby. *Our* baby."

I melt against him, and all the anxiety over my stupid brother goes away. Archer has a way of doing that with everything bad. It fades away until he's the only thing left.

"I'm excited to feel her kicking."

"Her? Did you look at the results?" he rushes out.

"No. I've been tempted," I confess. After giving blood last week, I got the results yesterday. I had the nurse go over everything else—baby is fine—but didn't tell me the sex. I had her write down 'boy' or 'girl' on a card and seal it in an envelope. Knowing myself and how hard it would be to resist temptation, I had her use thick paper so I couldn't hold it up to the light and try to see what she wrote.

Because I did.

"If it turns out to be a boy you'll have to get used to saying he," Archer laughs. "But I have a feeling it's a girl too. Probably because you refer to it as one."

"I blame my mom for putting that idea in my head." I bend over, purposely rubbing my ass against Archer's pelvis as I pick up my underwear. "She's the one who said it's a girl. It'll be nice to know either way so everyone can stop calling the baby 'it.' That's too impersonal."

"Yeah, it is."

I get dressed, run my hand through my hair, and apprehensively open the bedroom door. Rufus is at the top of the stairs, looking at me and wagging his tail. The rest of the house is quiet, and I start to feel sick as we walk down the stairs. The nausea hasn't faded at all. I don't think it ever will.

"Dean?" I call softly, seeing him in the kitchen. He's bent over his phone, no doubt texting our brothers to tell them what he just walked in on. I put on a fake smile and resist the urge to slap him upside the head. Archer and I are together. He needs to fucking deal with it.

Dean flicks his eyes up for half a second. "Good. You have clothes on now."

"I'm sorry," Archer blurts. If I could elbow him in the gut without being seen, I would. "We didn't know you'd be here."

"Quinn fucking invited me."

"Yeah, I did." I wrinkle my nose. I kind of forgot, though

I didn't think he'd show up this early. Our plans were for the evening. "We had dinner plans though."

"I came over early because I thought we could hang out or something. I felt bad for getting mad at you before and wanted to make it up to you."

I bite my lip. "Do you still feel bad?"

"Nope."

"Dean. Stop."

He shakes his head. "I've seen more of you than I ever wanted to see."

"Be glad I wasn't on top."

Dean responds with a glare. "Hilarious, Quinn." He sits back, shaking his head. "You said this weekend would feel like old times."

"You've walked in on me having sex before," Archer tries to joke. "And I've walked in on you."

"That was college. And not my sister." He shudders. "I can't unsee that."

"You're the one who came upstairs," I remind him.

"I didn't know Archer was here. Where's your car?" he asks.

"Mom has it," I tell him. "Archer got here early to surprise me and—it doesn't matter. You're acting ridiculous. Look, I'm sorry, okay? We didn't know you'd be here, so we didn't close the door. It's not that big of a deal."

"How'd you like it if you walked in on me and Kara?" he counters.

"I wouldn't like it, but I wouldn't sit there pouting like a baby."

"I'm not pouting. I'm scarred for life." He makes a face like he's going to throw up.

"Oh my God." I let out a sigh. "It's not like you walked in on Nana having a threesome."

"I'd rather see that."

"Really?" I put a hand on my hip. "You'd rather see Nana naked and sweaty getting groped by two sexy men?"

"Who says they have to be sexy?"

I narrow my eyes. "You're such an asshole."

"I'm not the one fucking my best friend."

"Grow up, Dean."

"You can't get mad that I'm upset about walking in on you two. I don't care who you're with, Quinn, I don't want to see it."

"And I said I'm sorry! Maybe Owen was right, and you do want Archer all to yourself. Well sorry, he doesn't swing that way!"

"Quinn," Archer says softly, hand landing on the small of my back. He's been around us enough to have seen a fight or two between me and one of my brothers. He knows how over the top and dramatic I can get. Though Dean is just as bad if not worse. When the two of us get into it, it's like a scene from *The Real Housewives* or something. We'll keep going until someone cuts us off. Usually, I'm mad at him for a few hours—maybe a day—and then we'll be back to normal. Things haven't been normal between us since I told him I'm pregnant. I've never had a feud going with any of my brothers for this long.

"That's a fucking low blow, Quinn. Even for you," Dean shoots back.

"Really? Because you're acting like you're jealous Archer won't play a private game of *Operation* with you right now."

"Guys," Archer says, stepping in front of me and looking right at Dean. "Quinn and I are together. We're having a baby. Don't like us being together? Fine. But you have to accept it and move on. If not for us, then for this kid." He slips his arm around my waist. "Stress isn't good for the baby, and I know this whole thing upsets Quinn. We just want you to support us."

He's trying to make things better with his best friend, and Mom's words echo in my head. Dean was there for Archer when no one else was. Dean and Archer being friends is part of life. They have to be friends again. I know Logan and Owen are dying to start up the bromance jokes again at least.

I open my mouth to tell Dean I'm sorry for overreacting, more than ready to pull the pregnancy card, but quickly clamp my hand over my mouth and close my eyes.

"Are you going to be sick?" Archer asks, stepping in closer. Most people move away when someone looks like they're about to throw up—myself included—but Archer does everything to comfort me. Tears burn behind my closed eyelids.

I feel so strongly for this man right now.

"I think I'm okay," I croak out.

"Go lay down upstairs." He brushes my hair back. "Do you want crackers?"

I nod, keeping one hand over my mouth, and go back upstairs to lay down. I discovered over the last week or two, that if I lay really, really still, the nausea isn't as bad. Problem is, I can't lay down and be motionless most places.

"Is she okay?" I hear Dean ask.

"She's had bad morning sickness since the beginning," Archer answers. "It sucks but it's nothing abnormal. But... no. She's not okay. I told you, this stupid shit upsets her more than she'll admit." The pantry door creaks open, and all the dogs go running. "Get the fuck over it. We're family now." There's venom in his voice, and I don't want him to be mad at Dean too. Being angry at Bobby is enough negativity for this wonderful man to have to deal with.

I get into bed, getting under the covers this time, and feel like I'm about to burst into tears. I'm such an emotional wreck, and I have six months left of this.

"Quinn," Archer whispers, and just hearing his voice calms me. "You okay, babe?"

"Yeah. Just tired. Mentally and physically."

He gets in bed with me. "Take a nap."

"Will you snuggle with me?"

"Of course." He's holding the bottle of anti-nausea pills, and I reluctantly take one. Archer yawns, and it's then I notice how worn out he looks. It's more than the long shifts. It's the stress of Bobby, Dean, and being away from me and the baby.

"Tired?" I ask.

"Yeah." He lays down and pulls me with him. We get under the covers this time and keep our clothes on. "I was in surgery before I came."

"I thought you were going to sleep before you drove."

He shrugs. "I was too anxious to see you."

I roll over and sit up, hands going to his shoulders, and start massaging his stiff muscles. He sighs happily, eyes falling shut. It only takes a few minutes before he's asleep. I lay down next to him, and in his sleep, he reaches out and puts an arm around me, hand landing on my stomach.

SOMEONE KNOCKS ON THE DOOR. MY EYES FLUTTER OPEN AND I sit up, blinking rapidly to try and focus my vision. I was in the thick of my nap and feel all groggy now that I've been woken up.

"Hey, sis," Owen calls. "You decent?"

"Yeah," I mumble and go to the door. I twist the knob and pull it open.

"You look like shit," Owen says as soon as I open the door. He grins and pulls me in for a hug.

"I was sleeping," I grumble, hugging him back. "What are you doing?"

"Mom asked Dean to come up and get you guys, but he was worried he'd catch you in the act again."

"Oh God." I bury my face in my hands. "I knew he'd tell you guys about it."

Owen laughs. "I'm glad I missed it, but I would have liked to have seen Dean's face. He's been downstairs pouting like a baby since we got here."

"That's what I said!" I shake my head. "He's being more dramatic than me and I'm the pregnant one."

"You're starting to look like it too."

"Did he tell Mom?"

"Probably in hopes you'd get grounded."

I let out a snort of laughter. "Why did Mom want us? Is dinner ready?"

"She says it is, but you know how Mom is. We'll sit around talking for half an hour before things are even close to being ready."

"Are Wes and Jackson here too?"

"Just Jackson. We picked him up on the way."

"I'm going to let Archer sleep," I say and close the bedroom door. "He was in surgery before he drove here. I know he's tired."

"So sweet," Owen teases and holds out his hand, letting me go down the hall first. The kitchen is bustling, and Jackson runs to me, jumping into my arms for a hug.

"Is Uncle Archer here?"

"Uncle Archer?" I raise my eyebrows and look at Mom. "Yeah, he's here. He's upstairs sleeping."

"Why's he sleeping? It's not dark yet."

"He works at night sometimes and is tired."

"Daddy works at night," Jackson says. "Does Uncle Archer work with Daddy?"

"Uncle Archer is a surgeon. He does operations," I add in case he doesn't know what a surgeon is.

Jackson's eyes widen. "Does he cut people open?"

"Yeah."

"Cool!"

I laugh and set Jackson down. He's getting heavy. Dean, Kara, and Logan are sitting at the island counter, eating the appetizers Mom always sets out as she's making dinner. It's nothing fancy, just chips and dip along with various cut up vegetables.

Logan flicks his eyes from me to Dean and makes a face, trying not to laugh. I shake my head, too irritated with Dean to feel embarrassed. Though it's not like it's a surprise Archer and I are sleeping together. I'm pregnant after all.

"Quinn!" Mom exclaims. She drops the spoon she's holding and rushes over.

I freeze, thinking she's going to tell me there's a spider in my hair or something. "What?"

"You have a bump!"

"Oh." My heart is still racing. I hate spiders. "Yeah. It just popped up overnight."

Mom puts her hand over my stomach. "You'll be able to feel the baby moving soon. It's the best feeling. Though it can get quite painful, especially in the end."

"I'm excited."

"You should be. I can't wait for tomorrow! But if you want to tell me what it is—"

"Mom," Logan interrupts. "She doesn't know either."

"I really don't. Neither does Archer," I assure her.

Mom takes her hand off my stomach. "Where is Archer?"

"Sleeping upstairs."

Logan gets up and goes to the fridge. "Why is he so tired?"

"Yeah," Owen goes on. "He must be pretty worn out."

"Stop it, you two," I say through gritted teeth.

Logan grabs two beers and gives one to Owen. "I don't know what you're talking about? I'm asking a simple question." He's not looking at me as he talks, but at Dean. Dean is staring at his phone, pretending to be so into whatever he's reading he doesn't hear them.

"Right," Owen says. "What *was* Archer doing earlier?"

Mom, who's oblivious to everything, picks up the spoon and goes back to the sauce she was stirring on the stove. "He told me he came from work. He was checking on patients."

"Yeah," Owen snickers. "I'm sure he was doing thorough exams."

"Seriously," I warn, shooting him my best *shut the fuck up* look. Taking a spot next to Logan, I reach over and grab a carrot. "How's wedding planning going?" I ask Kara, though that's a sore subject on its own.

"Good." She sets the bridal magazine she's looking at down and fakes a smile. If I haven't given birth by the time their wedding rolls around, there's a good chance I'll go into labor during the ceremony. She perks up, happy to talk about the wedding. "I finally picked the colors and I think I found my dress."

"Oh, that's exciting. Do you have a picture of it?"

"I do!" She pulls out her phone and comes around, not letting Dean see.

"It's gorgeous," I whisper. "You're going to look stunning."

"Thanks." She goes back to her spot and opens the magazine, showing me centerpiece ideas she likes. "I'm starting to go into panic mode though. We don't have much time and there's so much to do."

"You know we're here to help with whatever."

"Thanks," she says again. "We're leaning more towards something low-key yet elegant."

"I like that idea."

Kara smiles and looks down at the magazine again. "So far, we're thinking of having the ceremony in the late afternoon, then do pictures, a cocktail hour, and then the reception."

"That'll be really nice."

"We hope so. If only the weather would be nice then, right?"

"It can snow in March," Owen says.

"Everything is inside, so we should be fine," Dean finally speaks for the first time.

"I saw the new renovations to the venue on their website," I say. "It's so pretty."

"It's like a fairytale!" Kara agrees.

"I forgot to ask you, Quinn," Mom says and turns the burner off. "Is Jamie coming to the reveal tomorrow?"

"Yeah, she'll be here."

"I'm so excited for another grandbaby!" Mom beams.

Kara purses her lips together, annoyed talk of her wedding was interrupted with baby talk. It's going to be that way until the baby is born, and I can totally understand both her and Dean's frustration with it. It's their day, and they deserve to have it be about them.

Then again, I shouldn't have to downplay anything just

to spare their feelings. I sigh, putting my hand on my stomach. Can't we just all get along? Though really, having Dean's panties all in a wad over the fact his wedding and my due date are two days apart is nothing compared to the strained relationship between Archer and Bobby.

12

"Look at you!" Mom coos, going right for Quinn's belly. Quinn grins and bears it, and I mouth *sorry* to her, knowing she doesn't like to have her stomach touched. "That's a definite baby bump. She's so precious, Archer." Mom steps away, throwing her arms around me. She wasn't always overly affectionate, but seeing your eldest son repeatedly knock on death's door does something to you.

"She is," I agree. "I think I'll keep her."

"How are you feeling?" Mom asks Quinn, following us into the house. We're having dinner first, and Mrs. Dawson went all out with the food. This wasn't supposed to be a big ordeal. Quinn and I wanted our family and that's it, but it's grown to more of a party-party than a small dinner party. We woke up this Saturday morning to Mrs. Dawson bustling about the kitchen, starting the cooking and cleaning early.

I didn't expect my parents to come all this way down from Michigan, but Mom insisted she and Dad needed the break. Which they do. I haven't asked about Bobby but haven't been told he's dead or in a coma yet, so that's something.

"A little better," Quinn tells her. "Still sick, but it's worth it, right?"

"Oh, it is. And I feel like I should warn you. Both my babies were big. Archer was nine and a half pounds."

Quinn makes a face and I laugh, wrapping my arm around her waist. She's wearing a pale pink dress. It's form-fitting, showing off the little baby bump she has going on. We go into the house, and I reintroduce my parents to Logan, Owen, and Weston. They've only met once or twice before.

My phone rings, and I'm sure it's the hospital.

"Need to take it?" Quinn asks, looking at the caller ID.

"Yeah. I have a patient not doing well."

"Go." She motions to her dad's office. "It's quiet in there."

"Thanks," I answer, stepping into the office. Instead of bad news, the nurse is calling with current lab results and wants to know if I have new orders for her. I go over a few things, happy with the small progress my patient is making. When I go back to the party, I find Quinn in the kitchen, talking with both her mom and mine. She smiles as soon as she sees me and my heart swells in my chest.

"How's your patient?" she asks, reaching for my hand.

"He's doing better. I just had to go over lab work and give a few new orders."

"We were talking about you, you know," my mom says.

"Uh-oh. Do I want to know what you were saying?" I step closer to Quinn.

She laughs and tips her head up to mine. "We were just saying how proud we are of you."

Mom leans in. "I might brag about my son the surgeon, just a bit." She winks, and Bobby's words come crashing down on me. Yeah, I'm fucking proud of myself too. It takes hard work and dedication to get through med school. It takes skill and talent to be able to slice people open, remove and rearrange internal organs, and have them not only live but leave in better shape than when they came in.

I'm a good doctor.

I should be proud.

Dammit, Bobby.

Mrs. Dawson smiles and looks at Quinn. "It's nothing to be ashamed of. I brag about this one to anyone who'll listen. Though I have the hardest time explaining what she does."

Quinn laughs. "I have a hard time explaining it too. I've settled on calling myself a professional super nerd. But really, Arch, I am proud of you."

"Yes," Mom agrees. "And now you're almost done."

Quinn laughs. "Until he gets that trauma fellowship, which I'm sure he will."

The smile disappears from my mother's face. "More school? Even with a baby on the way?"

"It's not as long as a residency, right?" Quinn asks, and her hand subconsciously lands on her belly.

"Right. It's typically a year or two."

"Would you stay at the same hospital?" Mrs. Dawson asks.

"No. I'm not sure where I'd end up. I'd love to get in at a trauma center. The more injuries, the better. For learning, I mean," I say slowly, trying not to notice the way my own mother is looking at me. A year or two doesn't sound long compared to what I've already been through, but missing a year of my child's life...being away from Quinn...is it worth it in the end?

"I DIDN'T GET A CHANCE TO TELL YOU CONGRATULATIONS," Mom says to Dean. We're halfway through dinner and I'm getting full already. Everyone is crowded around the dining room table. It's just like college when Dean and I would make the drive here just for dinner. I put my hand on Quinn's thigh and turn to look at her. Maybe tonight I'll tell her—finally tell her—just how much she means to me.

She wants to take things slow, and I think we are. We're finding out what we're having today and are bordering on the second trimester. I don't know exactly what Quinn wants to expect. Whose last name is the baby going to take? Does she want to move in together?

If I get the fellowship, then that might not matter...

"Thank you," Dean says, taking Kara's hand to show off her ring.

"So when is the big day?"

Dean reaches for his water. "March sixteenth."

"Oh." Mom's eyes widen. "The day before Archer's birthday." And two before Quinn is due. Thank you, Mom, for not bringing it up. "How nice. Are you having it around here?"

Kara gives her details, and Dean does his best not to look up across the table or at anyone else for that matter. Jackson slides out of his chair and crawls under the table, ignoring Weston telling him not to, and comes over to Quinn.

"Hey, buddy," she says and sits him on her lap. He leans over, gently poking Quinn's belly. Then he looks at me and Quinn's belly again.

"Is that what Uncle Dean is mad?" he asks.

"What do you mean?" Quinn turns her head down to look at him.

"I heard Uncle Dean say Uncle Archer put a baby inside

you. But how? Did it hurt? Did you swallow it like a watermelon seed and now it's going to grow big and big and bigger?"

Quinn's mouth falls open and she looks at me for help. I have no idea what to say either, and I'm becoming more and more aware of everyone else staring at us.

"If she swallowed it," Owen starts, "then there wouldn't —" He cuts off when Logan kicks him hard under the table.

Quinn's cheeks are turning red, and everyone from her grandma to my dad are staring at her. Weston twists in his chair, glaring at his younger brother. "Why don't we let Uncle Dean explain this one since he's going around talking about it."

"Okay," Jackson says with a smile and looks at Dean. "Where did Uncle Archer get the baby? Why is it in Winnie's belly? Why didn't he just give it to her?" His brows furrow together and then he looks horrified. "How does it come out?"

Everyone sits in stunned silence for a good thirty seconds.

"Excellent questions," Mrs. Dawson says, getting up. She goes around the table and takes Jackson from Quinn and goes into the kitchen, saying something about chocolate.

"Really?" Kara whisper-yells at Dean, narrowing her eyes. She shakes her head and grabs her glass of wine, downing the whole thing in one go. The tension between the two of them is tangible, and Quinn is going back and forth between staring daggers at Dean and looking so embarrassed she might cry. Everyone is quiet, and as each second goes by, it's getting more and more awkward.

"So Archer," Logan starts, pushing his food around on his plate. "Do doctors really wear Crocs or is that a TV myth?"

"I do in surgery. They're comfortable and don't stain easily."

"Stain?" Jamie asks, looking past Quinn at me. "What are you walking in that'll stain your shoes?"

"It's not what I'm walking in. It's what might leak or splash on me during surgery or when I'm taking care of patients after. The worst I had was a wound drain somehow falling apart and splattering all over me."

"Gross," Quinn says, making a face. "How does that not gross you out?"

I shrug. "It just doesn't. I changed after, of course. Wound drains smell."

Owen shakes his head. "And I thought cleaning up puke at the bar on Sunday mornings was bad."

Quinn's mom and Jackson come back to the table. "Sounds like I'm missing a lovely conversation." She looks pointedly at the twins. "Though I will admit I was curious about the shoes too. You're on your feet for so long."

"What was your longest surgery, Archie?" Mom asks. "Ten hours?"

I nod. "That's my longest so far."

"Serious question," Mr. Dawson asks. "What do you do if you have to use the bathroom during an operation."

"You scrub out and go. If a surgery is rather long, there's usually another surgeon in there anyway. And during long procedures, I tell my team to take breaks if they need them. I'd rather have a nurse step out for five minutes than pass out from being dehydrated. It's usually hot in the OR."

Mr. Dawson playfully elbows his wife. "Still think those romance doctor shows are realistic?"

"Archer won't watch those with me," Quinn says with a laugh. "He critiques it the whole time."

Nodding, I smile at Quinn. "It drives me crazy."

The conversation comes back to the table, and the awkwardness fades away. Once we're done with dinner, Mrs. Dawson and my mother clear the table. I offer to help but am shooed away, being told to go sit with Quinn who started feeling sick. It was the first time in a while she ate everything on her plate and having a full stomach can make anyone not feel well.

Quinn is in the living room with Jamie, and I sit on the couch next to her. Quinn rests her head on my shoulder and I drape my arm around her body.

"You know what's weird to think about?" Quinn starts, stretching out her legs. "Like ten or twelve years ago, we could have been in this very spot. All of us."

"We used to bicker over who got to sit by you," Jamie laughs.

"I know," I tell them both. "I already told Quinn, but you two were obvious back then."

"I thought we were so sly," Jamie laughs. "It's crazy how things turned out."

"Yeah, it is." I lean over and give Quinn a quick kiss. She closes her eyes, and after a few minutes of resting, she feels better enough to get up and fix her hair before we open a box full of either pink or blue balloons.

As soon as Quinn leaves, my dad comes and sits next to me.

"Mom said you're thinking about a fellowship?"

"Yeah. For trauma surgery."

"Are you sure that's what you want to do?"

"It is," I assure him.

Dad just nods, and I'm sure he's thinking the same thing as Mom...which is what I'm thinking now.

"Where's Quinn?" Kara asks, coming into the living

room. "The box is out, and I can't promise Mrs. Dawson won't accidentally open it."

I laugh. "She went to fix her hair. I'll find her."

I leave the living room and get cornered by Quinn's grandmother, who openly hit on me the last time I spoke with her.

"Hello, doctor," she says and eyes me up and down. "Come here."

"I, uh, I need to find Quinn," I stammer.

"She can't know what we're doing."

Oh God.

"What?"

"Keep your voice down." She grabs my hand and pulls me forward. She's too old to be this strong. "Act natural if anyone comes in." We go into Mr. Dawson's office and Nana shuts the door behind us. I spent over ten years in school yet nothing has prepared me for this.

"Quinn is my only granddaughter," Nana starts. Wait. Quinn has two female cousins. "Well, the only one who's dating a man I tolerate. I more than tolerate you." She winks and reaches into the little sequined purse she's carrying. "Which is why I want you to have this."

I blink, staring at the ring in Nana's fingers. "It was mine," she says softly. "It's nothing fancy, and the ring won't fit Quinn. But I want you to have it, take the diamonds and make it into something Quinn would like."

I take the delicate ring, unable to say anything.

"I can tell you love her." Nana curls my fingers around the ring and pushes my hand away. "And call me old-fashioned—what have you—but you knocked her up. You should marry her."

Yes, she is old-fashioned. The problem isn't me not

wanting to marry Quinn. It's me not knowing if Quinn wants to marry me. Not yet at least.

"Take your time." Nana zips her purse. "But not too much time. I don't have much longer left to live." She gives me a wink and leaves the office. I'm stuck, rooted to the spot with Nana's ring clutched in my hand.

Blinking, I shake myself and put the ring in my pocket, a little worried I'll lose it. I have to take another minute to collect myself, and then I go find Quinn. She and Jamie come down the stairs as I'm coming up. Quinn's hair doesn't look any different to me, but she's glowing, and seeing her makes me feel like I did the first time I laid eyes on her.

Only now, she's mine.

I grab her by the waist and pull her in for a quick kiss. Fuck going slow. Quinn is mine...and I want her to be mine forever. I can feel the ring in my pocket, and I don't think I can go any slower. I want to propose to her tonight.

13

QUINN

I hate being the center of attention. Why did I agree to this? I can feel everyone's eyes on me, and my heart gets a little fluttery knowing at least four cameras are trained on us right now.

"Ready?" Archer asks, looking into my eyes. His are glimmering, and I think mine are too. I nod, and he puts his hand over mine. I'm supposed to be looking at the camera, smiling and making a point to have a nice photo taken. But I can't look away from Archer. He guides my hand, going to the pull tab at the top of the box. It rips open, and the cardboard flaps at the top of the box slowly push up and the first balloon pops out.

It's pink.

We're having a girl.

Archer wraps his arms around me, pulling me into a tight embrace. We kiss, and I forget everyone is watching and taking pictures. Standing here with him makes me feel like we're a family, and for a moment, I forget we're going home in opposite directions.

"My only daughter is having a daughter," Mom says, coming in for a hug. "Now I can start shopping."

"Don't go crazy, Mom. We still—" I cut off before I let myself finish the sentence. I don't want to think about it yet because it scares me, though it's not the unknown that's making me nervous this time around.

I know what I want, and *that* scares me.

Jamie acts as our unofficial photographer, and I hold the pink balloons to one side while Archer stands on my other, with his hand resting on my stomach. We spend a few minutes taking photos and then go into the kitchen for dessert. I stand by the counter, admiring the food but thinking I won't be able to eat any of it.

Archer comes up behind me, arms going around my waist. He slides his hands over my stomach and kisses my neck.

"You were right," Archer says, lips against my flesh. "We can start calling the baby Emma."

"Emma." Tears fill my eyes and I turn around in Archer's arms, lip quivering. "You like the name?"

"I do. I've been mentally calling her that for a while to see if I'd like it. Now it fits."

"Oh," I croak out, and tears roll down my cheeks.

"Are you crying?" Owen asks, eyes wide. He's across the counter from me, filling his plate with cookies and brownies. "You never cry."

"I've been crying a lot lately," I admit with a laugh.

Archer tightens his hold on me. "Whatever you do, don't bring up endangered species."

"I'M HAVING DEJA VU."

Archer pushes off the ground, sending the glider back. The heat of the day hasn't worn off yet, despite it being after dark. The sounds of a country night surround us, and the dogs run and sniff around the yard.

"We sat here and talked," I say, resting my head on Archer's shoulder. "That night I spilled the drinks on myself at Getaway and you took me home."

"Oh yeah. We did sit here."

I tip my head up. "It was the first time we had a real conversation. Want to know something silly?"

"Always."

"I thought you were going to kiss me that night."

"I wanted to kiss you."

"What?" I heard him correctly but need to hear him say it again.

"I wanted to kiss you that night."

"Why'd you pussy out?"

Archer laughs and kisses me now for good measure. "I wasn't sure you'd want me to. And I knew if I kissed you once I'd want to do it again." He runs his hand through his hair. "You said you thought I was going to kiss you, but did you want me to?"

"I did."

"Then why did you pussy out and not kiss me?" he says with a laugh.

"You gave off some very mixed signals. Up until the night this little girl was conceived. And then after."

"Yeah, I'm still sorry—"

"It's okay, Arch," I say quickly. We've moved past our issues with that. There's no need to bring them up now.

"Actually, Quinn," he says slowly. "There's a story behind that, and I want to tell it to you."

"I do like stories. Does it have a happy ending?"

He smiles. "I'm going to ask you a question at the end, and what you say will determine that."

I cock an eyebrow. "You're confusing me just a bit, Dr. Jones."

"Sorry," he says with a laugh. "I'm not a good storyteller, but I want you to hear this."

"Okay. Can I pee first? I'm ruining the mood, but I'm pregnant. I pee a lot."

"It's only going to get worse."

"Yay." I roll my eyes, kiss him, and hurry into the house to use the bathroom. When I go back outside, Archer is sitting by the pool. His shoes are off, and he's rolling up his pants.

"We can go in," I say. "The water is warm and it's humid out. It'd feel nice. You brought your suit, right?"

"I did. You only reminded me a dozen times."

"I haven't been swimming in a while. I'm looking forward to it." I sit next to him and stick my feet in the water. "Unless you want to skinny dip later."

"I like that idea."

"You know, I've never had sex in a pool before." I wiggle my eyebrows.

"And you shouldn't, especially when pregnant. You're likely to get a UTI if you have sex in a pool, hot tub, or lake."

"You're back to Dr. Fuddy-Duddy again."

"Hey, health and safety are important to me."

I laugh and loop my arm through his and look up at the star-studded sky. Everything feels perfect right now, and I know without a doubt that I'm in love with Archer.

And for the first time, I think he's in love with me too.

"You said we never really talked before," he starts. "There's a reason for that."

"Is it a good reason?"

"In retrospect, no." He kisses me, and the moment his lips are against mine, I melt. When his tongue slips into my mouth, I'm a goner.

"Maybe we can tell stories later and have sex now."

"You couldn't get more perfect if you tried," Archer mumbles, kissing me harder. Desire swirls inside of me. It would be really obvious if Archer and I both went upstairs together. Part of me doesn't care.

Fuck, this long-distance thing sucks. We're finally together after over a week apart and we're at my parents' house. I could always pretend to be sick and Archer is coming up to take care of me.

"Is your car unlocked?" I ask between kisses.

"I think so. Why?"

"Want to have sex in the back?"

"Yes," he says with no hesitation. We begin to untangle when the sliding glass door opens.

"Aunt Winnie!" Jackson calls. "Daddy said I can tell you goodnight."

"I'll be right there," I tell him and pull my feet from the water.

"Are you swimming? I want to swim!" Jackson's eyes light up and he comes running.

"No, Jackson!" I scramble up, but there's no way I can get to him in time. Wes sprints out of the house as well, seeing Jackson head right for the water.

"Jackson!" Wes yells. "No!"

Jackson can't swim, but that doesn't stop him from jumping right into the pool.

14

ARCHER

J ackson slips under the surface of the water and doesn't come back up. Quinn screams, and I jump in, diving down and swimming across to grab Jackson. I hook my arm around him and push off the bottom of the pool. He's thrashing, doing everything he can to get himself to the surface, and hits me in the face a few times. I bring him up out of the water, and Weston takes him from my arms, bringing him out of the pool.

"What were you thinking?" Weston asks, eyes wide with fear. Jackson coughs up water, and Wes holds him tightly against him. I pull myself up out of the water, eyes on the kid. "Are you okay?"

Jackson is still coughing, and being hugged tight by his father isn't helping. Quinn comes around, crouching down to Jackson. Mrs. Dawson comes outside, panicked.

"What happened? I heard someone scream."

"Jackson jumped in the pool and Archer saved him," Quinn says, letting out a shaky breath. "Is he okay?"

"I think so," Wes says, both hands on Jackson's shoulders. I've seen that look of fear and worry in parents' eyes before. My own kid isn't born yet and I already feel like I understand it more than I did before. "Don't ever do that again," Wes tells Jackson and stands, holding the boy in his arms and sits in a lounge chair. Jackson is crying, which is a good sign. At least he's getting oxygen.

Mrs. Dawson grabs two towels that were hanging to dry on the fence and gives one to me and one to Wes.

"Thank you," Wes tells me, wrapping Jackson up in the towel. "He came out to tell Quinn goodnight. I didn't think he'd jump in."

"I thought they were swimming," Jackson tells him, trying to stop crying.

"That doesn't mean you can jump in. You can't swim without floaties. You are lucky Archer got to you so fast."

"Thank you," Jackson chokes out.

"Of course, buddy," I say. "Don't do that again. You scared us all."

Wes smoothes back Jackson's hair and kisses his forehead. Quinn takes the towel from my hands and drapes it around my shoulders.

"Thank God you got to him so fast." She pulls the towel tight as if she's worried I'm cold. It's hot and humid out tonight. Jumping in the water felt good.

"I was close."

Quinn cups my face and stands on her toes to kiss me. "You're going to make a good dad."

"I hope so." I rest my hand on her stomach.

"Well, I know so."

"And you'll be a good mom. You know all the words to every Disney song."

Quinn laughs, some of the tension leaving her. She takes a glance at Jackson, who's still snug in Weston's arms. "I don't know if that's a qualifying factor for what makes a good parent, but I'll take it."

Quinn takes my hand and we go over by Jackson. He's sitting up now, eyes still red from crying and getting pool water in them.

"Are you going swimming, Aunt Winnie?"

"Not tonight," Quinn tells him, sitting on the lounge chair next to him. "Maybe we can go swimming in the morning, but only if you have your super cool shark floaty on first, okay?"

"Okay," he grumbles. Quinn puts her hand on his shoulder and flicks her eyes to her brother. "Are you okay?"

Wes shakes his head. "I've seen some pretty...pretty messed up stuff," he starts, and I'm reminded of his service to our country. "But seeing him go under like that..."

"Hey, he's fine," Quinn assures him.

"Thank you," Weston tells me, eyes drilling into mine. He's eight years older than Quinn, and the two of them look the least alike out of all the Dawson siblings. Their personalities are probably the most different too, with Quinn being quirky and easygoing and Weston being serious and rigid. He stepped in and gave me advice multiple times before, and has been a better older brother to me than my own.

"Of course," I say back. We stay outside for another minute or so, and then Quinn leads me upstairs to change into dry clothes.

"Do you want to shower with me?" she asks, reaching behind her and unzipping her dress.

"Do you really have to ask?"

She giggles and lets the dress fall to the ground. "Seeing you act all heroic is a turn on."

"Everything is a turn on to you right now."

"That is true." She unhooks her bra and lets out a breath of relief as soon as it's off. "I'm going to have to go bra shopping soon. I swear I've gone up a cup size already."

"Your tits are going to be huge when you're breastfeeding," I say without thinking. We haven't talked about it yet. We haven't talked about anything post-birth. "I mean, if that's what you want to do. If not, that's fine too."

She turns on the shower and grabs two towels from the closet between the two sinks. "What do you think I should do?"

I don't know if she's testing me or just honestly asking for my opinion. "If you're able to breastfeed, then I think you should."

"And if I'm not able to?"

"Then you feed formula. As long as they're getting fed, it's fine."

She rakes her fingers through her curls. "I haven't really thought about it."

"I know, babe. And that's okay. But we do need to start thinking about—and talking about—these things."

She nods and tests the water, seeing if it's warm enough to get in yet. I strip out of my wet clothes and put them in the laundry basket in the closet. "I know. And even though I really like how firm and perky my boobs are, I do want to try breastfeeding."

"I like how firm and perky they are too."

"Are you still going to be attracted to me when I'm nine months pregnant?" She gets into the shower and I follow after her.

Warm water pours down on us. "I'll always be attracted to you. And this might be weird, but knowing I knocked you up is kind of a turn on."

"Really?" Quinn wiggles her eyebrows. "Because you did this." She puts my hand on her stomach.

"See?" I motion to my dick. "You're starting to turn me on."

"What are you going to do about it?" She purposely drops a bottle of body wash. "Oh no. I dropped the soap. I should bend over and pick it up."

"You know what dropping the soap implies, right?"

"I do. And I'll totally be your prison butt-bitch."

Laughing, I take Quinn by the waist and turn her around. She locks her arms around my neck. I kiss her, and the need to be inside her takes over. I push her against the shower wall, being careful not to slip. Quinn puts one foot on the edge of the tub, aligning her pussy with my cock.

And then someone knocks on the door.

"Sorry to interrupt," Weston calls from behind the door, "but I need the kid soap."

Quinn and I untangle. "Right now?" Quinn asks.

"Yeah. Jackson threw up all over himself and he has a thing about getting shampoo in his eyes."

Quinn picks up the bottle, shakes off as much water as she can and tosses it by the door. "You can grab it," she calls. The bathroom is a jack-and-jill style, with doors going to both Quinn's old room and the one Jackson stays in. Wes opens the door just a crack and grabs the soap for Jackson.

Something isn't right. The kid inhaled water. Now he's throwing up.

"What's wrong, Arch?" Quinn asks, picking up her own shampoo. I make a face, not wanting to worry her just yet.

"Probably nothing."

"But it could be something?"

"Yeah, it could be." I take the shampoo from her and quickly wash my hair. We finish the shower in record speed, and I throw on boxers, athletic pants, and a white t-shirt. Quinn is still getting dressed and is brushing out her hair when I leave the room, hoping Weston hasn't left yet. They're about to, and Jackson looks a bit out of it.

"How's he doing?" I ask, eyeing the kid.

"He's worn out."

"Is he normally this tired at nine-thirty?"

Weston shakes his head. "He's usually a night owl," he says and then his eyes cloud with worry. "Why? Is something wrong?"

"Sit down. I'll be right back," I tell Weston and rush out to my Jeep to grab the stethoscope I keep hanging from my rearview mirror. Both Mr. and Mrs. Dawson are standing in the kitchen with them, sharing the same look of worry. Quinn comes down right as I'm listening to Jackson's lungs. And I hear what I was hoping not to hear.

I let Jackson take my stethoscope, using it as a distraction. I deliver bad news more often than I'd like. There's never a good way to say it, and sugarcoating it does no good in the end.

"He needs to go to the hospital," I say. "He has water in his lungs."

———

"WHAT'S TAKING SO LONG?" QUINN ASKS, LOOKING AT THE time on her phone. We're in the ER waiting room, and time is crawling. "Can you go back there and speed things up?"

I shake my head. "I don't have privileges at this hospital. It's not like it is on TV. You can't just say you're a doctor and start giving orders."

"I guess that's a good thing."

I take her hand, wishing I could ease her anxiety.

Another few minutes tick by, and Logan and Owen hurry in. Quinn fills them in on what's going on, and we wait together. Fifteen minutes later, I'm feeling anxious too. Finally, Quinn gets a text from her mother, who's in the exam room with Wes and Jackson.

"Mom said the nurse didn't seem too concerned and said that lots of kids are sick right now with a virus. They still haven't seen the doctor."

Only two people were allowed to go back with Jackson. Wes was obviously one of them, and the other was Mrs. Dawson.

"Ask your mom if I can switch her out," I tell Quinn. I don't have any authority here, but I'm sure I can get things moving along faster. Quinn fires off a text and a minute later, Mrs. Dawson comes into the waiting room.

I go back, finding Jackson curled up in Weston's lap. He looks peacefully sound asleep, which is what makes this so dangerous.

"How's he doing?" I ask, coming into the room.

"He's really agitated," Wes tells me.

"It's because he's not getting enough oxygen." I look around for the nurse. "Did they take his vitals?"

"He threw a fit when they tried."

"So they didn't?"

"The nurse is coming back."

I grit my teeth and sit on the bed next to Wes, taking Jackson's arm in my hand. He groans and tries to pull his arm away.

"Hey, buddy," I say gently. "It's Archer. I have to check for something, okay?"

Jackson struggles a bit more but finally stops, slitting his eyes open just enough to see me. I check his pulse; his heart is racing. Someone knocks on the doorframe while I'm checking Jackson's fingers for signs of cyanosis.

"You're new," the nurse says, rolling in the little machine that takes vitals.

"He needs his O2 checked, and probably have some administered," I tell her, unable to help but go into doctor mode.

"I'm getting to it." The nurse is middle-aged and smells strongly like cigarette smoke that she's trying to cover up with perfume. I would not allow that if she worked on my team.

"He's been here for half an hour and his oxygen hasn't been checked yet."

"We needed to give him time to calm down."

"He's agitated because he's not getting enough oxygen."

The nurse plops a folder on the desk and turns to me, hand on her hip. "Look, sir, I appreciate your concern for your son, but please leave it to the medical professionals to take care of him."

My son? I turn my head to Wes and—ohhhh. She thinks we're a couple. I don't even care to correct her. It doesn't matter.

"He needs a chest X-ray, an IV, and oxygen." I look at Jackson, not wanting to freak him out. "And I am a doctor. I'm a surgeon at Indianapolis General and I'm here visiting family."

The nurse purses her lips and nods, muttering something and going out of the room. Right away, the ER doctor comes in, and after talking with him for a minute, we get Jackson taken care of. I text Quinn, telling her Jackson is going to have a chest X-ray and then be admitted overnight for observation.

Half an hour later, Jackson is settled in his room. The

whole Dawson crew is here now, and they all crowd in to see him. He's tired and still has a risk of developing pneumonia, but he'll be monitored closely for the next twenty-four hours. I step out of the packed room, and Dean comes into the hall with me.

"Hey," he says.

"Hey."

"Wes said if you hadn't caught the early symptoms there's a good chance Jackson could have died in his sleep."

"Dry drowning has that risk. It makes kids tired and you think they're just sleeping like normal."

Dean looks down at the floor, probably overwhelmed by how close they could have come to losing Jackson.

"I'm sorry I've been an ass," he finally says.

"I'm sorry too."

Dean takes in a slow breath. "It's still weird as fuck, but my sister seems really happy."

"I'm really happy too." I lean against the wall. "This wasn't just some hookup that turned into a mistake. I've liked Quinn for a while."

Dean flicks his eyes to mine "Why didn't you say anything?"

"I knew you'd act like a fucking twat about it."

Dean gives me a half smile. "You weren't wrong." He leans against the wall opposite me. "How long's a while?"

"Years." Twelve years to be exact. I wanted Quinn the first time I laid eyes on her back when I was eighteen and she was fourteen. Sharing that tidbit of info can come later. Way later. If I ever share it at all.

"I didn't know."

"I made sure you didn't."

"Look," I start. "I get that it's weird. But we're together

now. We're having a baby. Quinn puts on a tough face, but I know it upsets her that you aren't supportive."

"I do support her. And you. You…I support you both."

"Then tell her."

Dean nods. "But being due two days before my wedding?"

"Like we planned that. We didn't even plan to get pregnant." If I wanted to be petty, I'd point out Quinn's due date was determined weeks before they picked a wedding date anyway.

"Want to get coffee?" Dean asks, pushing off the wall.

"Yeah, that sounds good."

We start down the hall, not sure where we're going. Dean's not really going to get coffee this late at night but is using it as an excuse to talk. Which is fine with me.

"So, are you two going to get married or at least move in together?"

"I don't know," I answer honestly. "Quinn wants to take things slow. Obviously we hadn't been together long before we found out she was pregnant." We weren't really together at all. She got pregnant the first or second time we ever had sex.

"I know you'll do the right thing," he replies. "Just don't hurt her. I'll be forced to take her side, you know."

I laugh, suddenly seeing a bit more into why Dean freaked out so much. It's not just about the betrayal of the unspoken bro-code, but the fear of things becoming awkward between us if Quinn and I don't work out.

"I'd want you to."

We reach the end of the hall and stop, looking at the map of the hospital tacked to the wall by the elevators. This place is small and dated. I'd hate working here after being in a big and busy hospital full of the newest medical equipment.

"They're going to tear this place down," Dean says distantly as we turn around, realizing there's nowhere in here to get food or coffee. "No one is supposed to know yet since it hasn't been approved, but we put in a bid to work on the new hospital."

"New hospital?"

"Yeah. The plans are huge. It'll be replacing this hospital and the one in Newport. It goes to the city council next week."

"And if it gets approved?"

"Then construction crews will be picked, and we'll break ground right away. Why, are you interested?"

"More curious," I say, which is true. A brand-new hospital full of brand-new equipment would be nice.

Raising our child in the safe town of Eastwood would be even nicer.

15

I lean back in my chair, wiping tears from my eyes. A logical part of my brain tells me I need to stop. But for some reason, I lack all self-control and don't click away. Someone knocks on my office door, and I look up, prepared to hide behind my monitor if need be.

But it's just Marissa, and I wave her in.

"Oh my God," she says and comes around to my desk. "Stop watching those clips of dogs greeting their owners after they come home from the military."

"But it's so sweet!"

"You have mascara dripping down your face."

"I didn't wear any today."

She hikes an eyebrow. "Then it's yesterday's leftover mascara."

I grab a tissue from my desk drawer. "That's likely." I wipe my eyes and close the viral video. "Did you come in here just to yell at me?"

"I wish I did." She looks behind her, making sure no one is lingering by my door. "I heard Raul and Mike talking."

"They talk all the time."

"About you," she presses. "Someone started a rumor about you being pregnant and now everyone is curious. Raul wants to throw you a baby shower."

"No showers at work. You know I feel weird when people buy me presents. And why would they think that?"

Marissa widens her eyes. "The weird food. The way you get teary-eyed at pretty much everything now. And yesterday you wore that Valentino cape dress and it totally showed off your bump. Which really just means you should give it to me until you're not pregnant anymore. Or just forever."

"It is a really nice dress. It makes me feel like a fancy, sexy superhero."

"And it's also sold out at Nordstrom."

"Fine. You can borrow it. What weird food? I haven't eaten anything weird."

Marissa looks at the plate on my desk. "Is that a hot dog wrapped in cheese that you're dipping in ranch?"

"Maybe. But that's not weird."

"Oh, no, not at all. In fact, I got one from that food truck down the street, uh, *never* ago."

"All right. It's weird. But I'm finally starting to get my appetite back." I subconsciously wrap my fingers around my left wrist, making a face.

"Yes! Another thing to yell at you about."

"Huh?"

Marissa points to my wrist. "I was in your office when you were on the phone with Archer yesterday, remember? He told you to stop taking the brace off."

"Oh, right. It's hard to type with it on and it's just so annoying."

Marissa laughs. "I'm sure it is." She sits in the chair across from my desk. "He's coming into town tomorrow?"

"Yeah. He's off Thursday through Saturday."

"How are you holding up with this long-distance thing?"

I pick up my hotdog and dip it in ranch. Okay, maybe I am getting a few weird pregnancy cravings. "It's not fun, but I guess it's okay. I mean, I did want to take things slow."

"You're such a terrible liar, Quinn. Even to yourself."

"I'm not lying."

"Bullshit. You want to *take things slow*? Really?"

I let out a breath. "We should take things slow. I don't want him to be with me just because I'm having his baby. We weren't dating when I got pregnant."

"But you're dating now, and even you have to admit Archer has gone above and beyond for you."

"Yeah," I say, unable to keep the smile off my face. "He has. And that's why it scares me. This is new and exciting... what happens if it fizzles out?"

Marissa shrugs. "I'm not one to give relationship advice since I've been chronically single since I turned twenty-one, but isn't that always a risk with a relationship? You do romantic things to keep it going. You've had a crush on Archer for years. Your feelings aren't going to fizzle out."

"I know *mine* won't." I rest my hands on my stomach, feeling so much love for my little Emma. "I want things to work between us," I start, knowing the truth's been inside me this whole time. "And I'm worried I'm forcing something that wouldn't otherwise be there. Does that even make sense?"

"Yeah, and I see your point. You're a practical person— most of the time. But love isn't practical. You've liked Archer since you've known him, and you told me he said he liked you before you two hooked up. So yeah, you got pushed into a relationship, but the feelings were there on both sides."

Tears prick the corners of my eyes, and I wipe them

away, annoyed with myself for how emotional I become thanks to all the hormones. "Thanks, Mar. You're right."

"I usually am." She gives me a smirk. "Now, tell me what you really want."

"I want him to tell me he loves me, for him to get a job in Chicago, and for us to move in together and eventually get married," I blurt.

"See? How hard was that. Now...do you think Archer knows you want that?"

I shake my head. "Maybe. I don't want to freak him out or anything. He really wants a fellowship to do trauma surgery and he can't really pick and choose where he'll get placed."

"How does that make you feel?" Marissa asks, doing her best Dr. Phil impression.

"I'd rather him be done with school so we can be together," I say, sticking with this honesty thing. "But it's only a year or two and it's his dream."

My phone buzzes and my eyes widen when I pick it up. "It's a group text from Dean. To me and Archer."

"Ohhh!" Marissa leans forward. "What does it say?"

I open the message and quickly read it. "He's asking if certain dates work for the bridal shower because he wants to make sure we both can go."

"Wow, progress! All it took was Archer saving your nephew's life to get him to turn around."

"I know, right?"

"Speaking of, how is Jackson?"

"Much better. He came home from the hospital yesterday and is having a hard time resting because he just wants to play."

"That's good!"

I nod. It's Wednesday afternoon, but Jackson jumping

into the pool still feels like yesterday. "It still freaks me out how fast things happened. He was only underwater for a few seconds and could have—"

"Stop. You're going to start crying again. He's fine."

"Right. He is." I wipe my eyes for good measure, just in time because Raul knocks on my office door, asking if I could go over some coding with him.

"Yeah, I'll be right there," I say with a smile.

"Thanks, boss lady." He smiles back and looks down at my hotdog. "Interesting lunch."

"You're right," I whisper to Marissa as soon as Raul leaves. I'm going to have to talk to HR sooner rather than later about arranging for my maternity leave anyway. And people are going to find out in time. I unlock my phone and open Instagram. I have an oddly high number of followers thanks to an article *Forbes* did on me right after I sold the app to Apple. I'm not that interesting of a person, but I do find the best funny memes to share.

I upload my favorite picture of Archer and me from this weekend, heart fluttering when I look at it. We're standing by the pink balloons, and looking lovingly into each other's eyes. My hair is tucked awkwardly behind my ear, but we both look so happy.

So in love.

Archer's hand is on my stomach, and his smile is genuine. Man, I miss him. Tomorrow is too far away. Long distance sucks.

"We cannot wait for spring. Hashtag thirteen weeks. Hashtag baby girl," I say out loud as I type.

"Don't forget hashtag blessed."

"And grateful. Please. I might be basic, but I know enough not to flaunt it around on social media," I laugh and post the photo. But I really do feel those things.

ME: I TOLD YOU, I'LL GET FIRED IF I DO THAT.

    Logan: Come on, sis. Live a little.

    Weston: As an officer of the law I must remind you... it's only illegal if you get caught.

    Me: Guys, I don't know...I really like my job.

    Owen: You'd be the coolest sister ever if you did this.

    Me: I'm already the coolest sister.

    Logan: Dean's only getting married once.

    Owen: That's debatable. I still don't see how Kara puts up with his ass. Think of it this way, Q: it's the only bachelor party we're throwing for him.

    Me: Maybe...it's risky. We're still working bugs out of the prototype. I wouldn't want you guys to get hurt.

    Dean: You guys are assholes. Mom told me the Batmobile isn't real and all that footage is fake.

I CRACK UP, READING DEAN'S TEXT TWICE. WE'VE BEEN GOING at this all day, with my other brothers trying to convince me to let them take the Batmobile out for the bachelor party.

WESTON: IT TOOK MOM TELLING YOU IT'S NOT REAL FOR YOU to get it? Jackson never once bought into it.

    Owen: And he's fucking THREE YEARS OLD

    Logan: hahaha you're never living this down, bro

I SEND A CAREFULLY DOCTORED PHOTO OF ME SITTING BEHIND the wheel of the Batmobile to the group text, still laughing as I imagine Dean's pouting face right now.

ME: I GUESS IT'LL JUST BE ME IN THIS BAD BOY THEN. So
long, suckers!

Logan: He's believed this for FOUR FUCKING
MONTHS, guys

Owen: I didn't think we could keep it going for
that long.

Weston: Q and I get all the credit.

Dean: Again. Assholes.

SOMETHING FLUTTERS IN MY STOMACH. I PUT MY PHONE DOWN,
smile still on my face, and put both hands over my belly. Did
I just feel Emma kick? My phone chimes again and again,
and I know I'm missing a slew of texts from my brothers. I
keep my hands pressed to my stomach, waiting for that
feeling again. Deciding it's just gas—I did have a burrito for
lunch—I pick up my phone again and catch up on the texts
from my brothers.

There's another from Jacob, asking if we can get together
when he's back in town. I bite the inside of my cheek, not
sure how to answer. I have no issue grabbing lunch with
him if we're with other people from work. And I don't mind
talking to him. We have a lot in common, and he does know
my family. We're better at being friends and fell flat
romantically.

He was a practical boyfriend. I was moderately
attracted to him, we worked in the same field, and lived
near each other. It made sense to date him. I gave it a shot,
and while I can't say it was terrible, there just wasn't a
spark.

I have more than a spark with Archer. We have a raging

fire. But we don't have much in common. We work in total opposite fields. And we live hours apart.

"Love isn't practical," I say out loud. And then it hits me what I just said. *Love*. I'm in love with Archer.

Tapping my fingers on my desk, I start to type a reply to Jacob. He still follows me on Instagram, so he has to know I'm pregnant and with Archer. I delete what I'm typing and start again, finally agreeing to have a 'working lunch' with him the week he gets back. He responds with a smiley face and I go back and read my message, wondering if I was too callous. I don't want to lead him on...this is only this hard for me, I'm sure.

Silencing my phone, I go back to work, wrapping up a final system check on a program we're launching next month. I find a few things to tweak, make notes, and go back through it again.

I have to stop to pee for the second time since lunch. If I wasn't so damn thirsty all the time, I'd lay off beverages until I got home. It's getting a bit annoying to use the bathroom more than normal, and I know it'll only get worse.

When I get back to my office, I see I missed a call from Archer. I sit back in my chair, put my wrist brace back on and call him.

"Hey, babe," he says right away. It sounds like he's outside near a road. "How's work?"

"It's all right. I'm busy, but it's going by slow since I know I'll get to see you soon. Are you done with surgery?"

"I didn't get to do it. My patient ate three hours before he got here. We had to reschedule the operation."

"Wow. Way to listen to doctor's orders."

"I know. And it wasn't like a quick drink of water and something small to eat. He went out to breakfast."

I let out a snort of laughter. "I'm glad you found out."

"It was obvious. He had bacon stuck in his teeth."

"So does that mean you're done for the day?"

"It does. Or it did, I suppose. I'm already in Chicago."

"Are you serious?" I bring my hand to my chest, smiling like a fool.

"I am. I've been here a while, actually. I tried to find a spot to park close to your apartment. It took a while, but I wanted to surprise you."

"That's twice in a row you did. I need to step it up and surprise you," I say, very glad now I got new lingerie to wear for him tonight. "Where are you now?"

"Almost to your office building."

My eyes fill with tears and I shake my head at myself. "I've missed you."

"I've missed you too. You're almost done with work, right? I don't want to interrupt your day."

"I am. I have like half an hour left and I'm wrapping up for the day. I can't believe you're here!"

"Believe it, babe. How's Jackson doing? Dean said he came home from the hospital."

"You guys are talking again?"

"We are. He called and asked if I wanted to come to the bachelor party."

"That's great! You're going, right?"

"If I can. The party is in April, and by then, I'll officially be a surgeon and no longer a resident."

"Right! You're done at the end of the year."

"I'm counting down the days," he says with a laugh. I don't know why I more or less forgot about him finishing his residency before Emma is born. In my mind, the two happened at the same time. But he'll have a new job before she's born, which is good, right?

"Jackson's doing well. Thanks to you."

"You all can stop thanking me. I'm a doctor. Noticing illness and injury is part of my job. Though it has been a few seconds since I brought up that I'm a doctor. I can see how you could forget."

"You better wear a name tag that says Dr. Jones on it or something."

"I'll add in MD and the fact that I'm a surgeon. I don't want people thinking I just have a lowly PhD or something."

I laugh and move to the window, looking down at the street far below. I won't be able to see Archer walking in, but it's still interesting to stop and people watch from this far up.

"We can't have that, now, can we? Are you almost here?"

"Impatient?"

"Just a little," I say with a laugh. "I thought I felt Emma kicking today. Is it too early?"

"It's unlikely but not impossible. It'll be another few weeks before you can externally feel her kicking." The sounds of traffic fade. "I'm in your building."

"You might lose service in the elevator. Come up and I'll meet you in the lobby. See you soon."

We hang up and I save what I've been working on. I quickly straighten up my desk and do a quick check of my appearance, using my phone as a mirror. I go into the lobby, just in time to see Archer get off the elevator.

I rush to him, throwing my arms around him and pulling him in for a kiss, not caring who sees. Archer kisses me back hard, tongue pushing into my mouth.

"That gets better every time," he breathes, breaking away.

"It really does."

He slowly brings his hands down my arms and rests one on my stomach. "I missed her too."

The fluttering feeling comes back as if Emma knows her

daddy is right here with us. Smiling, I lead Archer back into the office with me, ignoring the blank stares Rene and Charlene are giving us right now. I introduce him to a few coworkers, and then he sits in my office talking with Marissa while I finish my work.

When I'm done for the day, Archer and I walk out together, and he takes my hand as we walk the few blocks it takes to get to my apartment. He grabs his bag from his car and lugs it upstairs and inside.

Neville circles around Archer, meowing to be picked up almost immediately after we walk in.

"Hey, buddy," Archer says, cradling the cat to his chest. "You remember me?" He takes off his shoes and goes to the couch, sitting and petting Neville, who's purring loudly. I cross the room and go into the kitchen to get a can of food for the cats, and I realize this is exactly what I want.

Archer and I together, raising our child together as a family.

16

S miling, I take Quinn's hand. "Things are quite different now than the last time we walked up and down this river."

"You're not kidding," she says back with a laugh. We just got done with dinner and are enjoying the night out together.

"Though one thing is the same."

"What?"

My heart is in my throat, but this time I'm not nervous. "I was in love with you then, like I am now."

Quinn stops short, grip on my hand tightening. Her lips are slightly parted with shock, but her eyes are sparkling. "What?"

I pull her close, heart thumping away. "If you're not ready to say it back, that's okay. But I've been wanting to tell you for a long time. I love you."

"I love you, too."

"Really?"

"Yes," she says with a laugh, blinking back tears. "I knew I was falling but was scared you didn't feel the same."

"I do, babe. I really fucking do."

Unable to keep my lips off hers any longer, I lean down and kiss her deeper than I should be kissing her in public, but I can't help it.

"Wait." She breaks away and for a split second, I think she's going to tell me she takes her words back. "You were in love with me that night we hooked up?"

"I've been in love with you for even longer than that." I take her hand again and lead her to a bench. We sit, and I wrap her in my arms. "Do you remember the first time we met?"

"When you came home with Dean?"

"No, when Dean was moving into the dorm."

"Oh, yeah. I do now. I thought you were cute."

"I thought you were too," I confess for the first time ever. "I didn't realize you were so young. You had on a tight black dress and your tits were practically falling out. You looked older than fourteen."

"I forgot about that. I bought my first pushup bra the day before and Jamie and I were going to talk to seniors down at the lake. My dad found out and made me come with them to Purdue. I was so mad."

"I was all for making a move until I found out you were four years younger than me."

"That wouldn't have gone over well with my brothers."

"Not at all. You were a minor."

"But then I wasn't," she starts.

"Trust me, on your eighteen birthday I thought about it. I've always been insanely attracted to you, Quinn. And then I got to know you—and your family. Things got complicated. I didn't tell you how I felt before out of respect for Dean. He's more of a brother to me than my own brother. Hell, Logan, Owen, and Wes are too. But then I saw you again the weekend of Dean's engagement party, and it was so hard not to kiss you."

"Is that why you were such an asshole?"

"I wasn't an asshole."

She snickers and rolls her eyes. "Sure you weren't."

Running my hand over her hair, I chuckle. "Fine, and I have no excuse for it. I didn't know how to deal with it. I wanted you so much it was frustrating."

"I know the feeling." She cups my cheek in her hand and locks her eyes with mine. "I had a major crush on you as a kid, that apparently you knew about."

"I did, and it didn't help my situation. Especially when you were walking around in your bikini flirting with me. You were older then, but still a minor. And still Dean's sister."

She laughs. "I'm sorry for giving you blue balls. I can make it up to you tonight."

"I'm going to take you up on that offer."

"I can put on a bikini too, but I don't look the same as I did when I was fourteen, you perv."

"I was really conflicted after I found out you were so young."

"I bet. Though if it makes you feel any better, one of Weston's friends used to hit on me. And he *did* know about our age difference."

"Gross. At least we're only four years apart, not eight."

"I know, right? That guy continued his love for younger girls and ended up being one of the first people Wes ever arrested."

I laugh. "Interesting turn of events. So, hypothetically speaking, if I had asked you out years ago, would you have said yes?"

"Depends on when you asked." Her eyes sparkle again.

"I went through a very dark period where I thought I was in love with Andrew Winslow."

"I remember that. You spent a lot of the summer locked in your room crying."

"Being a teenage girl is rough. Are you sure you're ready for this?" She puts her hand on her belly again. "If she's anything like me she might be a little dramatic."

"A little?"

"Hey, now. At least I have other redeeming qualities."

"You do." I put my lips to hers again. "Want to head back?"

"Yeah. I'm getting tired and we've only had sex once so far today."

"We do have to prepare for the rest of the week apart." We get up and start walking, and as much as I'm enjoying being out on a date with Quinn, we're both ready to call it a night. She's tired and I'm exhausted. I was in surgery all night with back-to-back emergencies, slept for three hours on the breakroom couch, and then had my scheduled procedures this morning.

I cannot wait until I'm not a fucking resident anymore.

I put my arm around Quinn as we walk, going a few strides together in silence.

"Hey," I start when we come to a stop at an intersection. Cars fly by, and I don't think the drivers so much as notice people standing on the sidewalk. My first thought is how scary it would be to have Jackson walking on this sidewalk. It'll be even worse to have our own kid.

"Yeah?" Quinn tips her pretty face up to look at me.

"I love you."

I'VE GOTTEN SO USED TO SLEEPING FOR JUST A FEW HOURS here and there that sleeping through the night seems weird. Sometimes I wake up in a panic thinking I missed a shift or didn't hear my phone ring. It's rare I don't have to go in for an emergency appendectomy or cholecystectomy on my on-call nights. Pure exhaustion is what helps me sleep through the night, and even then, it still feels weird.

But when I woke up with a start at four a.m., all it took was one look at Quinn to calm my nerves. She said she gets up around eight to be in at work by nine, and will leave around three or four since it's Friday. As we settled in to sleep last night, she was telling me about some new code she was writing, and another program the company is about to launch.

She gets so excited when she talks about her job. She has good hours, a great work environment, and makes decent money. I can't blame her if she doesn't want to cut back on work when Emma is born. She has as much right to work full-time as I do. Still, we need to talk about it.

Instead of closing my eyes and trying to go back to sleep, I sit up and look at Quinn. She's so fucking beautiful. Careful not to disturb her, I get up and use the bathroom, and then go into the kitchen to get something to drink. The cats all follow me in, meowing loudly.

"I'm not feeding you," I tell them, flicking my eyes back to Quinn's room, hoping they don't wake her up. I open the fridge and pull out the orange juice. I pour myself a glass and go to the window, watching the early morning light bathe the already busy city.

"Arch?" Quinn's voice comes from behind me. She's standing in the threshold of her bedroom, blinking her eyes open. She's wearing a Minnie Mouse t-shirt and black panties. I'm confident in saying she could literally put on anything and I'd find her sexy.

"Did I wake you?"

"No." She yawns and pulls her arms in around herself. It is a little chilly in here, and her pert nipples are starting to push against the thin fabric of her shirt. "Or maybe? I don't know. I just woke up and you weren't there."

I finish my orange juice and put the glass in the sink. "I'm still on my work schedule this week. Sleeping for more than four hours in a row is weird."

She yawns. "You must really like surgery to put up with that schedule."

"I do. Being a surgical resident is more of a lifestyle than a job," I tell her seriously. "I won't always be this busy, I promise." I wonder if she's thinking about how hard it'll be for me to be involved in Emma's life. If we're apart, it will be hard. I won't lie to her or myself. It's hard enough seeing Quinn for a day at a time.

"Good. You deserve more time to yourself. What's your schedule like when you get home?"

"I'm on-call this weekend, which means I'll be in removing infected organs for sure. And then I have shifts Monday through Thursday."

Quinn takes my hand. "Come back to bed. Sleep while you have the chance."

"I do get to sleep while you're at work today."

"That is true. And I hope you do sleep. I worry about you driving all the way back to Indy."

I worry too, but I'm not going to tell Quinn that. Though when I do leave, I'll be well-rested at least. I drank so much coffee on the way here my stomach hurt. But I needed it to stay awake.

We get back into bed, and Quinn snuggles up with her head on my chest.

"Pretty soon I won't be able to do this," she says.

"Emma will be in the way."

"I can still sleep on my back, right? My OB said it's okay until twenty weeks, but should I stop sooner just in case?"

"Twenty weeks is standard. If it makes you feel better— mentally, I mean—you can stop sooner. You're not abnormally large or anything, so I'm not worried about pressure on the vena cava—the blood vessel that can get constricted."

"Okay, good. You're like my personal walking-talking version of Web MD."

I laugh. "I glad I spent eight years in college and another six as a resident to be as qualified as Web MD."

"Well, that was silly. Clearly you only needed a couple of nights to look through that website before you could diagnose anyone complaining of a headache with either the Black Plague or a tumor."

Laughing again, I kiss the top of her head and run my fingers up and down her arm until she falls back asleep. I start to drift off too, thinking of us living together as a family. The ring her grandmother gave me is in my bag, but since we just told each other we love each other, I think it's best to wait.

Until the next time we spend a weekend together, that is.

I rest my hand on Quinn's belly and fall asleep, dreaming about Quinn and Emma. Things start off normal and good like it should be in a dream, but then quickly shifts to weird as fuck. Emma is really a puppy, and I have to go back to med school because it was discovered I somehow missed a class.

"Archer," Quinn says, waking me up. I blink, shaking off

the weirdness but not looking into it too much. Dreams don't mean shit. She reaches over me and picks up my phone from the nightstand. It's on silent and vibrates one last time before the call goes to voicemail.

Quinn's face tightens when she looks at the name on the screen. "It was your mom."

17

QUINN

A rcher doesn't need to say it for me to know: his mom calling at dawn can't be a good thing. He sits up and takes the phone from me.

"Are you going to call her back?"

"I will later. You should go back to sleep so you're not tired. I fucked you hard before we went to bed. Didn't you say I wore you out?"

He's trying to lighten the mood, I know. And he really did wear me out. How he functions so well on so little sleep is beyond me. While I appreciate his efforts to downplay this for my sake, I know he shouldn't.

"Something could be wrong with—"

"I'll call her later. Lay down and I'll rub your back."

"I won't be able to sleep. Because now I'm worried."

Archer lets out a sigh. "I didn't want him to take up any of your time or energy, Quinn."

"Yeah, but he is and he will. He's your brother, Archer. He's messed up and made bad choices, but you said it yourself. He can't help it and has a disease."

"It's not an excuse."

"I know it's not. And I don't *want* to worry, but I do. I worry for you."

Archer looks up at me, dark circles under his eyes. This beautiful man needs a break.

"I'm fine."

"Arch," I say gently. "You know what I mean. He's your brother and no matter how mad you are at him, I know you care deep down."

He nods. "I'll call her back."

I adjust my pillow and lean back against the headboard, putting one hand on Archer's thigh.

"Hey, Mom," he says into the phone. "Yeah, I was sleeping. It's okay. What's—" He pauses for a few seconds. "Again?" His eyes fall shut and he shakes his head. "I'm in Chicago with Quinn. I'll call Sam and let him know. Thanks. Mom, no. It's not your fault."

I swallow hard, not sure if the lump rising in my throat is morning sickness or a sick feeling knowing what Archer and his parents have to go through over and over again.

"Call me if you hear anything." He hangs up and tosses the phone onto the mattress. "Bobby left rehab again. My mom thought he might come to Indy and see me again."

"Oh, wow. Is he allowed to do that?"

"Leave rehab?"

"Yeah."

"It wasn't court ordered or anything, so yeah, he can leave of his own free will. He needs to go to court ordered rehab," Archer grumbles. He brings his hands to his head, rubbing his temples and leans back. "It's fine, Quinn. Please don't worry. You have enough going on and you don't need to be stressed."

"I know," I say softly. "I care about you, Archer. I love you. Your family is going to be mine too—in a sense I mean.

Since Emma will go to family events on your side as well as mine."

Fuck. I'm making things awkward, which is something I'm good at. I didn't mean to insinuate that Emma will be at his family events because we're splitting custody or whatever.

"And I'll be there too," I add. And I really do hope I am there with Archer. I'm so in love with him. I can't imagine ever not being in love with this man.

"Yeah. You're right." His eyes fall shut. "I should call Sam and let him know there's a chance Bobby heads south again."

I sit up, intending on grabbing Archer's phone for him. But the sick feeling comes back and I clamp my hand over my mouth, scrambling out of bed just in time to throw up in the toilet. Archer hurries in after me, gathering my hair and holding it out of the way.

"It came out my nose," I groan, taking the towel Archer hands me. "I'm in the second trimester. Is this ever going to stop?"

"Yes. I'm sure it will." He smooths my hair back. "There's barf in your hair. I'll start the shower."

"Call Sam first."

Archer's face tightens, and he shakes his head. "It can wait. It takes hours to drive down from Michigan to Indy. Bobby doesn't have money or up-to-date ID to buy plane tickets."

"Okay."

Archer pulls me to my feet and starts the shower, getting fresh towels from the linen closet. I rinse out my mouth and strip out of my clothes. I'm up several hours before I need to get up for work, and I know I'll be tired later. But I can tough it out for Archer.

Archer washes my hair, and while a wash-the-vomit-out-of-your-hair is anything but sexy, there's a certain intimacy between us right now. I close my eyes and tip my head up, rinsing my hair. We finish showering in silence, and while I'm getting dressed, Archer says he's going to make breakfast.

I put clean pajamas back on, brush and dry my hair, and go into the kitchen to find Archer sitting on the floor petting the cats. He's holding a piece of bacon and they're swarming him, meowing and rubbing against him in hopes for more.

"Eggs and bacon? You spoil me, Arch."

He looks up, breaking off another piece of bacon for Luna. "You deserve it. And I've never seen cats beg like this."

"Oh, they're terrible. Neville wasn't that bad until he moved in with us. The girls are a bad influence," I laugh. "They never got over being alley cats, I think. They act like they have to eat everything or they'll starve to death."

"They're definitely not starving."

"I know." I pick up Bellatrix. "They're all fat."

Archer breaks up the rest of the bacon and gives it to the cats before getting up. He washes his hands and takes our plates, bringing them into the dining room.

"I rarely eat in here," I tell him. "It's nice."

"This whole place is nice. I still can't get over the view."

"That's what sold me on it. And it's close to work. Can't beat that."

"No, you can't."

I put another fork full of eggs in my mouth, watching Archer's face. Now would be a good time to bring up living arrangements post-baby. We're talking about my apartment after all. I finish chewing and take a drink of water, trying to plan out in my head what I want to say out loud.

Problem is, I don't really know what I want, other than

us being together. The reality of us having separate and opposite careers screams at me. Archer's worked so hard to get to where he is, and he wants to keep going to further his career. And I've busted my ass to rise up in the company I work for, and have to prove myself over and over that I'm just as smart and capable as the men I work with.

Archer likes his job.

I like my job.

But I love him.

One of us is going to have to compromise.

"Are you feeling sick again?" Archer asks, and I realize that I stopped eating.

"No, just tired. And deep in thought."

Archer picks up the last piece of his bacon. "About what?"

"If I should go back to work after I have Emma."

"Oh. I've wondered about that too. What do you *want* to do?"

I shake my head. "I don't know. I like my job, but I think I'm going to like being a mom too."

I always knew I would get married and have kids someday. I tried not to let myself think too far ahead and risk feeling sorry for myself since I had no prospects in sight, but I imagined being home with my children like Mom was home with us. But now I have a job I really enjoy, and I don't know what to do.

"If it helps," Archer starts, picking up his coffee. "You don't have to work. I'm still a resident now, but once I get a job, I'll make more than enough to support us all."

I smile, but his words make me realize how much we have to talk about. We never discussed finances or anything serious like that. Though those are topics usually discussed before getting married, when debts and assets combine.

Archer and I aren't getting married, though having his baby is more binding. I can't divorce him from being Emma's father.

"I don't want you to feel obligated to support me."

"I don't," he says right away, setting his coffee down. He looks into my eyes and my heart flutters. "I want us to live together," he says and looks relieved as soon as the words leave his lips. Has he been wanting to say that for a while too?

"You do?"

"Of course. I love you and love waking up next to you. I like making you breakfast and taking a shower with you. And when Emma is born, I want to be there. Yeah, she wasn't planned, and things aren't exactly worked out yet, but I love you and I love her, and I want us to be a family."

"Me too," I tell him, not sure why I dreaded this conversation as much as I did. We're at the tip of the iceberg with a lot left to discuss and figure out, but at least I know for sure we're on the same page.

Archer phone rings, and we both tense. He grabs it, lips pressing into a thin line. "It's the hospital."

"On your day off?"

"I never really get time off," he sighs. "Don't worry, they can't make me go in or anything today. I'm already maxed out on hours." He flashes a smile. "But I did tell the nurses to call me with progress on patients."

"You're a good doctor."

He answers the phone, going over a progress report with a nurse and gives an order for a medication increase.

"So what happens if you're like out of the country on vacation?" I ask when he hangs up.

"There's always someone on call. On the weekends it's usually other residents. I know which surgical resident is on all this weekend." He makes a face. "That's why I asked the nurse to call me."

I laugh. "So this might be a stupid question, but I'm gonna ask it."

"Shoot."

"Med school is hard. Like really hard. So how does a not-so-good doctor get to the point of performing surgery?"

Archer laughs. "I'd like to know that myself. Some people are book smart and might do really well in something like family practice but can't handle the stress and pressure of anything more urgent."

"Makes sense."

"And not all med schools are created equal." He finishes his coffee and yawns. "We have time to lay down. You've already showered and eaten breakfast. Want to go back to sleep?"

I take another bite of eggs and nod. Going back to our conversation about living together is ideal too, but we have limited time and that's a big topic to discuss. Still, I know I'll be distracted at work and can't be held responsible for searching for houses for sale in the suburbs.

"YOU'RE IN A GOOD MOOD. DID YOU GET LAID BEFORE YOU came in or something?" Marissa asks a little too loudly. A few others in the breakroom turn and look at me.

"Yes," I say, noting the surprise in their eyes. I might be a nerd, but I'm not a prude. Obviously. Though as Marissa pointed out this morning, what I know is my baby looks like I ate too much for breakfast to anyone who doesn't know me. "Archer is in town. Though it's more than that." I add granola to my yogurt and grab another bowl to fill with fruit.

There were complaints about our breakfast spread being 'unhealthy'. Instead of pointing out that everyone in the office should be happy we even provide food in the morning, we simply added healthier options. The company has money for it, after all.

Waiting until we're in the hall and headed to my office, I look around and make sure no one is in earshot. "Archer told me he loves me and wants to live together so we can raise Emma as a family."

"That's great!"

"I know!" I smile, feeling my whole heart swell up inside of me. I focus on the happy, purposely ignoring the fact that wanting something doesn't mean it's going to happen. We still live miles and miles apart. Archer has no idea where he's going to end up. He could be in school, so to speak, for another one to three years.

"And we talked about me going back to work after Emma is born."

Marissa turns to me, face paling. "Are you not coming back?"

"I honestly don't know. I feel really conflicted." We go into my office. "I love it here. But I also know I'm going to love being a mom. Archer said he's happy to provide for us too. I mean, he'll make a very decent living as a surgeon. It's not like we couldn't afford for me to stay home."

She snickers. "You'd make a good trophy wife."

"We're not married."

"Not yet." She raises her eyebrows.

"Easy tiger," I say, holding up my hand. I flip it around. "No ring."

She laughs. "He's crazy about you. I could tell just from the two minutes we were together. I bet he'll put a ring on it before the baby pops out."

That weird squirmy flutter is back, and I put my hand over my stomach, gently pressing down as if that'll help me feel Emma moving. "Being crazy about each other isn't the same thing as having a relationship and getting engaged."

"I'd ask if you were drunk, but I know how serious you are about avoiding anything bad for the baby."

I make a face. "Why would you think I'm drunk?"

"Because you're not making any sense. He's crazy about you. How is that any different?"

"Because as much as I love Archer—which I really truly do—how can he know this is what he wants?"

"Uh, because he said he fucking loves you." Marissa takes a bite of her donut. "Stop doubting yourself."

I nod, putting both hands on my stomach. "I know I am. But I'm trying to be practical. It's not just my heart on the line here."

Marissa nods and puts her food on my desk. "Do you think Archer is going to flake out or something?"

"No. I just..." I close my eyes in a long blink. I've been keeping this from everyone, even myself, since Archer and I started dating. "I don't want him to regret this in a year, ya know? I don't want Emma to think we're a family and then have us split up."

"Are you worried *you're* going to regret this in a year?"

"No. But I need to be realistic. People who get married just because they're having a baby together don't always have the best relationship. We're not living together. He doesn't know the bad side of Quinn Dawson yet. While I love to believe I'm perfect, I'm sure there are plenty of little things about me that will annoy him. Like my obsession with cats. Or the way I put off doing laundry until I have to wear bikini bottoms as underwear."

"Don't you think he has weird things too?"

"Yes, I'm sure he does. What if they annoy me too much?"

"And what if they don't? I totally get what you're saying about people trying to make things work after an accidental pregnancy, but it's not like you and Archer are some random hookup. You've known the guy since you were fucking fourteen years old."

I take a moment to let that sink in. There's no one safer than Archer. I might not know the nitty-gritty, but I know him. I've known him for years. And he's known me.

"You're right."

"What?"

"You're right."

Marissa smiles and I realize she only asked 'what' so I'd repeat myself and say she was right twice. Laughing, I shake my head and pick up my yogurt, wanting to eat the granola before it gets soggy.

"Okay, fine. I do trust him. I'm scared things are too good to be true. He seemed really set on being a family and living together, and mentioning how he'd have a job makes me think he's leaning away from the fellowship and more toward getting his big-boy job. Hopefully here in Chicago or...or..."

"Or?"

"In Eastwood."

Marissa's eyes widen. "Eastwood?"

"Don't hate me."

"I could never hate you. Unless you quit your job, had a beautiful baby and moved to the quintessential town featured in every Hallmark Channel movie."

I purse my lips, staring at her. "Then I guess you might hate me. Though it's a small chance. Very small. The hospital in Eastwood is small, and I don't think Archer would be happy there. And he mentioned a while ago that the smaller the surgical team, the more on-call hours he'll have. Bigger hospitals have bigger teams and more people to pool from for on-call shifts."

"That makes sense."

I nod. "He really likes being a surgeon."

"I'd hope so, after a million years of school. But he likes you more."

I smile again. "Yeah. I think so too."

I hang up the phone and rub my temples. I wasn't expecting that. Not at fucking all. I'm still a little stunned. Raising my arms above my head, I stretch and roll my neck. I'm used to standing in the same position for hours and didn't realize I've been sitting and hardly moved for the last hour and a half.

I go to the window, giving myself a moment to process everything, and look down at the city. I'm in Quinn's kitchen, and the view is amazing. In my younger years, I would have loved to live here. I'd feel like a fucking baller up in this place, with its large white kitchen and lakefront view.

But now...now I'm questioning raising a child in a place like this. Not because I don't think it's fitting, but because I know how Quinn grew up in a small town, and how I watched them, an outsider looking in, and thought the Dawsons were fucking perfect.

I press one hand against the cool glass, staring at Lake Michigan until my vision goes blurry. Recalling everything I said in the last half hour, I don't have any regrets, which is a first.

"I think that went well," I tell Neville, crouching down to pet the fat orange cat. "Better than I expected."

My eyes fall shut and I sit on the floor, leaning against the window. I'm tired and want to try to get a few hours of sleep before Quinn comes home from work. I need to catch up on my sleep for my own sake, but mostly, I want to go out and have fun with Quinn tonight before I have to leave and get back to work in the morning.

Physically, I'm worn the fuck out. Mentally, I'm even more exhausted, but it's going to be damn hard to turn my brain off. My best bet is to jerk off in the shower and collapse into bed, dreaming of Quinn. If I'm really lucky, I'll stay asleep until she gets home from work and she'll wake me up with her lips around my cock.

With Quinn, I know it's possible. She's everything I could ever want, which is why the phone call that just ended is all the more important to me. I already turned down one job, and I'm having anxiety over it. What if I don't get offered another? Or if the only other job I'm able to land is hours away?

I squeeze my eyes shut, thinking of Quinn's pretty face. I can't let myself fall into negative thinking. I got through med school and all of my residency with the belief I'd land my dream job.

And working at Rush Hospital is a dream.

I'd be in Chicago. With Quinn. We'd be able to live together. Raise Emma as a family. I'll propose and eventually we'll get married and have more babies. I meant it when I told Quinn I'd be happy to support her.

I went through years and years of schooling and surviving off shitty-ass food and little sleep to be able to save lives and help others. But I'm also going to really fucking enjoy the salary that comes along with it. Though truth be told, I know I'll still work long hours even if I can become an attending and have my own residents to assign to weekends and holidays.

Yawning, I pick up Neville and go into the bedroom. Quinn's pajamas are on the floor, and I smile, thinking of her slender body and ample breasts. They most definitely have gotten bigger, and I'm almost surprised at how turned on I am by her growing belly. Knowing that my baby is inside of her, that I knocked her up, is a strange turn on, one I'm not sure I should openly admit to anyone but Quinn or not.

The tip of my cock tingles and I climb into bed with the thought of Quinn's tits on my mind. I pull the covers over me, smelling a mixture of Quinn's perfume and her conditioner on the pillows. I press my face in and breathe deep.

And now I have a boner.

Closing my eyes, I reach down, pushing my hand down the front of my boxers. I take hold of my cock and pump it up and down once. Twice. I moan into the pillow, missing Quinn so bad it hurts.

I'm pathetic, aren't I? I just saw her an hour ago and I'm already missing her to the point of jerking off to her memory. Though there's something about Quinn that turns me into a horny teenager all over again. At least this time it's legal.

I turn on my side, slowly rubbing my shaft. My eyes are shut, and I know once I come I'll be able to pass out and get some decent sleep until Quinn gets off work. I press my face into my pillow, wishing Quinn was in bed with me.

And then my phone rings.

Blinking and sitting up, I hope it's Quinn and I can get

just a few seconds of sexy talk out of her so I can come. But it's not Quinn. It's my fucking mother. I squeeze my eyes shut and exhale heavily. My phone is still ringing, but I'm not in the right headspace to talk to my mother right now.

I catch it on the last ring, putting the call on speaker and laying back down.

"Hello?"

"Hey, Archie. Did I wake you?"

"I'm in bed, but no. Did you find him?"

"I didn't, but the cops did."

"Good." Shit. I didn't mean to say that out loud. Or did I? "I mean, good he's been found. How is he?"

"He's high on something."

"How'd he get caught?"

"He was with that friend he calls Cuddy. I don't think that's his real name."

"Oliver Milstead," I tell her. I went to school with his younger sister. One of seven, Oliver and his siblings fit the stereotype that comes to mind when you say 'meth-heads.' When Bobby started hanging with Oliver, shit hit the fan. I'd love to blame Oliver, say he got my brother hooked on drugs, but the disease was always inside Bobby. He'd been pushing on the door his whole life. Oliver simply gave him the key.

"Right. That man. He was cooking in his garage. Bobby was over at the house at the time."

"Jesus fucking Christ."

"Archer," Mom scolds.

I pinch the bridge of my nose between my fingers. "Is he still in jail? Do you need bail money?"

"No, but thanks, honey. He's out and is home resting. I'm looking up new rehab facilities, ones not in the area. One of

Cuddy's cousins was in the same place with Bobby and convinced him to leave."

I grit my teeth, beyond irritated at how Mom acts like Bobby is the victim here, coerced into doing bad things against his will. "Thanks for letting me know."

"Of course, hun. How's Quinn? You said you were in Chicago, right?"

"I am, and she's good. She's at work right now."

"Have you two decided what you're going to do about that? Work, I mean, after the baby is born."

"Sort of. We've did decide that we're going to move in together."

"Oh, that's wonderful! But, uh, where are you moving?"

I close my eyes again. "I'm not sure. It depends on where I get a job. I just had a phone interview with someone from Rush. I'll find out if they want me to come in for a real interview in a week or two."

"Why do they have to take so long? They either want you, or they don't, and they know that right away."

I find myself smiling. "I wonder the same thing."

"So you two want to stay in Chicago?"

"Yeah," I say right away even though I haven't talked at length about it with Quinn. "She likes her job here."

"Chicago is nice. And you're closer to us there than you are in Indy."

"It is nice," I say with a yawn.

"I don't want to keep you, Archie. You sound tired. Get some rest, okay?"

"I will. Let me know if anything changes."

"Okay, love you, hun."

I hang up and lay back down, trying for half an hour to go to sleep. I can't turn off my fucking brain, so I end up turning on the TV and watch two hours' worth of TV before finally passing out.

———

QUINN'S LIPS PRESS AGAINST MINE, STIRRING ME FROM SLEEP. I'm dreaming about her and have a hard time distinguishing between what is real and what's a dream. It feels the same when we're together.

"Morning, sunshine," she whispers, and I wrap my arms around her waist, pulling her close to me. She falls into bed, and I spoon my body around hers.

"I missed you," I grumble, not ready to wake up just yet. It feels like I fell asleep only minutes ago.

"I missed you too."

"What time is it?" I ask, face in her hair.

"Like two-thirty. Have you been asleep this whole time?"

"Not the whole time." I'm not sure when I finally fell asleep, but it had to be around eleven. Or even noon. I'm taking years off my life being so tired all the time.

Quinn rolls over and rakes her fingers through my hair. "Go back to sleep."

"We can go out."

"Later. I'm tired too. And I think I felt Emma moving again."

"I love you, Quinn," I whisper, tipping my head up just enough to kiss her. And then I let my eyes fall shut again. Two hours later, I wake up, hot and sweaty. Quinn sleeps with a lot of blankets, and I don't know how she doesn't swelter in her sleep. I kick off the comforter and roll over, feeling relief from the ceiling fan above us, and close my eyes again.

Quinn rolls over, hand landing on my chest. "Archer?" she grumbles. "Are you awake?"

"Kind of," I say, slitting my eyes open. "Are you?"

"No."

Silently laughing, I take her hand and rub circles in her palm until we both fall back asleep, not waking until one of the cats jumps onto the nightstand and knocks Quinn's water bottle over. I startle awake, and Quinn feebly swats at Luna. This must happen often.

"Rise and shine, babe," I say to her with a smile.

"Morning," she says back, rolling over and wrapping her arms around me. "I didn't mean to sleep for so long."

"You needed it."

"So did you."

"Yeah. It feels good to lay down and do nothing. I'm aware of how lame I am, so no need to point it out."

Quinn laughs. "I sat in my comfy office chair all day and I still like to lay down and do nothing."

"My mom called," I start. "Bobby got arrested."

Quinn opens her eyes and pushes up on her elbow. "Shit."

"It's okay. It's a good thing, actually. He was with some loser who was cooking meth in his garage. It could have been a lot worse."

"He's okay?"

"For now."

She runs her hands through her hair and sits up. I realize for the first time that she's only wearing a camisole and white underwear. Whatever she has to say might be lost on me.

"I was thinking about what I said earlier, about how Bobby is family and you'll always care and all that."

"Yeah?" My eyes dart to her nipples.

"It's okay to cut off toxic family members, and if you think Bobby is toxic, then I support you in cutting him off."

"He's more than toxic. He's a festering pile of—" I stop, seeing Quinn's face. "He's still my brother, I know. And yes, I'll be upset when the day comes and he finally kicks it. But only for my parents."

Quinn's frown deepens. "If that's how you really feel, then okay."

I sigh. "It's not. I wish it was though."

She nestles her head back against my chest. "I did tell you I like honest-Archer best."

"I feel like an asshole when I'm honest about Bobby," I admit. "I do care about him because he's my brother, and he wasn't always a piece of shit. I'll be sad when he dies, but sometimes I wish it'd just happen already." I've never spoken these words out loud before. I've barely let myself even think them. "Every time my phone rings I wonder if it's *the call*. And if it's not his death my mom's calling about, then it's something he did. He's killing himself and there's no way around that. But he's going to take someone down with him too. Maybe it's driving under the influence or selling laced weed to kids. All Bobby does is destroy, and waiting for the end is worse than going through the final never-ending chapter."

"That makes sense," Quinn says quietly. "Living with the fear of never knowing what's going to happen would make me anxious."

"In a perfect world, he'd recover. But the world isn't perfect, and I know the odds of someone coming back from something like this."

"It's not impossible," Quinn adds, tracing her fingers up and down my chest. She flattens her hand and slowly drags it down, fingertips slipping under the band on my boxers.

"Instead of going out for dinner, I was thinking I could cook for you and then maybe we could go out for dessert."

"Sounds good to me."

"Have you had The Cheesecake Factory cheesecake before?"

"I have not. I'm guessing it's good?"

"It's so good." She pushes herself up, kissing me before getting out of bed. "Do you like chicken enchiladas?"

"There's not much I don't like. I'm easy like that."

"You are easy, Dr. Jones. I got in your pants on our first date, remember?"

Laughing, I slap her ass as we get out of bed, catching her around the waist. I pull her in and kiss her neck, dreading leaving already. I go into the living room, cats following, while Quinn uses the bathroom. The cats won't stop meowing, and I know enough now to know they're expecting dinner at this time.

Going to the cabinet where Quinn keeps the cat food, I don't see Quinn walking out of the bedroom. I close the cabinet and turn. The can of cat food slips from my fingers.

"Holy shit." I blink, slowly running my eyes over Quinn. She's wearing dark purple lingerie and she's so right about her tits getting bigger. They're close to spilling out of the thin lace.

A bit of color rushes to her cheeks, which only adds to the appeal. "I was going to wait until later to put this on, but you keep surprising me. I wanted to surprise you for a change."

I take a few seconds to look her up and down again, memorizing every curve of her body. "This is a good surprise."

Her shy smile turns coy, and she walks right past me,

heels clicking on the hardwood floor, and bends over to get a pot from a cabinet next to the oven.

"Sit down," she says, putting the pot on the burner. "Part of your surprise is getting to watch me cook. Well, if that's something you'd like." She turns to me, cheeks flushed again. "I'm not very good at this."

"You're perfect."

19

QUINN

"I think we should make this a regular Friday-night occurrence," Archer says. We're sitting on the couch, naked and snuggled together with our feet propped up on the coffee table and plates of food on our laps. "I like eating naked."

"I do too, and I have to say I did a good job on these enchiladas."

"They taste just like the ones your mom makes," he tells me, knowing that's a compliment. My mom is a great cook.

"The recipe is pretty easy to follow," I confess. "It's not like a four-course fancy meal or anything, though I think the preparation gives this meal five stars."

"You could have made me Ramen noodles and it would have been five stars."

Laughing, I take my last bite and put my plate on the coffee table, reaching over to get my water. Archer gets up to get a second helping, and I shamelessly watch his ass as he walks into the kitchen.

Once we're done eating, we lounge around a bit and then get dressed to head out. The weather turned overnight, and the air has a cool crispness in it that always excites me. I love the fall.

"Are you hungry for dessert yet?" Archer asks me.

"Oh hell no." I pat my stomach. "I'm still not used to eating full meals like this."

"I'm glad you're able to again. See?" He gently nudges me. "There is light at the end of the tunnel."

"Yeah. I'm excited to get to that end too. Who do you think Emma will look like?"

"I imagine her to look like you."

"Me too. And if she were a boy, she'd look like you."

"That's how I imagined it too," he says with a chuckle. "I hope she has your green eyes."

"Is that possible? I don't remember anything about genes from the bio class I took in high school."

"Yeah, it's possible, but she's more likely to get brown eyes from me. So, sorry." He gives me a smile. "I think the percentage is around thirty-eight for green and fifty for brown."

"That's higher than I thought you'd say. I do like having green eyes, but I like yours too. Our child will have dark hair, right? How do dominant genes work?"

Archer's eyes light up. "You really want me to explain it? Because I will."

"Sure. But don't get mad if I don't follow along."

"I'm happy to repeat myself. I told you, biology fascinates me."

ARCHER COMES TO A SUDDEN STOP, STARING ACROSS THE street. We're making our way down Michigan Avenue on our way to the Cheesecake Factory.

"See a ghost?" I ask him.

"That's Dr. Crawford."

"Who?"

"The trauma surgeon I wanted to talk to at the convention."

"Oh! Should we go say hi?"

He shakes his head, looking almost starstruck. "He probably doesn't remember me."

I look across the street, guessing Dr. Crawford to be the stuffy looking old man walking next to a thin woman in a red coat. "They're going into Gucci. Let's go in."

"To Gucci?"

"Yes," I say with a laugh. "I really like their handbags, and it's been a while since I've gotten a new one."

Archer takes my hand as we stop at the crosswalk. "Okay. I guess it won't hurt to see if he remembers me."

"Exactly." Cars zoom by, and a couple of minutes later we cross and enter the store.

"Good evening, Ms. Dawson!" one of the clerks says, looking up from behind the counter.

"How long is a while?" Archer asks, raising his eyebrows. "They know you by name here."

"I'm very memorable."

He smiles and steals a glance at Dr. Crawford, who's standing behind his wife looking bored. I walk past the purses and over to the display of belts the doctor's wife is looking at. Buying a five-hundred-dollar belt to fit my pregnant belly isn't something I can rationalize, but I could always buy one for later, right? Anything to try and get Archer an in with the doc.

"I have that one," I say to whom I assume is Mrs. Crawford. She's holding a black leather belt with gemstones on the logo. "I always get compliments on it."

She runs her fingers over the colored stones. "You don't think it's a little young for me?"

"Not at all! I think it'd look great on you."

She smiles. "Thank you for saying that." Her eyes go to my purse on my shoulder. "I see you have great taste."

"It's more like an addiction," I laugh, and she does too. I turn away from the belts, lusting over pretty much everything in this store, and see Archer looking at shoes, and probably choking over the price tags.

"Find what you're looking for?" he asks, coming over. His hand settles on my hip.

"I found too much." I look behind him. "You'd look really good in that suit, you know."

He smiles and shakes his head. "Give me a year—or two, probably two—to make more than I do as a resident and then we'll come back here."

"Deal. Are you going to talk to him?"

"I don't want to be awkward."

"You won't be." I step forward. "Actually, I do need a new fancy professional outfit to wear when I go talk with those professors from MIT."

"Already?"

"I'm giving a speech at graduation." I shake my head. "Unless I chicken out. But that Professor Slughorn guy I told you about has been emailing me about coming in and talking to his class this semester."

"You should do it," Archer encourages. "Like you said, you're in the minority being a successful woman working in the technology field."

"True. And I haven't been back to MIT since graduation. It'll be kinda fun to see the campus again."

"Excuse me," Mrs. Crawford says. "I don't mean to

eavesdrop, but did you say you're giving a commencement speech at MIT's graduation ceremony?"

"She did." Archer smiles at me. The way he's looking at me right now makes my heart skip a beat.

"Our son is graduating high school this year and that's his top choice."

"It's a great school."

"You went there as well?"

"I did," I say with a smile. "And I loved it. It opens so many doors and the education is priceless. What's your son's area of interest?"

"Algorithms and code or something like that."

"That's what I do!" I say a little too excitedly. But hey, if Archer looks cute when he talks about genes, maybe I look cute too? "I work at IGH now overseeing software development as well as creating codes for high-profile clients. Having that MIT degree definitely helped me land the job."

Mrs. Crawford says, "Barry, this young woman went to MIT. Maybe she has some advice for John."

Dr. Crawford comes over, a pleasant smile on his face. "Sorry to bombard you while shopping," he starts. "We're more than a little excited. Not to be those parents that brag, but John is a smart boy."

"No worries. I don't run into too many people around here looking to apply to MIT. It's exciting!"

"We're not ashamed to be *those parents*," Mrs. Crawford says. "We're very proud of our son and take any opportunity we can to help him."

Archer tips his head down to me. "I think we'll be like that too."

I put my hand on my stomach. "I think so too."

Dr. Crawford's eyes drop to my middle. "Are you expecting?"

Mrs. Crawford elbows him sharply in the ribs. "You can't ask people that!"

Archer and I laugh. "I am," I tell him, and Dr. Crawford looks at Archer, and a spark of recognition crosses his face.

"I know you," he starts, still staring at Archer.

"We've met before," Archer starts, "at a conference in June."

"Dr. Jones from Indianapolis," Dr. Crawford recalls. "Yes. I do remember you. You made quite an impression on Dr. Miller."

"A good one, I hope," Archer says and we all laugh.

"Yes, she spoke very highly of you. If I recall correctly, you're finishing your surgical residency this year and are interested in a trauma fellowship."

It's all I can do not to make a weird squeaking noise of excitement. Archer wants this fellowship so bad. It'll be long hours, hard work, and functioning on little sleep. But if he's in Chicago, we can live together. He'll be crazy busy busting his butt to become a trauma surgeon, but we'll be able to raise Emma as a family under one roof.

"Yes, I am interested."

"You're sure you want to do that with a little one on the way?" Dr. Crawford raises his eyebrows. "It's long hours."

"It can't be worse than what I'm working now, can it?" Archer says back with no hesitation.

Dr. Crawford laughs. "I don't miss my days as a resident. Though at least now you've been capped on your hours. Back in my time, there were no regulations."

"I've heard horror stories. The first attending I worked with scared a resident out of the program."

"If stories can scare a resident, he has no place in surgery in the first place."

"That was my thought too. And all the stories in the world can't prepare you for that first time shit goes south."

Dr. Crawford laughs. "My first day of med school I had two patients die. Completely unrelated and total freak accidents."

"That's one hell of an orientation. One of the first surgeries I observed, the surgeon perforated a bowel. None of us were prepared for that smell."

Both Archer and Dr. Crawford laugh, and I find it oddly sexy to hear him telling what I guess would be considered doctor jokes.

Mrs. Crawford shakes her head and leans into me. "He'll talk about surgery all day." She rolls her eyes. "How long ago did you graduate? You look so young."

"Four years ago."

"And did you start at IGH right away? John has mentioned that company a few times, so I know it must be good. I'm not the best with technology. I have a hard enough time with my cell phone."

"I had an internship there and after the year was up, they hired me."

"Oh, I didn't know they offered internships. What are the requirements?"

"A college degree for a paid internship, but we do have unpaid interns who basically shadow and help with small tasks. It's not the most fun, but it looks good on a resume or college application. I can give you my email if you'd like and maybe we can set something up."

Mrs. Crawford thanks me over and over, and saves my email address in her phone. Archer and Dr. Crawford are still talking about surgery and difficult patients. I get back to shopping, purposely taking my time so Archer has more time to talk with the doc.

We're finally on the same page. In love, wanting to raise Emma as a family. I don't think marriage is that far off, though I still want Archer to take his time and make sure this is really what he wants to do.

My mind jumps ahead of me, to accompanying Archer to fancy dinners with the Crawfords. We're married and have at least two kids at home. Mrs. Crawford talks to me about MIT, and Archer and Dr. Crawford compare days in the OR.

I blink and shake my head. I don't do fancy dinners like that. I'll go out on a hot date, don't get me wrong, but playing the pretentious wife—yeah. That's not me. I like designer shoes and purses, with the occasional accessory thrown in, but that's not me and it never will be.

I'm small town born and raised, coming from a large family who had to cut corners and coupons to get by. My dad's business didn't take off until my senior year in high school, and when I sold that app, I had no idea what to do with all the money.

I paid off my student loans. And Dean's. And Logan and Owen's. Weston's were taken care of thanks to the US Army, but I would have paid those off too. I gave myself an allowance and then stuck half the money in a savings account and had an investor help me with various investments. It's nice having disposable income, I won't lie, but the fancy, stuck-up, I'm-better-than-you-because-I-have-money life isn't for me, and I sure as hell won't let Emma grow up thinking that.

Several minutes later, I go to the register and pay for a new pair of shoes. Archer comes up behind me, followed by the Crawfords.

"If you change your mind about the fellowship, you should consider applying at Northwestern," Dr. Crawford tells Archer. "I'd love to have a surgeon like you on my team."

"I will consider that. Thank you," Archer tells him. They shake hands, and Mrs. Crawford thanks me again. Archer keeps a neutral face until we exit the store and make it a good few yards away.

"I have a good feeling about this fellowship now," he says with a smile.

"Me too. I know it'll be crappy hours again, but if you're here, it'll be okay."

He tips his head down to mine, pressing a kiss on my forehead. "Yeah. It will be."

"NOW THIS IS FUCKING AWESOME." ARCHER GOES TO THE EDGE of the rooftop, making my anxiety shoot up, and looks out over the city. There is a patio on the roof of my building, and while it's usually occupied, we're some of the only people up here right now.

"It is. But, uh, can you come away from the edge?"

Archer places his hands on the thick cement railing. It comes up past his waist but still makes me nervous. "Does this freak you out?" he asks and leans forward just a bit. I squeeze my eyes closed. He laughs and comes back. "Babe, I'm fine. But I won't scare you. Raising your blood pressure isn't good for Emma."

"So when I'm not pregnant you plan to freak me out?"

"Oh, totally. I might pull a Michael Jackson and dangle Emma off a balcony or something."

I swat his arm, pursing my lips. "I would kill you."

He laughs again. "How'd you do it?"

"It'd probably be a messy heat-of-the-moment type of kill."

"One of the benefits of being a doctor is knowing how to kill people and have it be untraceable."

"That's the whole reason you went to med school, isn't it?"

"Yep. That's what's in that storage locker, but the way."

"Ah-ha," I laugh. The first time I stayed with him in Indy, I joked about going through his personal possessions, but the majority of incriminating evidence was stored away. "I knew it."

He pulls the blanket around us both and holds me close. We brought the cheesecake to the roof to eat and haven't gone back inside yet. It's breezy and cold up here tonight, making it perfect for snuggling.

"I miss the stars," I say distantly, looking up. "I don't see them too often here."

Archer moves my hair back out of my face. "You miss Eastwood, don't you?"

"Yes and no. I miss my family and that small-town feeling, as lame as that sounds. But I like it here."

I like it here because I like my job...which takes me back to the whole being a stay-at-home mom or not. If I decide to stay home, then I'd like to move back to Eastwood. I have Marissa here and a few others from work that I hang out with occasionally, but that's it. Would I be lonely? I can't see myself joining a moms group or anything like that, and there's only one other couple with a baby in the building. Everyone else who lives here is either single or much older.

"I like Eastwood," Archer says. "And it's not lame to like the small-town feeling. I like it too. Ever since I was eighteen, it's had this sense of safety for me. For obvious reasons." He exhales heavily. "Going back is always a reprieve."

"Yeah," I agree, mind whirling. If I lived in Eastwood, I'd have my whole family around to pitch in with Emma too. Mom took Jackson one night a week when he was a newborn to let Wes and Daisy catch up on sleep. Daisy was already on the verge of flaking out, but that one night where she and Wes got to sleep without interruptions probably kept her from going crazy sooner rather than later.

I'd have built-in babysitters when Archer and I went out on dates. Mom would be just minutes away and able to come over whenever I need her. Other than family, there are other reasons I loved Eastwood growing up, and the pro and con list is heavily skewed with pros.

But the hospital in Eastwood is half the size of the one Archer is at now. He wouldn't be happy there.

"Getting tired?" he asks.

"Kind of. I'm feeling sickly full."

"Me too. I shouldn't have had that third piece."

"I could hardly finish my one and only piece," I say with a laugh.

Archer kisses my neck and goosebumps break out along my flesh. "Let's go in."

He gathers our stuff and I stand, wrapping the blanket around my shoulders. We go back into my apartment and strip down to our underwear and get into bed.

Archer is leaving in the morning, and we won't see each other again for another week. He has to work next weekend, but I'm coming down to see him anyway. I want to have sex since it's going to be a good while until he's naked and on top of me, but dammit, I'm tired.

Yawning, I nestle against my pillow. Archer takes me in

his arms, pulling me against his chest. I resituate and listen to his heart beating, slow and steady.

"Babe, if you're tired you should get ready for bed."

"I'm not tired," I grumble.

"Convincing, Quinn." He tightens his hold on me and kisses me again. "Come on. You're going to have an even harder time getting up if you wait."

"I know. I don't want to stop snuggling." I let out a breath, knowing he's right. He gets up first and helps me to my feet. I'm feeling a little sick again and get ready for bed as quickly as possible. I cuddle up under the covers, waiting for Archer to get in bed.

He's sitting on the side of the bed, checking something on his phone.

"Want to know something pathetic?"

"Sure," I answer, opening my eyes.

"I have a week of vacation in late October. I forgot about it."

"How do you forget about vacation?"

"I scheduled it at the beginning of the year. We should do something."

That perks me up. "Like what?"

"Go somewhere. Just the two of us. Are you able to get off work?"

"It's a month away, so it shouldn't be a problem. I don't take vacations often either. We could go on a babymoon."

"Babymoon?"

"It's a word that basically means a couple goes on vacation before the baby is born. A last hurrah, if you will."

"I like that. What about Hawaii?"

"Heck yes! Have you been? I haven't."

He shakes his head. "I've always wanted to go. Or we

could do Disney. Oh wait, you can't do rides. I'll still go if you want to though."

"I'd be sad not to go on Tower of Terror and Space Mountain if I'm in Disney. But I do think we should take Emma there for her first vacation."

"Sure. You can pick where to go. As long as I'm with you, I'm happy. Also, I don't have a passport."

I laugh. "Get one. Aruba is gorgeous and not in a hurricane zone. Fall is hurricane season for a lot of tropical places."

"Good point." He turns off the bedside lamp and spoons his body around mine. "Pick a place and give me the info. I'll book everything."

"Hawaii sounds so nice. Laying on the beach in a bikini is my kind of a vacation."

"Mine too," he says, snuggling in closer. "Night, babe. I love you."

I put my hands on top of Archer's, heart so full it could burst. "Love you too."

I cried when Archer left this morning. I didn't mean to, and I tried really hard not to, but I'm full of so many damn hormones I can't help it. Our goodbye lasted longer than it should, and he had to speed to make sure he's home in time for his call-shift.

He got up early, and after lying in bed worrying about him falling asleep while driving, I called him, and we talked for half an hour. After that, I ended up falling back asleep, and now that I'm up again, I'm keeping my phone by my side. Archer should be arriving at his place in the next half hour or so, and he promised to call as soon as he got in so I know he's okay.

Not wanting to risk sitting around my apartment feeling sorry for myself the rest of the weekend, I get dressed and go get out of the house, going to the pet store for cat food and litter. I usually order everything off Amazon because what's the point of advancing technology if I'm not going to use it, right?

I've been ordering groceries for the last year and I don't think I can ever go back. It's just a pain lugging everything from my car to the elevator. A couple on the floor below me have a collapsible wagon, and I used to think it was silly. Now I think it's genius.

Mom calls as I'm lugging the heavy cat litter down the hall, and I wait to call her back until I'm inside and the litter is in the foyer, where it'll probably stay for the rest of the day at least.

"Hey, hun," Mom says when I call her back. "How are you feeling?"

"All right. The morning sickness is slowly fading. Emphasis on the slow."

"You're in the second trimester. It should be gone soon. Hang in there."

I put the phone on speaker and go to the sink, washing my hands. "Yeah. I'm only fifteen weeks. I still have so far left to go."

"It'll go by faster than you think," she says and pauses. I know what she's waiting for, and I throw her a bone and just say it.

"Archer and I talked about living arrangements after Emma is born. We're going to move in together."

"Ahh, yay! That's what I was hoping to hear. Is he moving in with you?"

I grab a piece of cheesecake and sit on the couch. "It still depends on where he gets a job, but he's applying to the different hospitals around here." I stick my fork into my cheesecake. "And yesterday we ran into some famous doctor, or something who I think runs the fellowship Archer's hoping to get into."

"That sounds promising."

"I think so too."

"We miss you around here. Both of you. Jackson asks for

Archer every day. That boy hasn't forgotten who saved his life."

"We might be able to come in like two weeks. Archer works next weekend, and I'm going to Indy to see him."

"It'll be nice once you two are in the same city."

"I know. I don't like this long-distance thing. I miss him."

"Have you thought more about the baby shower? I know you said Archer is done with his residency at the end of the year and will start a new job right away."

"That's the hope."

"Does he know his schedule far in advance?"

"I'm actually not sure how far, but I think so."

"Let me know. I was thinking we could do it mid-December. You'll be close to the third trimester, so I know it's a little early, but it's not like we're doing it next week. And if we have it on the fifteenth or sixteenth, it's far enough from Christmas it shouldn't be an issue."

"That could work. I'll ask Archer about his schedule the next time we talk."

"Great. And if that doesn't work, then we can plan for the end of January."

"We'll know where we're living by then."

"Are you taking time off work after the baby is born?"

"I'm not sure," I start and tell her pretty much everything Archer and I talked about. Mom thinks I should be a stay-at-home mom, which is appealing in a way but makes the feminist in me question if it's oppressive. Though in the end, I suppose the most anti-feminist thing is going against what I *want*. And I'm leaning more and more towards wanting to be home with my baby.

"Whatever you decide will work out," Mom goes on. "It makes me happy to hear you and Archer talking long-term.

I don't want you to be with him just because you're having his child, but raising that baby as a family is the best thing."

"Yeah," I say, not totally agreeing with her. Raising the baby in a happy, healthy home is the best, not forcing a relationship so she can have two parents in the same house. "He's a great guy. I've always thought so."

Mom laughs. "I never would have thought you and Archer would end up together. But yes, he's a good guy and we like him. And it seems like Dean's coming around."

"Finally," I stress. "He's been a total baby about this."

"You have to understand—"

"Mom," I interrupt. "I get he's your kid and all, but come on."

"Fine," she agrees with a huff. "He's always been my dramatic child."

"So dramatic. Anyway, Archer and I are going on vacation together next month."

"While pregnant? Are you sure that's a good idea."

I'm so glad Mom can't see me roll my eyes right now.

———

"Morning," I say to Raul, walking into the break room Monday morning. I woke up and didn't feel sick today, which is enough of a small victory for me to talk to everyone in the office today.

"Hey, lady." He adds slices of cucumber to his water. "Look at that little baby belly."

"It popped more overnight, I swear."

"You're going to be all belly, I can see it now. My sister was small like you before she got knocked up. Looking at her from the back, you couldn't even tell she was pregnant."

"My feet might give me away." I make a face and look

down at my brand-new Gucci shoes. They fit like a glove at the store. And early this morning while I was sitting at my desk. But after standing and talking for just ten minutes, my ankles are looking a little puffy, and the straps of my heels are tight. *Sorry, gorgeous metallic gold heels.*

"Did you change your mind about letting us throw you a shower?" he goes on.

"I don't know," I say and get myself a cup of coffee. I add a tiny amount of regular and fill the rest up with decaf. "I feel weird knowing people are coming to a party for me and have to bring presents."

"That's the point of a shower. We all love you."

Rene and Charlene come in and stop talking almost immediately. They both look impeccable, and I don't understand how Charlene's bun looks equally done up and effortless at the same time.

"Isn't caffeine bad for the fetus?" Rene asks, eyes cold. Yeah, yeah. I get it. You're jealous. You only wrote a dozen emails to your sister saying how you wished Archer knocked you up instead of me so you could quit and be a doctor's wife. She really needs to learn not to send scathing emails about her boss on the company server...

"It's fine in moderation."

"Seems like a risk."

I force a smile. "It's not. My OB said it was fine and Archer—my boyfriend and the baby's father who's a doctor —also assured me it's fine." Maybe I'm being petty but fuck it. I'll blame it on the hormones.

"Right. I guess it's up to you in the end anyway."

"Yeah. It is." Raul catches my eye and raises his eyebrows. Most of the other people who work here fall into a similar category as me and were looked down on as nerds or dorks in high school and even college. It's weird how something that happened so long ago still holds an effect on me.

I take my coffee into my office and go through emails, responding to clients and scheduling meetings for the rest of the week. I need to clear my vacation time with the few people above me, making sure it's not going to interfere with anything we have going on. I don't think it will, and since I haven't taken any vacation yet this year, I doubt it'll be an issue.

I really do have it good here, which is going to make it harder to leave. I don't think there are many other places that are so up-to-date with the latest trends and technology while still being laid back and easygoing like this. I have no doubts I'll enjoy being home with Emma, but I'm sure going to miss this place.

Tapping my pen against my planner, my mind starts to drift. I'll be faced with opposition to whatever I choose. If I decide to be a stay-at-home mom, there will be plenty of people who will tell me I should contribute to my family by holding a job. And if I decide to come back to work, I won't hear the end of it from others who think it's the mother's place to stay home and raise babies.

In the end, it comes down to what I want to do, and that's all that matters. Trouble is, I'm still not sure what I want to do. Looking down at my belly, I shake my head.

"I'll figure it out," I tell her. "We still have time."

Taking a drink of coffee, I get to work, reviewing a file and finding errors right away. It's not an easy fix either, because changing one part creates change in other areas. Sighing, I lean back in my chair and give myself a minute before going and talking to those working on the project.

This part of my job isn't something I'll miss.

My phone dings with a text, lighting up from inside

my purse. I roll my chair over to get it instead of getting up. It's from Dean, texting in the group with Archer and me.

Dean: Have you picked a date for the baby shower yet? Kara keeps bugging me about our wedding shower and doesn't want it to be close to your party.

Me: Why does it matter if they're close together?

Dean: IDK. Kara thinks it'll be too much for our side of the family or something.

Me: Mom's not throwing the bridal shower. That makes no sense.

Dean: Can you just pick a date?

Me: We're thinking December. Archer knows he'll have a weekend off before Xmas

Dean: Are you sure on that? You don't want to switch it?

I send an eye rolling emoji, having a feeling Kara is on the other side of his texts, telling him what to say. Dean felt betrayed by Archer, worried he lost his best friend, which is why he acted like an ass. Kara was on our side at first...and then realized her wedding isn't going to be the center of attention. Which is funny since she said she doesn't like having all eyes on her.

Weddings bring out the best of us.

Me: If you want to have your shower in December, then just say it. Archer and I really don't care when we have it. I'm sure we can find at least one weekend off together before Emma is born to have a shower. Right, Arch?

Dean: Okay. Thanks. Kara is freaking out about next semester in school. She's turned wedding planning into a part-time job.

Me: So this small, casual wedding is no more?

Dean: There are more people on the guest list then I actually know.

I laugh and shake my head. I don't understand why people freak out so much over a wedding. I get that it's a big deal and it symbolizes something huge. Love should be celebrated.

But not at the expense of going into debt.

Dean: Also, Kara doesn't know what to do about the bachelorette party

Me: Aren't her sisters planning it?

Dean: Yeah, I mean she doesn't know if she should invite you or not. You can't do anything.

Me: I can do lots of stuff.

Dean: You know what I mean, sis...

Me: I do. Tell her she doesn't have to invite me. We can go out and drink another time.

Dean: Good plan. Another question...

Me: Yeah?

Dean: Do you still want to be in the wedding party?

I blink once. Twice. Three times. I know he's only asking because Kara's hoping I'll say no.

Me: I want to be in it if I'm welcome.

Dean starts typing and stops to delete what he wrote several times. I look at my phone, waiting for him to respond. Now I know this is all Kara. Even if Dean didn't want me in the wedding party, there's no way in hell he'd risk the wrath of our mother. She's going to be pissed.

Shaking my head, I put my phone down and get back to work. Five minutes later, Dean calls.

"Calling to kick me out of your wedding?" I ask. I'm being catty, but it's Dean.

"Shut up."

"Then why are you calling?"

He sighs. "Kara is worried about you being super pregnant at the wedding."

"Super pregnant? Nice."

"Well, you either will be, or you'll have a newborn."

"I know."

"Right now, we have an even number of bridesmaids and groomsmen, but we can't assume you'll be there."

"So you'd rather not have me?"

"No," he rushes out. As annoyed as I am with him, I do feel a little bad for the guy. This wedding is turning levelheaded Kara into a bridezilla. "I want you there. But if you don't want to be there, it's okay too."

"Gee, way to be subtle."

He laughs. "Yeah, that did sound bad. What I mean is, I don't want you to feel bad if you can't be there. I know you and how you feel bad about everything."

"That is true, but I really don't think I'll feel bad if I'm pushing out a baby the day of your wedding. It's not like I'm bailing because I'm too lazy to go." I pick up the pen again and start tapping it against my desk, not realizing how much this is upsetting me. "You can't punish me for being pregnant."

"I'm not!"

"It feels like you are. And let me remind you that my due date was determined before you picked your wedding date. You're acting like I chose when I got knocked up just to spite you."

"That's not true." Dean lets out an exasperated sigh. "I'm sorry, okay?"

"Okay."

A few seconds of silence tick by. "Mom said you and Archer are going to Hawaii?"

"I think so. We're going somewhere in October. We still have to pick a place."

"That'll be nice. Get a chance to relax before the baby comes and all."

"That's our thinking." I subconsciously rub my belly. "Are you still weirded out by us?"

"Yes," he says honestly. "But it's cool too. My best friend is the father of my niece. He's family now."

"Right. It'll make holidays more fun for you to have him there."

"It will, and I think we'll have to bust out some of our old traditions. You might not know about them."

I laugh. "I don't think I want to."

"Hey, sorry to cut you short, but Dad and I have to head out and see a client."

"Thanks for calling."

"Of course, sis."

We hang up and I feel a little better, though it still stings to know Kara is more concerned about having an equal number of bridesmaids and groomsmen in her photos than having me there.

Getting up to pee, I force myself to talk to Mike and Samantha, who incorrectly coded the new program. They took the news better than I hoped. There were no tears at least.

My phone dings when I sit back at my desk. It's Archer, replying to the group messages. He was in surgery and missed it all, but doesn't care about dates either. He calls right after that, and I answer on the first ring.

"Hey, babe. Are you okay?"

I know exactly what he's asking about. "Yeah. Dean called and tried to explain. Kara is obsessing over things being perfect and is worried I'm going to go into labor at the altar or something."

He chuckles. "If you're still pregnant by then, it's entirely possible."

"Oh my God, don't even say that. How's your day going? You're out of surgery already? It's early."

"I just finished my second procedure for the day. I started at six a.m."

"I am not a morning person."

"I've noticed."

I prop my feet up, trying to hold off on taking my shoes off. They're just so pretty. "I'm going to look up resorts and plane tickets during lunch. Want me to send you options?"

"Sure. I'm looking forward to seeing you in your bikini all week."

"Baby bump and all."

"You're still sexy, Quinn."

I smile. "I'm glad you think so."

"I do. And I keep thinking about you in that lingerie. I should have taken a photo."

"I did take one. Want me to send it to you?"

"Do you really have to ask?"

"I'll send it then."

A page goes out for Dr. Jones, echoing through the phone. "That's me," he says. "Gotta go. Love you."

"Love you too."

I quickly send the photo, smiling when I think of Archer's face when he opens the text. Setting my phone down, I get back to work, only making it so far as pulling up a new file before Archer texts me back. He's at work and can't send me a sexy photo back, but just a selfie of him in his scrubs is enough for me. I flip my phone over but don't just see Archer's name.

I see Archer's name next to Dean's...in the group message we were just texting in.

Oh God. No. No, no, no, no. I didn't—I mean I couldn't—but maybe. I madly unlock my phone.

"Oh my God."

I did. I sent a sexy photo of myself to Archer *and my brother*. I might as well start digging my own grave now because I'm officially dead.

"Fuck." I start typing something only to stop. What the hell do I say after this?

Archer: Thanks, babe, but I don't think Dean wants to see that. Sorry, buddy. Don't really wash your eyes with bleach. It could make you blind.

Me: Delete this whole thread, Dean. Now.

I space out my words, trying to bury the image so he won't see it when he opens the text.

Me: Don't

Me: Even

Me: Look

Me: Just

Me: Delete

Archer: What are you doing?

Me: Burying the image. OMG OMG

Archer: So you don't want me to screenshot it and send again?

Me: NO

I set my phone down, laughing to keep from crying. Sucking it up, I call Dean. His phone rings. And rings. And rings.

And then my mother answers. I don't know if this is a blessing or a curse.

"Hey, honey! Dean's out on a job with Dad. He left his phone at home."

"Hi, Mom." If I could internally cringe any harder, I'd turn inside out.

"They won't be back until later. Is something up?"

"Uh, not really."

"It's good to see you two talking again," Mom says.

I close my eyes, bracing myself for what I'm going to say. There's no point in denying it, in acting shy and trying to pretend like Archer and I are waiting until marriage. I'm pregnant, for fuck's sake. "Mom, I need a favor."

"Sure, hun. What is it?"

"I accidentally sent a sexy photo of myself to Dean and Archer when I meant to send it to only Archer. Obviously. Can you delete it?"

A few seconds of stunned silence tick by. "Oh, well, you shouldn't send images like that, Quinn. You of all people know what happens on the internet does not stay on the internet."

I don't bother telling her that statement doesn't quite make sense. "Mom, please?"

"I don't want to see it. Can you hack in and delete it or something?"

"If I could, I wouldn't be asking you this very embarrassing favor. Just open the texts and delete the thread. You won't see the picture. I buried it with text."

"Okay." Mom pulls the phone away from her ear. My heart is thumping and I'm pretty sure I'm just a ghost right now after I died of embarrassment. "It's gone."

"Thanks, Mom."

"That's something I never thought I'd have to do," she laughs. "Especially not from you."

"I know." I shake my head at myself. "I was trying to send it fast and wasn't paying attention. Archer, Dean, and I have had a group chat going for a while."

"That's good news. Those two need to get along."

"It's not Archer who's not getting along," I say, automatically becoming defensive. "Dean's the drama queen, remember?"

"Be nice to your brother, but yes, I remember. And it's a good thing he left his phone because this wouldn't have gone over well."

"Oh, I know. I need to get back to work. Thanks again, Mom."

I hang up and put my head in my hands, and then text Archer, double checking that it's only him I'm texting. I resend the picture and tell him that I had to ask my mother to save me.

I'm never going to live this down.

It takes a while to get back into the groove of things for work, but by lunch, I've moved past my stupid mistake. I go to find Marissa so I can make her walk with me to get hotdogs.

Jacob is walking in as I'm leaving my office. Oh, shit. I forgot I told him we could have lunch sometime when he came back from out of town. Is it too late to turn around and pretend I forgot something in my office?

"Quinn! Hey!"

Yep. It's too late. "Hey, Jacob. How was the trip?"

"Decent. San Francisco is a nice city. Are you still able to grab lunch?"

He came all the way from his office, and I technically did tell him yes. "I, uh," I mumble, looking around the office. We're surrounded by people and I don't want to embarrass the guy. "Sure." I'll let him down gently. "Did you have anywhere in mind? I was going to grab a hot dog from the vendor on the corner. We can sit in the courtyard and eat."

"I actually made us reservations at Mickey's."

Mickey's is a little authentic Italian place a few blocks from here. They have the best cheese ravioli in the city. And it's also where we went on our first date.

"Mickey's?" I echo. "I haven't been there in a while."

"I figured so. It's hard getting a table there."

"Yeah, how'd you manage that?"

"I helped Mick's son build a robot for his science fair. I have priority seating any time now."

"Ohh, look at you, you baller."

He leans back and narrows his eyes, nodding. I laugh and look back at my office. "Let me grab my purse then."

"Okay, great."

I debate on asking Marissa to 'invite herself' along to save me from any potential awkwardness. But I owe this to Jacob. If he's going to try and ask me out again, I want to be the one to let him down easy. We didn't have a passionate, wild, love and lust-filled relationship, but we're friends.

We get into the elevator together, neither speaking, and stand against the mirrored wall to let the little space fill with others. I put my hand on my stomach, bracing for the slight drop to make my stomach flip-flop.

"How are you feeling?" Jacob asks, flicking his gaze to my hand.

"Better now that I'm—wait, you know?"

"That you're pregnant?" he asks with a laugh. "I liked your announcement photo on Instagram."

"Oh yeah. You did. So you know Archer and I are together then, right?"

"I assumed so. I mean, you are pregnant."

My brows pinch together. "So you're not..."

"Trying to take you out on a date?" He laughs again. "No. I mean, if you'd let me take you out, I would. Archer's a lucky guy." He takes a step closer. "I have a business opportunity and we want you?"

"Are we finally building life-sized animatronic dinosaurs?"

"Close. Dragons."

"Even better."

He smiles and flicks his eyes to a few of my co-workers. I nod, knowing that this isn't something we can talk about in the elevator. The ride down takes forever, and my feet are aching by the time we're out on the sidewalk.

"I worked on a project for Henry Gibbons last year."

"I remember." Henry Gibbons is an environmental engineer who's made some great advancements in protecting the oceans.

"He wants to start his own company with a focus on energy saving."

"And he wants me?"

"Yeah. You're the best at what you do, and we need someone who can develop and write code."

"Then you came to the right person."

Jacob smiles. "Nothing's been set in stone yet, and we're just spitballing but need to get a team more or less established before we go through with things."

"Go on."

"He has office space in Lincoln Park, and during the start-up phase we'll have to meet several times a week, but this will eventually turn into something you can mostly do from home. It's a ways out—we're still looking for investors —so don't worry about giving me a yes or no to this. Just let me know if you're interested."

Writing code from home and developing advancements in technology that can help save the world? "Hell yes, I'm interested."

21

I zip up my suitcase and haul it into the living room. I'm on call tonight and then I'm home free, ready to spend a week on the Hawaiian coast with Quinn. Everything is ready, and I plan to sleep as much as I can until I have to go in. Then it's come back here, take a quick shower and drive to Chicago so Quinn and I can board the plane together.

The last time I went on a real vacation was my senior year during my pre-med schooling. Dean and I went to Miami for spring break, stayed in a shitty-ass motel and almost got hustled by a pair of twins. Can I even consider that a vacation?

"Did you pack the ring?" Sam asks, coming out of the kitchen.

I turn, giving him a surprised look. "You know about it?"

Sam's eyes widen. "I was giving you shit. You really bought her a ring?"

"Not quite. Her grandma gave me her ring to propose with."

"Are you going to?"

I run my hand through my hair and sit on the couch, reaching for my wallet on the coffee table. The ring is inside, and I've been constantly worried about losing it.

"I don't know."

Sam hikes an eyebrow. "Weren't you just telling me yesterday how you're all ready and shit to start a family and live together."

"Yeah. And I am. I want to marry her. Hell, I've known she's the only one for years."

"So what's the fucking problem?"

I let out a breath. "What if she says no?"

Sam laughs. "You're joking, right? She's in love with you and is pregnant with your child."

"That doesn't mean she wants to get married before the baby is born."

"So don't get married before the baby is born." Sam grabs the TV remote and sits on the lounge chair opposite me. "You're overthinking this. You love her. She loves you. If you want to propose, then fucking propose."

"I think the ring is too small."

Sam makes a face. "Give it to her now and upgrade later. You'll be able to buy a big rock in a year or two."

"True, but I mean the actual ring. It won't fit on her finger."

"Get it resized. Or is that bad to do with rings with sentimental value? I don't know this shit."

"I don't either. Her grandma suggested using the diamonds in another setting, but it feels wrong to take the thing apart."

Sam nods. "Just ask her. I want to throw you a bachelor party."

I chuckle. "I'll do it just for your sake then. But no, we're not going to try and recreate *The Hangover*."

"You're no fun, man."

"We'll do that for your wedding."

Sam lets out a snort of laughter. "I don't plan on settling down anytime soon. Don't forget, I'm younger than you." He turns on the TV. "One more year of residency and then I'll be making bank and can use that to impress the ladies. Only one-night stands for me."

"You're such a standup guy."

"Please," he retorts. "If you hadn't knocked Quinn up that's all she'd be to you."

It'd be easy to get mad at him and say Quinn's always been so much more to me, that we'd find our way together somehow.

But maybe we wouldn't.

I lived for years with a hole in my heart years ago? Would we be married with children already? Dwelling on what-ifs does no good. But thinking about the future does. And I'm not going to stand back anymore.

I'm proposing to Quinn on our trip.

I CHANGE OUT OF SURGICAL SCRUBS AND GRAB MY SHIT FROM my locker. I got three and a half hours of sleep before I got called in. I've been in back-to-back operations since, and I'm not sure if I'll be able to make the four-hour drive without falling asleep behind the wheel. I'm going over everything in my head and assuming traffic is moving like normal, I can get in a good power nap before making the drive.

I have a missed call from a Chicago number. There's no voicemail, and a tiny bit of panic flashes through me that something happened to Quinn. I call her cell right away, and she answers on the third ring.

"Are you okay?" I rush out.

"Yeah, why?"

"Someone with a Chicago area code called and my first thought was that something bad happened to you."

"That's kind of sweet. I'm fine, I promise. I just got up and am straightening up my apartment before we leave. I'm so excited!"

"Me too. This will be the longest time we've spent together."

"I hope you still like me at the end of the week," she jokes.

"It would take a lot for me to stop liking you, babe. And even more for me to stop loving you."

"Okay, you just earned major points with that one."

"I'll be sure to cash those in at some point this week."

"I'll be disappointed if you don't. I'm assuming you're at work, right? You said you had a missed call."

"Yeah. I've been here all night."

"Oh," she says, sounding a little disappointed. "Are you too tired to drive?"

"Nah, I'll be fine."

"I don't believe you," she says back right away. "Take a nap. I'd rather miss our flights than have you fall asleep behind the wheel. If you died, Archer, it would kill me."

"Stop thinking about it," I tell her, knowing she'll start crying. This new emotional side annoys her, but I find it charming. "I have time for a short nap, and I'll grab some espresso on the way."

"Naps make me feel more tired sometimes."

"The trick is not letting yourself get to REM sleep. You have to wake up before then."

"Right. I think I've heard that before. Go home and rest. Call me when you leave, please?"

"I will. Love you."

"Love you too."

I tuck my shirt into my pants, put on my belt and grab my lab coat, needing to do rounds on my patients before I can leave. I have at least twenty minutes of paperwork too, which is my least favorite about being a doctor.

A sense of relief comes over me when I step out of the hospital. I haven't been away for more than two days at a time in too fucking long. I speed home, take a quick shower, and crash in bed. The pressure to sleep keeps me from falling asleep, and when my alarm goes off to get up, I'm finally feeling tired. I set it again for another fifteen minutes and close my eyes.

Those fifteen minutes go by fast. Yawning my way out the door, I get back in my Jeep and head out. I get coffee on the road and talk to Quinn for the first hour. I make a pit stop for more coffee at the halfway point and walk around a bit to try and keep myself alert and awake. It's cloudy, and the farther north I go, the more it looks like a bad storm is about to rain down on us.

Quinn calls again about forty-five minutes later to make sure I hadn't fallen asleep at the wheel and says it's raining in the city with a storm forecasted to come in right around the time we're supposed to take off.

Traffic slows thanks to the rain, and I get to Quinn's with only minutes to spare before we have to leave for the airport. But when she answers her door in just a silk robe, I assume our plane has been delayed.

I don't waste time asking questions. I roll my suitcase to the side, close the door, and pick her up and kiss her.

"Good morning, Dr. Jones," she says, throwing her arms around me. "How was the drive?"

"You were on the phone with me most of the time," I say with a smile, kissing her again. I shift my gaze down, first noticing her bare breasts and hard nipples. "Emma has grown."

Quinn nods. "I feel it. And she's been kicking up a storm. It still feels squirmy and not kicky."

"Kicky?"

"It's a word. I think. I told her you were coming."

"That's not an appropriate thing to tell a baby." I raise my eyebrows and Quinn laughs. "How much time do we have?"

"Two hours. But the flight will probably get pushed back even more." She wrinkles her nose. "Though I'd much rather have the flight delayed ahead of time than to get there and sit on the runway for hours."

"Me too." I slide my hands down Quinn's ass. "How do you want to spend our time?"

Her full lips curve into a smile. "Remember the first time you kissed me?"

"I will always remember that."

"And what came after?"

"I believe you did. At least two times."

She nuzzles her lips against my neck. "I want to do that again."

"You don't have to tell me twice."

"ARCHER," QUINN WHISPERS, BREATH WARM ON MY SKIN. I passed out after we had sex and have no idea what time it is. The sky is still dark and cloudy, and rain hits the tall windows in her bedroom. If the promise of paradise wasn't on the horizon, I'd be tempted to stay here all day.

This is as close to perfect as anything.

"Is it time to get up?"

"Yeah. The storm passed, and I think the rain will let up enough for us to take off."

"One more minute?"

"Sure." She presses her lips to my neck and lays back down, running her nails up and down my arm. It takes more than one minute to pull myself out of bed. We get dressed and I help Quinn remake her bed. She says bye to her cats and feeds them a can of food before we do a quick double-check that we have everything and head out.

Quinn is beaming as we get into the elevator.

"Excited?" I ask, taking her carry-on bag from her. It's surprisingly heavy.

"What gave that away? Are you?"

"Yes. And right now, I'm excited to sleep on the plane."

"That's so sad, Arch," she says with a laugh. "I can't sleep on planes. I'm totally jealous that you'll pass out."

"I've learned to sleep anywhere simply for survival. After you work so many thirty-hour shifts, you sleep when you can wherever you can."

She pats her stomach. "My little energy sucker might help me fall asleep this time around though. It's been a while since I was on a plane for more than four hours."

The elevator stops two floors down, and an older couple gets in.

"Hello, Ms. Dawson," the man says.

"Hi, Mr. Keller. And Mrs. Keller. How are you?"

"We're good, thank you. Getting ready to brave the rain," the wife says, bringing her hand up to her hair. "Are you going on vacation?"

"We are," Quinn replies, tipping her head up at me. "Hawaii."

"Oh, you'll love it!" Mrs. Keller coos. "Our daughter went before her baby was due too. That whole babymoon thing wasn't around when we had our kids." She darts her gaze to me. "I didn't realize you two moved in together."

"We haven't yet," Quinn admits almost shyly. "This is my boyfriend, Archer. Arch, this is Mr. And Mrs. Keller from two floors down."

Mr. Keller shakes my hand. "Nice to meet you. That's a fine young woman you've got there."

I put my free hand on the small of Quinn's back. "She sure is."

"Have a fun trip." The elevator slows as it gets to the main level. "Nice meeting you, Archer," Mrs. Keller tells me. "Hopefully we'll run into you again."

"I'm sure you will. I'm hoping to get a job in the city."

"He's a doctor," Quinn tells them. "A surgeon, actually."

"Wow, how nice."

The doors open, and the Kellers step aside, letting us out first. Quinn already requested an Uber to take up to the airport, and one should be here any minute now.

"I wasn't going to bring up the whole doctor thing," I tease. "But you couldn't resist, could you?"

"It's almost like your sense of identity will fade away and you'll forget who you are if you don't constantly remind people of your MD status."

I laugh and push my suitcase against the wall as we wait. "Now, don't panic, but I didn't pack my lab coat or scrubs."

She dramatically gasps, bringing her hand to her mouth. "Now I might forget who you are." She slides her suitcase over by mine and looks outside for our ride. She checks the status of our fight, and when I look at my own phone for an update on the weather, I see I have four emails.

Call me OCD, but I can't stand when I have unread emails. I don't understand how some people let their mailboxes fill up and have thousands and thousands of emails just sitting there.

Read them or delete. It's not that hard. And yes, I'm aware what a pointless thing it is to obsess over.

I open my email, expecting all four to be junk. Three are, but the forth isn't.

"Dr. Crawford emailed me about the fellowship," I say, madly scanning the email. I read it so fast I miss information and have to go back and start from the beginning.

"What did he say?"

"I got in."

"What? Are you serious?" Quinn jumps up with excitement and throws her arms around me. "That's amazing! I knew you'd get in. We have double to celebrate on vacation now! When does it start? I can't wait until you're here with me!"

I blink, reread a particular part three times, and feel like someone just dunked me under water.

Icy cold, dark water.

Because this is both good and bad. This is tearing me in two and I haven't even made up my mind, yet alone said it out loud.

I want to live with Quinn and Emma. I want us to be a family, and I really and truly believe we will. I want to marry Quinn and have more babies because I know our kids are going to be fucking awesome kids with the best mother anyone could ask for.

But I also want this fellowship and know a few years can

go by fast but can also feel like hell. And a few years of Emma's life is full of firsts and difficult times. I don't want to miss out on that.

"Arch?" Quinn asks, sliding her hands down my shoulders and stopping at my biceps. She gives them a squeeze and looks at my phone. "What's wrong? I thought you'd be happy about the fellowship."

"I am," I start. "But it's in Boston."

"Boston?" I echo even though I heard him right the first time. "As in east coast Boston?"

"Yeah," he says, not looking away from his phone. I can see the conflicting emotions on his face, and I hope he looks up and says it's not worth it after all because his family is here in Chicago.

But he doesn't.

"I think our ride is here," he says instead, and grabs my carry-on bag, hiking it up on his shoulder. I flip my hood on to keep my hair dry and wheel my suitcase out, and the word *Boston* repeats through my mind over and over. I've been to New York but not Boston. It's not a terribly long flight, but it's no quick trip either.

And Emma will be born by then. Traveling alone with a baby has to be difficult. I can't tell Archer not to go though, right? He's furthering his education, not taking a year or two off to party.

"Get in so you don't get wet," Archer tells me, acting as if everything is normal. It's far from it. He has a life-altering decision to make and it's not bothering him at all.

Maybe he's already made up his mind. He wants this, after all, and getting in is a huge accomplishment. "I'll get your suitcase."

"Thanks," I say distantly and climb into the back of the car. I pull my hood off and watch Archer quickly load the suitcases into the trunk. He slides in next to me, setting my carry-on in the space between us.

"Do you know how long the fellowship is?" I ask.

"Two years."

"And you'd start in January?"

"Yeah."

I nod, and I'm sure he knows what I'm thinking. He'll be hours away working long shifts. What happens if I go into labor? There's a chance he won't make it back in time.

I blink back tears. I should be proud of him. Really fucking proud. This is no easy feat, and he mentioned before how competitive the fellowship is. Only the best of the best get in.

Archer is the best.

He'll make a great trauma surgeon, saving lives and making the world a better place and all. Plus, being temporarily separated by distance isn't the worse thing. There are lots of military couples who handle long distance. Archer will be in Boston, not the Middle East.

Yeah...it's not that bad. We'll get through this and when it's over we'll look back at the hard times and see how it strengthened us. This will be good in the end. Archer will be happy, and most of the time, long-term success and happiness require some give and take.

But we'd just talked about him looking for jobs in the city and us moving in together. I go from feeling like we're on the same page to thinking he's jumping ahead into another book. On a different shelf.

If Boston is where he wants to go, then fine. I love him, and we'll make it work.

"So, what do you have to do about the fellowship?" I ask, picking at a loose string on the fabric seat of the car.

"Accept or decline."

"What do you want to do?" I tear my eyes away from my lap to look at Archer. The excitement has washed away, and he's back to looking strained and stressed.

"Let's not worry about it now. No talking about work, remember?" He smiles, but his lack of response makes me think he wants to take it.

Which is fine. And I know it's fine because I keep having to tell myself it's fucking fine.

"Okay." I reach over and take his hand. Feeling his skin on mine relaxes me, but I know there's no way I can let this go and not think about it until he comes to a decision. This is big and life-changing. For all three of us.

I WISH I COULD DRINK. IF I COULD SUCK DOWN A MARGARITA right now, I so would. And then I'd probably be able to relax and not constantly wonder what Archer's going to do about this fellowship.

We just woke up on our first official full day in Hawaii, and it couldn't be more beautiful. I'm standing on the balcony of our hotel room looking out at the ocean trying to find my fucking zen.

The fact that I'm not jumping for joy for Archer makes me feel so guilty it's like the morning sickness has come back full force. I *am* proud of him. I *do* want him to take the fellowship position.

But I want that position to be in Chicago. Maybe it was

naive of me to assume he'd get in at Northwestern since we ran into Dr. Crawford and his wife. That's where he works, after all, and he and Archer have emailed a few times and I even brought it up to Mrs. Crawford when we met for lunch to talk about MIT and internships.

I don't think it's terrible that I'm upset to think about Archer moving far away though. Anyone who's in love would have hesitations about their better half moving states away.

Archer steps out behind me, and his hands settle on my waist. "That's one hell of a view," he says, lips brushing against my neck as he talks.

"It is. You might have a hard time getting me to leave."

"We can become permanent vacationers and forget all responsibilities." He slides his hands around to my middle. "For a few months at least."

I close my eyes and lean back against him, inhaling deep. The sun is already warm but the breeze coming in from the ocean makes the weather perfectly enjoyable.

"Nah, we can stay here and just change Emma's name to Moana. She'll like the island life."

"Maybe she'll grow up to be a pro surfer or something. She'll need to do something that'll make a lot of money to support her deadbeat beach bum parents."

I laugh, spinning in his arms. He grips me tighter and plants a kiss on my lips, making my heart do a skip-a-beat thing.

"We can start her young. Some of those athletes go pro before they can drive."

"That's my plan," he says, and I laugh. Leaning down to kiss me again, he brushes my hair out of my face. It's hanging down my back in loose waves, and I'm debating twisting it up into a bun. The constant ocean breeze is amazing but makes for messy hair.

"You are so beautiful," Archer whispers. "I love you so fucking much."

"I love you, too." I hook my arms around his neck, heart lurching and wishing I could put Boston out of my mind. But I can't because not knowing if he's going to be miles and miles away is killing me.

I don't want him to go, and though I'm not going to tell him that and let that sway his decision one way or another, I feel guilty over it, like I'm a bad girlfriend.

I can support him and not be happy about it, right? It's not permanent, by any means, and just because we'll be living apart—still—doesn't mean things will fall apart between us. We'll keep doing what we're doing now, and by the time the fellowship is over, we'll have so many frequent flyer miles we can come back here and not have to pay for airfare.

There. Much better. I just need to keep a positive outlook and—who am I fucking kidding? It's going to suck. I'm going to hate being away from Archer, and he'll hate being away from us. He'll support me every way he can, but I'll still be alone at night with a newborn.

Unless I quit my job and go to Boston with him, because I could. I don't *have* to work, and can move out with him. We can rent a cute little house close to a park, and Emma and I can go visit him at the hospital for lunch. Moving far away from my family will hurt, but not being with Archer will hurt more.

"Are you okay, babe?" Archer asks. "Did your morning sickness come back or something?"

"No." I look into his brown eyes and smile. "I'm still jetlagged I think. And hungry."

"Let's go get breakfast before you feel sick."

"I think I'm okay," I tell him, a little afraid of jinxing myself. Right around the end of my seventeenth week, the morning sickness went away. Waking up with an empty stomach makes me feel a little nauseous, but it's nothing like it was before.

We step back into the room and Archer closes the balcony door. I run my fingers through my hair and fix the tie on my beach coverup.

"Should I put on a regular dress?" I ask Archer.

"Aren't you wearing one?"

"No, this is a swim coverup."

He raises an eyebrow. "I don't get the difference."

"This one is a little see-through."

"I didn't even notice and I'm always checking you out."

I laugh and grab the beach bag. "Okay, that's good enough for me then."

"Walk in front of me," he says with a smile. "Let me check out this see-through dress."

"What's on the agenda for today?" Archer asks once we're seated for breakfast. We're on an outdoor patio with the resort pool on one side and the ocean on the other. I cannot get over how pretty everything is here.

"Beach time, a couple's massage, and then a luau. It's supposed to be really good according to what I read online."

"I've never had a professional massage," Archer says as he looks over the menu.

"You'll love it."

"What exactly does it mean 'do a couple's massage' over a regular one?"

"We're just next to each other. Usually you do the same things, but mine has to be altered since I'm pregnant." I glance at the drink menu. "Order a mimosa for me. I just want to smell it."

Archer laughs. "I can do that."

I look out at the ocean, watching people drag kayaks through the sand and into the water. There were a few things I couldn't do that I wanted to—like kayak and go horseback riding—due to being pregnant. There were mixed reviews online about whether it was safe or not, but Archer and I decided or err on the side of caution.

"So, the fellowship," I start, looking down at my menu. "Have you thought about it at all?"

"Nope."

I put the menu down. "Really?"

"Really. I meant it when I said we shouldn't think about work. Let's focus on us and how fucking amazing it is here."

I smile and nod, wondering how I can focus on us when I don't know where we'll be. I don't want to be away from him.

"Us. Right. Well, we are doing the perfect Quinn and Archer vacation with food, sleep, and sex."

"It's the perfect relationship," Archer says with a smile. "Doesn't hurt that you're a total hottie."

I laugh. "We are good together and—" I cut off, hand flying to my stomach.

"Are you okay?" Archer starts to get up.

"Yeah. I felt a kick. Like a real kick." I move my hand, feeling it again. "Whoa. That's weird. But cool."

"You know the whole process of conception and birth fascinates me."

"Oh, I know. You had me watch that Miracle of Life video with you like we were in a middle-school sex ed class."

"You never watched the end."

I shake my head. "I don't want to see someone give birth until after I have."

"That might be a good idea," he laughs. The waitress comes to take our food order. When she leaves, silence falls over the table. I'm trying hard not to think about the fellowship, and I have a feeling Archer is too. But he's right not to bring it up.

We're in paradise together with no responsibilities. The week will be over before we know it, and then it's back to reality.

"You're looking a little red," Archer tells me, setting his book down. We've been on the beach for a while, and I moved out of my shady spot inside the cabana to soak up some sun.

I sit up, readjusting my floppy hat. "I'm feeling a little warm." I stretch and go back into the shade next to Archer and grab the sunscreen. Archer takes it from me and rubs it on my shoulders. "Want to walk in the water with me? I'll cool off and we can explore the beach a bit."

"Yeah, that sounds good. Let's get something to eat first." He grabs a bottle of water and hands it to me. "You need to make sure you stay hydrated."

I twist off the cap and take a long drink. "You too, mister. You might be used to not taking care of yourself, but I won't allow that on my watch."

"Thanks, babe." He takes his own water and finishes it off. I stick his book in my bag and move it deeper inside the cabana. Taking only my phone and wallet with me, we go to a walk-up tiki hut-themed bar that serves snack foods as well as alcohol. We bring the food back to our reserved space.

We sit close together, cuddling up after we're done eating. Being with Archer feels so right. This is how we were meant to be.

Together.

Which makes not knowing what Archer wants to do about this fellowship hover above me like a dark shadow. Refusing to let it darken my mood, I get out my phone and take selfies of us together, and then snap a few pictures of the beach to send to Mom, who's been texting me all day asking for more photos.

Archer and I walk along the beach for a while, and then I lay out a bit more, careful not to overheat. We go back to our room a few hours before dinner to shower and get ready.

I stay in the bathroom to blow-dry my hair, and when I come into the room, Archer is already asleep.

Smiling at how he looks both sweet and sexy at the same time, I grab my phone and take a picture of him before carefully getting into bed next to him. The balcony doors are open, and the sound of the ocean below lulls me to sleep.

I wake up before Archer, needing to pee. When I get back into bed, I can't fall asleep. My phone is on the mattress next to me, and I go through the photos we took today while at the beach. I upload my favorite to Instagram and send a few more to my mother.

I log back onto Instagram to check and see who's liked my photo so far. Instead of putting my phone down and turning off my mind, I open an internet search and look up information on the fellowship.

The particular hospital in Boston is one of the best in

the nation, and I'm all the more proud of him for getting in. It hurts my heart to think of us being separated, but this is his dream. I don't want him to regret this, years later or to resent me or Emma for keeping him from following this path.

If he wants to go, I'll have to be okay with it.

23

ARCHER

"**A**re you doing all right, babe?" I ask Quinn, wondering if the sun is getting to her like it's getting to me. Though judging by the distance between us, she's doing just fine.

She stops, turning around and holds up her phone, taking pictures of our surroundings before taking one of me.

"I'm fine, just like I was the last time you asked me. You're a slowpoke."

I laugh. "You ran up ahead."

"I thought I saw a ferret."

"They're mongooses. Mongeese? They were brought here to help control the rat population but took over."

"Well, they're cute. I want one."

"I think they're mean."

"They just want love." Quinn puts her phone back in her bag and holds out her hand. I take it, lacing our fingers and pulling her in for a kiss. We're hiking today, on our way to see a waterfall. It's hotter today, and the comfortable breeze is gone now that we're in the thick of the woods. Still, being here with the love of my life is good for my soul. I didn't know how much I needed this until we got here.

Quinn makes it easy to enjoy life. To laugh and smile. To be happy. She's distracting, which is good because I'm having a really hard time not obsessing over the fellowship. We're on day three of our vacation, and other than Quinn bringing it up at breakfast, nothing more has been said about it.

Though I know we're both thinking about it.

Part of me didn't think I'd actually get in. It's an extremely competitive program, and after not hearing back for several weeks, I assumed I hadn't made the cut.

And it was a relief.

I could pick and choose my job—to an extent—from there on out. There are enough hospitals around Chicago that I'd get something, and Quinn and I could raise Emma together like we want to. We could talk about looking for a new place, maybe even one in the suburbs with a yard.

But if I go to Boston...I don't know what will happen. It's only temporary, but two years is a long fucking time. I don't want to be away from Quinn for two days, and Emma...I'd miss so much if I were in Boston. We'd see each other as much as possible, of course, but it wouldn't be the same.

Getting the fellowship and becoming a trauma surgeon has been part of my long-term plan since I got into med school. I want to do this, and I know I'll love working trauma.

"There's another one!" Quinn whisper-yells. "Come on, you have to admit it's cute."

"It's not hideous."

She laughs and starts forward again. We made it another few yards before I slow to a stop.

"Listen," I tell her, tipping my head.

She closes her eyes, lifting her chin to the sky. "Water."

"We're close to the waterfall."

Quinn's lips curve into a smile and we start forward again. I break a spiderweb out of Quinn's way at the last second. We're on a less popular trail, going to see one of the smaller waterfalls. We haven't seen anyone else out here in a while, which has been nice. The world seems to fade away when Quinn's with me like we're the only two left in it.

The path gets a little steep and slippery with wet rocks and mud. I keep a tight grip on Quinn's hand, but she doesn't need any help. Emerging through a thick of trees, we see the waterfall.

"It's gorgeous," Quinn breathes.

"It is," I say, but I'm still looking at her, watching her face light up as she takes it all in.

"Come here," she says, turning around. She gets out her phone and holds it up to take a picture of us kissing with the waterfall in the background.

"You're a terrible selfie-taker," I joke, taking the phone from her.

"I don't take too many selfies. And when I do, they're of me in lingerie and I accidentally send them to my brother."

We both laugh, and I take a photo. It's candid and probably my favorite of us so far on the trip.

"I can't believe I had to ask my mom to delete it for me."

"At least it wasn't your dad."

"Oh my God, I know."

We sit on the flat rock, feet dangling over the water, and eat some of the snacks we packed. Neither of us speaks as we eat, but it's not awkward in the least. Quinn finishes her water and puts the empty bottle in her bag.

"I have to pee."

"Go in the woods," I tell her, waving my hand at the trees behind us.

"Keep watch and make sure no one is coming?"

"Okay." I finish my food and get up, looking down the path. There's no one in sight. Quinn goes a few yards away just in case, and once she's out of sight, I carefully pull her grandmother's ring from my pocket. It's in a little velvet bag, but I'm still scared of losing it.

The question burns in my throat, and I've gone over and over what I want to say to her. Laughter echoes through the forest, and I quickly put the ring back. Quinn is making her way back and gets to me before another group of hikers comes to the waterfall.

Taking Quinn's hand, we start down the path going back the way we came. We have a fancy dinner later tonight...I can ask her then. Though that's a little cliché and Quinn doesn't like cliché. The pressure to make this proposal unforgettable is getting to me. Quinn deserves the best.

"There's another mongoose," I tell Quinn, pointing it out. "And yeah, I'll admit it now. They're cute."

"Let's take one home with us."

"That would not go over well with TSA."

"Fine. I'll just get another cat."

I put my arm around her. "You're turning me into a cat person."

Quinn smiles. "Now that's something to be proud of."

"Wow." My eyes widen when Quinn steps out of the bathroom. She just got done getting dressed and looks stunning in a low-cut white dress. "You're beautiful, babe."

"And you look pretty hot too, Dr. Jones." She makes a move to come in and kiss me.

I hold up my hand. "I almost forgot my accessories."

"Accessories?"

I reach into my suitcase, pull out my stethoscope, and hang it around my neck.

"No. You did not," Quinn laughs.

"We gotta make sure people know you're dating a doctor, right?"

She laughs again, throwing her head back. "I can't believe you brought that and didn't get it out until now."

I stride over and kiss her. "Is it turning you on?"

"Being able to make me laugh is one of the hottest things you can do." She runs her hands down my chest. "You'll have to give me a checkup when we come back."

"As a doctor, it's my duty to examine every single inch of you."

She takes the stethoscope from around my neck and puts it on, listening to my heartbeat for a moment.

"I love you, Archer," she says slowly, looking up into my eyes. She takes the stethoscope off and tosses it on the bed. I kiss her hard, feeling the ring in my back pocket. Cliché or not, I want to ask her to marry me tonight.

"And I love you." I kiss her once more and then break away, needing to stop now or else I won't be able to. She's pressed up against me, and letting her go proves to be difficult. I'm about to let her go when I feel something.

"Is that Emma?"

"You felt that?" she exclaims.

"Yeah." I put my hand on her stomach and wait to see if I'll feel it again. I don't, not now at least. Quinn moves my hand to the other side of her stomach.

"Can you feel that?"

I shake my head. "I didn't think I'd be able to feel her this early." I take my hand off Quinn's stomach and close the balcony doors. We need to get going before we miss our reservation.

The restaurant is outside on the beach, and our table is close to the water. The only light around the tables are from candles and tiki torches. Yes, this is the perfect place to ask Quinn to marry me.

We get seated and are looking over our menu when cheers erupt around us. I look up to see a guy down on one knee sliding a ring on his girlfriend's finger. Well, there goes that idea...

"I wouldn't want to get engaged in a public setting like this," Quinn tells me, looking back at her menu.

I guess I dodged a bullet here for sure then.

"Why not?"

"Everyone is looking."

"Oh. Good point." So, something secluded is better. We have plans tomorrow that involve a group, but I'm sure I can get her to go on a walk along the shore with me at night. My heart speeds up thinking about it.

"What are you getting?" she asks.

I haven't even looked at my menu yet. "I'm not sure. What about you?"

"Probably this one that I can't pronounce." She points to it on her menu. "Everything sounds good. I swear I'm going to leave here weighing ten pounds more than I did when I came."

"The food is good. Now I really don't want to go home to microwavable meals and Ramen noodles."

"Hey, you're almost done and then—" She cuts off, remembering that the fellowship is still up in the air. "I'm not the best cook, but that's mostly because I'm lazy. I have a lot of my mom's recipes so I could make us decent dinners if you're, uh, you're in town."

She folds her hands in her lap, looking out at the ocean.

"I'm proud of you," she says after a minute passes. "And I want you to know that I'm in favor of whatever you choose."

"You are?" I ask because I'm not even sure if I am. I want to take the fellowship and become a trauma surgeon. But not only is the fellowship far away, but I could work just as many hours as I do now as a resident.

"Yes. You've wanted this for so long."

I look at Quinn. "I have." But there's something I've wanted even longer: her.

"Today is our last day to stake a claim on the beach and never leave," I say, running a comb through my wet hair. "I'm not ready to leave in the morning."

"Me neither. I know my surgery schedule and it's back-to-back operations."

"I feel bad for you," I tell Archer, turning away from the mirror to look at him. "I have Sunday off before going back into work." I comb out a tangle, regretting keeping my hair down while we were at the beach today. "Will you work as much in the fellowship?"

"The workload will be more intense, and the hours will probably be similar."

His words make me cringe, but only on the inside. Archer needs a break. He deserves one more than anyone I know. "It's just two years," I say, trying to be optimistic. But two more years of working eighty hours a week sounds awful. Archer closes the balcony doors and lays down on the bed, turning on the TV. We spent the day on the shore, had an early dinner, and are going whale watching. Archer doesn't seem as excited as I am about it.

I get the tangle out and towel dry my hair the best I can before putting it in a French braid.

"Do you think it'll get chilly on the boat?" I ask.

"It might be windier than on shore. Bring the sweater," he answers, knowing what I'm thinking. He gets me, and I'm sad our vacation is coming to an end. Being with him this week has been so nice.

"I'll grab your jacket then too. Ready?"

"Yeah." He turns off the TV and looks me over. "I don't know how you look so good in everything you wear."

"You must have gotten too much sun or something. I'm in leggings and a tank top."

"If you haven't picked up on it yet, I think you look hot in anything."

I smile and go over to him. "I hope you always think so."

"I don't see why I won't."

"What if I get really bad stretch marks?"

"Then you get really bad stretch marks."

I raise my eyebrows. "You'll still find me attractive?"

Archer plants his hands on either side of my waist. "I know there's a stigma against gaining weight and not having perfect skin, but I love *you,* Quinn. And if you get stretch marks from carrying our daughter, I'll look at them and remember everything you went through in order to bring me Emma."

My eyes well with tears and I can't find any words to say. Besides, if I opened my mouth, sobs would probably come out instead.

"Any man who finds his girlfriend or wife or whatever less attractive because she bears the marks of pregnancy and birth is a fucking asshole." He slides his hands to my ass. "Yes, I very much enjoy how you look right now, but I know what your body goes through during pregnancy. Your organs shift around. Getting stretch marks is the least of it."

I blink back tears and straddle Archer's lap, hoping he doesn't make a move. I want to be close to him, but I'm not in the mood for sex. Which is nothing against him, but we've made love a lot on this vacation. My lady bits need a break. "You do have an appreciation for the arrangement of organs."

"I do. Probably more than the average person." He looks up at me, eyes a little glossy. "I've cut open a lot of people and have seen their insides. And it still blows my mind that something so incredible can grow inside of you."

I smile. "Out of context, that would be a very strange sentence."

He laughs. "A lot of what is said among surgeons sounds very bad out of context. Also, if you knew how small your uterus was before you got pregnant, you'd be amazed at what it holds at the end. It fits in your hand when there's no baby inside."

I make a face. "I never thought I'd date someone weirder than me, but I think you fit the bill."

Archer laughs. "But I'm weird in a sexy way, right?"

"Oh, for sure." I run my hands through his hair. As much as I want to go whale watching, snuggling in bed while he rubs my back is tempting too. "And you can lie and tell me I am."

"I always knew I'd end up with someone who loved robot fights, computer codes, and cats."

"Damn. You set the bar high."

Archer laughs and nuzzles his head in between my breasts. Shit. I think he's going to want to have sex. I don't understand how he has the stamina for it all the time. I love him with all my heart, but I'm tired, dammit.

"Would you think it was lame if we ordered room service and crashed after whale watching?" Archer asks.

"Hell no. That's my kind of night."

He tightens his grip on me. "I knew there was a reason I fell for you."

"Do you want to go for one last walk on the beach?"

I just sat down in bed and don't feel like getting up, but the look in Archer's eye can't be described as anything else but romantic.

"Yeah," I tell him and get up. "Should I change?" I'm still in the dress I wore earlier, and my hair is in a messy bun on the top of my head.

"No, that's perfect. You might want to bring a sweater." He smiles and rolls his eyes. "Only you would be cold on a tropical island."

"The night air has a bit of a chill to it. I was expecting it to be super humid all the time here."

Archer looks at me as if I'm crazy. "It is humid here."

"Not really."

"Have we been on the same vacation?"

I laugh. "I guess I'm comparing it to Disney World in the summer. That's brutal."

"I was thinking about that the other day, actually."

"About Disney?"

"Yeah. You said you wanted to take Emma for her first vacation. Maybe can go for her birthday."

I smile so big my face hurts. "That would be so fun!" I go into the bathroom to pee and brush my hair. I grab my sweater on the way out and walk close to Archer as we go down to the main lobby.

"Looks like someone is having fun," I say, looking at a group of girls stumbling about.

"A little too much," Archer notes, frowning when he sees them.

"Is Dr. Fuddy-Duddy coming back out?"

"He never went away." Archer takes my hand again and pulls me close. "You like him, don't lie."

"The responsible side of you is attractive, I'll readily admit it."

He goes in to kiss me and someone screams. I jerk up, looking at the source of the scream. One of the drunk girls has collapsed and is convulsing on the floor. Archer lets go of me and rushes over. I stand there in shock for a few seconds and then notice the bleeding. The girl hit her head on the way down.

Things happen in a blur after that: someone from the hotel says they're calling an ambulance, and Archer works on stopping the bleeding and attending to the seizing. He's focused, fully aware how dire the situation is, but isn't scared.

He's in the zone, and this is his element.

I force myself over, asking what I can do to help. Archer says there's not much we can do other than keep her stable until the EMT's arrive to take her to the hospital. And he does just that, and as I stand there watching him take care of a perfect stranger, I know without a doubt he has to take that fellowship.

I lean back in the uncomfortable airport seat, watching our bags while Quinn goes to the bathroom. We're headed back to reality, and something seems different between us. As much as I want to deny it, I know what it is. After taking care of that drunk girl last night, Quinn told me I need to take the fellowship. She said she can see that trauma and life-or-death situations are what I'm made for, and I can't disagree.

But I should. Because as much as I want to take the fellowship, it feels wrong telling her I'll reply with my acceptance as soon as we get back. Yeah...I want to be a trauma surgeon, but it's not like settling for general surgery is the shitty consolation prize. She's so encouraging and optimistic, hinting even that she'd move to Boston so we can be together. I want nothing more than to be with Quinn, but I know she'll hate it up east with me.

I'd be at work more than I'd be at home. She'd be alone most of the time with a newborn. She wouldn't have any friends to hang out with. Family wouldn't be nearby to help with Emma or give her a much-needed break.

She's resent me in the end, and nothing is worth that.

If I do go through with accepting the fellowship, the best thing to do would be for her to stay in Chicago and for me to go, and for us to try and maintain a long-distance relationship until I'm done.

It's a good thing I didn't propose, right?

I let out a sigh and turn my head down, not knowing what the fuck I'm doing. Neither is a bad option: take the fellowship or find a job in Chicago so I can be with Quinn and my daughter. But one is so much better than the other.

"Tired?" Quinn's voice comes from behind me, startling me a bit.

"Yeah, I guess."

"Me too. It's kind of funny how all that beach relaxing wasn't as restful as I thought it'd be."

I turn my head up and smile. "Being out in the heat wears you down. And we spent a lot of our sleep time having sex."

"I believe that was mostly your doing."

"You're just as much to blame here, missy."

Quinn laughs and my heart aches at the thought of not being able to hear that in person. And—fuck—I'll be hours away around the time she has to give birth. If I'm in the middle of a long shift, I can't just leave and hop on the first plane I can to the Midwest.

She rests her head on my shoulder. "We have the plane ride to sleep. Well, you can sleep at least. I'll probably be awake the whole time, which is okay. I've loaded up my Kindle and I'm ready to dive into this paranormal series I've been wanting to read for years."

"Years?"

"I wait until at least three books are out in a series to start reading. Cliffhangers give me literal anxiety."

I laugh and slip my arm around her, glancing up at the clock. Our plane is on time today, and we'll be boarding soon.

"Have you heard anything from your parents about Bobby?" she asks.

"Nope. No news is usually good news. I'll be generous and give him a few weeks before he fucks up again."

Quinn frowns. "You don't think he'll recover?"

"He doesn't want to recover."

"Oh, right. I guess you can't force it on him."

I shake my head. My parents have tried many times and it hasn't worked. Life isn't like a book or a movie. Not everyone gets a happily ever after or even an epic exit scene. Some people coexist with the rest of the world, functioning on a level of minimum survival, living for themselves and not caring what the fuck they do to other people.

That's Bobby.

"Do you have to write a formal letter or anything to let the fellowship people know you've accepted?" Quinn asks as she picks off her nail polish.

"No. I basically need to reply and say I'll be there."

"You should do it then," she encourages. "You're going to be great, you know."

I smile, but it feels forced. "Yeah. I know I'll enjoy it." I enjoy general surgery too. And I enjoy being with her even more.

"The two years will be rough." She takes my hand. "But we'll make it work."

Before I can say anything, we're called to line up to board. Quinn gathers her stuff and I grab her carry-on as well as my own. We're walking up when her phone rings, and she digs it out of her purse and answers. It's loud at the moment, and she steps away to hear better. She comes back right in time to hand the attendant her ticket.

"Was that your mom?" I ask, hiking my bag up on my shoulder.

"No, Jacob."

"Your ex?"

She nods. "Yeah. He's working with a few others to start up a new company and asked if I was interested. I am."

We walk down the terminal. "What would you be doing?"

"It's kinda complicated. To make a long story short, we'd be developing new software and using technology to help the environment."

"Sounds neat."

"Yes! There will be a lot of environmental research too," she says, looking excited. I swallow hard. I don't want to make her give that up. "And the best part is after the initial start-up phase, I'll be able to do a lot of the coding and development from an office at home."

"You could work from home?"

"Yeah. It would take a while before we got to that point though. We'll all be sharing an office in the Lincoln Park area for a while."

We get on the plane and find our seats. Quinn takes the spot by the window this time since I had it on the way to Hawaii. "So you'd be working with Jacob?"

"Yes. We'll be equal partners to the project."

I nod again. "Why did he ask you?"

She raises her eyebrows and I realize my question wasn't worded the best. "I'm good at what I do. Plus selling that app gives me street cred in the technology world and we're more likely to get big investors if they see my name. I've already proven that I'm able to turn a profit." She continues to explain how things would work, and how they're hoping to expand the company over the years and have it make an impact on the world. I always knew she was smart, but I didn't realize she was so business savvy as well. I can easily see her as a big CEO of an energy solutions company, creating new programs to save energy and bring clean water to underdeveloped parts of the world.

I can't take that away from her and have her move to Boston.

"So no, he's not trying to hit on me or anything," she concludes, going back to my question. "I made sure of it."

"You did?"

"Yeah. I basically asked him and made sure he knew we were together."

"That's good, though you have to admit it's a little weird to work with your ex."

She shakes her head in disagreement. "I don't think it's weird at all. If you worked with that one nurse you dated, I wouldn't think it's weird."

"But we're surrounded by other people. It's not like the two of us are performing surgery in my living room."

"Performing surgery in your living room isn't weird but working with an ex is?" She buckles her seat belt.

"You know what I mean."

"No, I don't. Because you're sounding really jealous and like you don't trust me, which hurts."

"I trust you, but I don't trust him."

"So you're saying he doesn't think I'm good for the job and is secretly trying to steal me back even though I'm pregnant with your child?"

"No."

"Then what are you saying?" She lifts her eyebrows and waits.

I shake my head and let out a breath. "I don't know. He's your ex and you admitted that he still likes you. I'm sure he'll hit on you."

"That shouldn't matter, Archer. I get hit on from time to time and it might be hard to believe, but I don't fall for just any guy who tells me I have a nice ass," she says, looking pissed. Her eyes fall shut and the anger fades away into something worse. She's hurt by my words and I hate it. "I love you and I thought we had a good relationship. But if you can't even trust me..." She turns, tears filling her eyes.

Her reaction is justified, and not without merit. I am jealous—just a bit. And I do trust her to be loyal, but yeah, I'm a little afraid she'll not want to do the long-distance thing while raising a child. I've wanted us to be together for so long the fear of it all crumbling apart around me is nagging.

"Babe," I start and take her hand. "I'm sorry."

She wipes her eyes and smiles. "Thanks." She gives my hand a squeeze and then lets go, getting her phone from her bag. "Want to look at vacation pictures with me?"

I lean closer. "Yeah. I do."

26

I hang up without leaving a message and set my phone down, feeling a little uneasy. I haven't talked to Archer since yesterday afternoon. Things still weren't quite resolved between us when we got off the plane, and it's making the missed calls seem like a bigger deal than it is.

I know Archer was in surgery throughout the night and is working again today. He doesn't usually call if he gets off in the middle of the night, not wanting to wake me up. Though given the way things are unsettled between us, it's making me worry. And when I worry, I tend to obsess and assume the worst is going to happen. That way if something slightly less traumatic actually does happen, I'm not as devastated.

"My bitch is back!" Marissa throws her arms up and comes into my office. "It was so boring around here without you last week. How was vacay?"

"Fun," I tell her with a smile. And it was, up until the plane ride home. Archer felt bad for insinuating he doesn't trust me, and I believe him. And a bit of jealousy is nice, if I'm being honest. But he has nothing to worry about, and what hurt the most was that I gave him well wishes to go follow his dreams in Boston and didn't even bring up the fact that he'd be away and alone and has the potential to stray.

Because I didn't even think about it.

I love him. I trust him. I've known Archer for years and have always believed him to be a good man.

"You have a sour look on your face." Marissa sits in the chair in front of my desk. "Are you feeling sick again?"

"No, thankfully." I let out a sigh. "Archer and I got into a weird fight-thing on the way home and it's still bugging me."

"Fight-thing?"

"It wasn't really a fight but was more than a disagreement and we're both at crossroads, and I don't know what to really think about it."

"Start from the beginning because you lost me."

I nod, so glad Marissa is here. She's not exactly a neutral party; she'll side with me nine times out of ten. That's what best friends do, after all.

"Archer got into a fellowship program to do trauma surgery, but it's in Boston. It's an intense program and he'll be there for two years."

"Oh, damn, that's both good and bad."

"Yeah." I shake my head. "I want him to go as much as I don't. He's wanted this and was aiming for it before this happened." I motion to my belly. "And I don't know what's right or wrong here. I feel bad telling him I don't want him to go. We've been talking about moving in together and it felt like we were on the path to becoming a family. But it's just two years, that's nothing compared to the rest of his life as a trauma surgeon. And it's not fair for him to change his plans for me when this has been his end game the whole time, right?"

"You're changing your plans," Marissa counters. "Once the baby is born you're taking at least some time off." She holds up her hand before I can interrupt. "And don't tell me it's because you're the mom. Do you feel like that's unfair?"

"No, but it's not the same. This fellowship is really competitive and if he doesn't do it now, there's no promise he'll get in again later."

"Okay...say you got into some sort of training program with Bill Gates or something. You'd go away for a year or two, but Emma would stay with Archer. Would you do it?"

"No," I say with no hesitation. "But I don't want to push my personal opinion on him."

"You guys are pretty personal though. Personal enough to have a baby."

I make a face. "I know. But I don't know, and that's the issue with this."

She nods. "So that's what your fight-thing was about?"

"No." I look at her, realizing I'm going to have to spill the beans about potentially leaving IHG. "Close the door."

"Ohhhh, this has to be some good drama." She gets up to close the door and comes back, sitting on the edge of the chair.

"Jacob approached me about starting up a new company, and when I told Archer he got a little jealous, which is fine, but it's making me wonder if we did rush into things because he has nothing to be worried about. It takes time to build up trust between two people, and we haven't been dating for that long, which makes me go back to feeling bad not wanting him to go to Boston because he should want to be with us more than he wants this fellowship." I blurt that all out fast, relieved when I finally say it out loud.

"Taking the fellowship doesn't mean he wants it more than he wants you," Marissa tries to reason.

"I know," I sigh. "And that's why I feel so bad wishing he'd decide on his own to stay here."

"You shouldn't feel bad about it. No one wants their boyfriend to go away for work."

I wrinkle my nose. "True. I'm faking my happiness, so I do feel bad."

"Don't fake it. Tell him how you feel."

"Then he might not take it."

Marissa widens her eyes. "Which is what you want."

"Yeah, but because he doesn't want to, not because he knows I don't want him to go."

Marissa shakes her head. "What's the damn difference?"

"The root of his decision?" I try, knowing I probably sound insane. "I love him and want him to be happy."

"Don't you think he wants the same for you?"

My phone rings before I can answer her. "It's Archer."

"I'll catch up later," Marissa says, going to the door. "I need to hear all about this new company you might leave me for."

Waiting until Marissa has closed the door behind her, I answer. "Hey, Arch."

"Hey, babe. How are you?"

"All right. I just got to work. You?"

"I'm just leaving work."

"You've been there all night?"

"Yeah," he groans. "I have a few hours to sleep before going back. I have a Whipple today, so I'll be in surgery for eight or so hours."

"What the heck is a Whipple? Sounds kinda kinky."

"It's a pancreaticoduodenectomy," he says.

"Oh right, one of those."

He laughs. "It's basically removing cancerous tumors from the head of the pancreas. It's a long procedure."

"Wow. That's intense."

"It is, and the pathology isn't the greatest for this patient."

"I'm not sure what that means either, but good luck? Is that the right thing to say?"

"I guess. It's just work for me, though this isn't as routine as removing a gallbladder."

I smile, imagining Archer in his blue scrubs. "Did you think about the fellowship any more?"

"Yeah...I think I should do it."

My eyes fall shut and I put on a smile, forgetting for a moment that he can't see me. "Great. It's such a good opportunity."

"It is. What about you? Have you heard anything more about your job?"

"No, not yet." Someone knocks on my office door. I move the phone away from my face. "Come in," I call.

"Do you need to go?" Archer asks.

"Yeah. I suppose I should work at work, right?"

Archer chuckles. "Right. I'll call you later. Love you, babe."

"Love you too." I hang up, and the uneasy feeling comes back. I don't want to drift apart after we finally got together.

"Your frequent flyer is back."

"Are you serious?" I look up from the paperwork I've been filling out for the last twenty minutes, knowing by the nurse's face she is.

"Popped stitches. ER sent him up."

"They can't do stitches down there?" I grumble.

The nurse rolls her eyes. "Apparently 'it's internal,' and he needs to see a surgeon. Like we can just put him in front of our other patients. Do you want me to send him back down?"

"No, I'll deal with it. Thank you, though."

I finish my paperwork and deal with the difficult patient, who had a hernia repaired a month ago and hasn't followed post-op instructions at all. He's been in three times since his operation. I do rounds after that, finish my paperwork and finally go home after a twenty-six-hour shift.

Another resident who's been in the program with me since the beginning got into a car accident and broke several bones in her hand. She's unable to operate and just thinking about it makes my stomach churn. It's a shitty blow to be this close to the end and have an injury that could prevent you from performing surgery ever again. Another resident and I had to pick up the slack this past week, and needless to say, I'm fucking exhausted.

It doesn't help the situation with Quinn. It's been nearly a week since we've seen each other and as every day passes, the tension grows. She's encouraging and understanding and thinks I should do the fellowship because there's no promise I'll get in again. I don't want her to think it's a decision I've taken lightly, but I've worked so hard to get here.

I call her when I get into my car, seriously wondering if I'll be able to make it home without falling asleep behind the wheel. The good news about working all these hours is that I'm maxed out for the week and can't work the weekend.

"Hey," she answers cheerfully. "How are you?"

"Tired but alive. You?"

"Tired too, but good. I'm packing to go back to Eastwood this weekend."

"Oh right, the downtown Trick or Treating is tonight. What's Jackson going as this year?"

"A Stormtrooper. And it's actually not too cold today. I hated having to wear a coat over my costume."

"Me too. We had snow on Halloween many times and putting that coat on ruined my look."

She laughs. "Yeah. It's seventy and sunny at home, which is exciting. It'll feel like a movie Halloween or something." She zips up her suitcase in the background. "How was work?"

"I'm finally leaving."

"Finally? How long have you been at the hospital?"

"Since yesterday afternoon."

"Arch, that's not good for you! Are you driving right now?"

"Yep. Want to talk to me until I get home? Make sure I don't pass out."

"That is not funny," she says pointedly.

"Sadly, I'm not joking."

"I thought you said someone was supposed to come in and help cover those patients."

I sigh. "They haven't yet. Some of these procedures should have been canceled but the hospital is money-hungry."

"Aren't they all?"

"It's what makes the world go 'round."

"Do you have the rest of the day off?"

"I do, luckily. I'm supposed to get ten hours off between each shift, but that doesn't always happen."

Silence falls between us, and I hate it.

"So, what do you want to do about the baby shower?" she asks. "My mom keeps bugging me. The easiest thing would be to have it before you leave."

"Yeah," I agree. "Dean's not going to be happy about that."

"Dean can deal. He and Kara can pick another weekend in December. They can pick any weekend they want since they both live in the same town." She sighs. "Sorry, I'm just frustrated today."

"What's going on?"

"My wrist hurts, and the round ligament pain is back. The cats spilled a food bowl over and I didn't realize kibble got under the fridge and now I have ants. But seriously, how do they get all the way up here? I'm on the tenth floor. I got spray and then realized it wasn't safe to use while pregnant or around the cats, so I've been vacuuming them up all afternoon. I tried to move my fridge but it's too heavy and I don't want to make those stupid ligaments hurt even more than they already do."

I feel bad I'm not there to help her. "Sam and I had ants when we first moved in. Get the traps that have poison inside. It won't hurt your cats but will kill the queen ant because the worker ants take the food back to their nest."

"Okay. I have to run out before I leave, anyway. I'm almost out of cat litter and I don't feel like dealing with that old lady at the pet store telling me how I shouldn't clean the litter box since I'm pregnant, but who else is going to do it?"

I could do it...if I were there. And Quinn has been cautious and safe, knowing how to avoid getting sick from cleaning the litter box.

"How bad is the pain?"

"It's not abnormal. I saw my OB yesterday and she said everything is fine."

"I didn't know you had a doctor appointment yesterday." We hardly spoke yesterday since I was at the hospital and didn't have a chance to check in. Guilt creeps over me. It's going to be like this again in the fellowship. "Everything went okay?"

"Yeah. I scheduled my mid-pregnancy ultrasound too but can reschedule if you can't make it that day. You do want to come, right?"

"Yes, definitely. When is it scheduled for?"

"November eighth."

"I'll check the schedule the next time I'm in."

"Great. Oh, and Jacob got good news about the new company. We're meeting on Monday to discuss names. So in like six months or so I'll be free to work from home. Any home."

I know what she's hinting at again, and I just can't do

that to her. I love her too much to drag her to Boston where she'll basically be alone with Emma.

"That's good." Exhaustion is pressing down on me, and I give my head a shake to try and stay awake.

"Almost home? I worry about you."

"I have ten minutes."

"Okay. I'm going to narrate what I'm doing for your entertainment then," she says with a laugh and goes about making herself something to eat.

"I'm parking now," I say with a yawn.

"You made it! Now just march up and take a nap."

"That's my plan. After I shower. I think I stink."

"You think?"

"I might have gotten used to the smell."

She laughs again. "Poor baby. You need to—ugh."

"You okay?"

"Yeah. Just that pain again. If I hunch over it's not that bad, but when I straighten up it's like someone's flicking rubber bands again. I'm fine though, don't worry. Before you go, would any Sunday in December work for you? What about early January?"

"You can pick a date. If I can be there, I will."

"You won't know if you have a day off?"

I pinch the bridge of my nose. "I can't promise anything. But that's okay. Do it whenever it's good for you, babe."

"But I want you there."

"I might not be able to," I say harsher than I intend to. I'm just so fucking tired. "And I don't have to be there either, right? Guys don't have to go."

"No, Archer, you don't *have* to be there," she says slowly. "But it'd be fucking nice to have the father of the baby the shower is being thrown for at the party."

"Quinn," I start and unlock my door.

"It's fine," she sighs. "I don't even know where I'm taking the baby stuff."

"To your apartment," I say without thinking.

"I thought that we...that I..."

"You'll hate it in Boston," I interrupt. Quinn doesn't say anything for a few seconds and I wish I could take back my words. I'm doing that thing again where I act like an asshole to avoid dealing with feelings.

"I'll talk to you later. Get some rest," she says and hangs up.

"Fuck." I take off my shoes and strip as I walk to the bathroom, taking a fast shower and debating if I should call Quinn back now or give her space. My phone is at one percent, and I take that as a sign to give her space.

I plug it into the charger and crash into bed as soon as I'm out of the shower. Not even two minutes later my phone rings and I spring up to grab it. But it's my mother, not Quinn.

"Hello?"

"Hey, Archie!" she says cheerfully. At least she's not calling with bad news. "How are you? We've hardly talked the last few weeks."

"I've been busy at work. What else is new, right?"

"You're almost done. Tell me all about Hawaii! I'm so glad you got to go and relax for a week."

"It was great."

"The last time we talked you mentioned possibly popping the question. I've been watching Quinn's Instagram and she hasn't posted much, but...did you?"

"No," I say with a sigh. "The timing didn't feel right."

"How could you have better timing than being in Hawaii?"

"It just wasn't."

Mom can sense the tension and quickly changes the subject. "You spent a lot of time in Eastwood. Are you familiar with the town much?"

"I know my way around. Why?"

"Your father and I were talking about moving there. He's able to get a transfer to New Port, which isn't far, and it's such a cute little town."

"I'm not following. Why are you moving?"

Mom lets out a sigh. "Every time Bobby comes close to cleaning up his act, he falls back with the same crowd. If we move away from the bad apples, maybe he'll stay clean long enough to make it a habit."

I rub the back of my neck, stress and sleep deprivation getting to me. "He's thirty-two years old, Mom. When are you going to let him go and start enjoying your life?"

"Never," she says without hesitation. "He's my child and I'll forever try to help him."

"But that's not fair to you."

"Even if I *said to hell with you* and threw him on the streets, I wouldn't be able to live. I'd worry. You'll understand when Emma is born, Archie. You'll do anything for your child."

"But you've sacrificed so much for him."

"And I'll keep sacrificing until there is nothing left. In a few months, you'll see. I promise you, after holding Emma for the first time, you'll just know that there's nothing you won't do for her."

I squeeze my eyes shut. We have to do what's best for Emma, no matter what...even if that means making tough sacrifices.

"Your tummy is big, Aunt Winnie."

"Thanks, buddy. But if you think this is big, just wait."

Jackson scrunches up his nose. "I still don't get how Archer put a baby in there."

"Hey," Weston says, shaking his head. "We talked about this."

I try not to laugh, knowing the reaction will only perpetuate the situation. "What did you say?" I quietly ask Wes.

"A lot of stuff that confused him even more. But I told him it's not polite to talk to women about things in their bellies."

"Good call. Raise him to be a gentleman." I put my hand on my lower abdomen, wincing as I straighten up.

"You okay, sis?"

"Yeah, I'm fine. I've been having more round ligament pain the last few days. My OB said it was more common in the first trimester, fades in the second, and comes back at the end. Some lucky people get it the whole nine months, and it looks like I'm one of those."

"Daisy had that," Wes says, not looking at me. He doesn't talk about his wife that often, not that I could blame him. She's a piece of shit for abandoning her son. "There's nothing you can do, right?"

"Right. If it gets really bad, I'm supposed to call my doctor."

"Can't you just call Archer?"

I sink onto the living room couch, watching Jackson run around my parents' living room pretending to be a Stormtrooper. "Yeah. He did an OB rotation but says he's limited in his knowledge."

"That makes sense. How is he?"

"Good," I say with a pressed smile. I haven't yet called him back, hoping he fell asleep after I got off the phone. His words bothered me, but I don't think he really meant it. I get cranky if I stay up too late. I don't imagine I'd be Miss Suzy Sunshine if I worked for over twenty-four hours. "Busy with work."

"He's almost done though, isn't he?"

"Kind of." I put both hands on my stomach. The eight-year age difference between Weston and I made it so we never really hung out like I did with my other brothers, but the fact that we're the only two with kids—well, soon to be a kid for me—is bonding. Wes is the most responsible out of all of us, myself included, and says it like it is with no sugarcoating. He'll be a good one to run this Boston issue by.

Jackson runs over, jumping onto me. His knee gets me in the gut and I gasp from pain.

"Did I hurt the baby, Aunt Winnie?" he asks, blue eyes wide with fear.

"No, it takes more than that to hurt her," I assure him. After the doorknob incident, I know.

"You have to be careful," Wes tells him. "That's your cousin in there. Give her a few years and then you two can play."

"I don't want to play with a girl." Jackson makes a face. "Girls are gross, and I like boy stuff!" He jumps back off me and pretends to shoot things.

I turn to Wes, raising an eyebrow. "I see you still have your work cut out for you."

He laughs. "Having another girl around here is going to be strange."

"We need more girls in this family."

"You are pretty outnumbered."

Mom calls us into the kitchen for a quick dinner before heading Eastwood's downtown Trick or Treating. I check my phone for missed calls, just in case, and set it on the counter. We eat and then attempt to leave but end up dealing with a fifteen-minute temper tantrum because Wes told Jackson he had to go potty before they could leave the house and Jackson refused to go.

"I see you silently judging," Wes says, picking up Jackson, who's flailing about and screaming. "But just wait."

I shake my head. "My daughter will be calm and collected at all times. Just like me."

Mom lets out a snort of laughter. "You were the queen of meltdowns. Karma is coming for you, hun."

Finally, Jackson uses the potty and wants to show me how he learned how to wash his hands while singing *Happy Birthday*. We're running late now, and Jackson doesn't remember where he put his plastic pumpkin he needs to collect candy. In a mad rush, we all look around the house and find it filled with crayons and stashed under Dad's desk in his office.

I carry Jackson outside and buckle him in his car seat. As soon as we get downtown, I'm hit hard with nostalgia.

"Why do you look sad, Aunt Winnie?" Jackson asks, taking my hand. I help him out of the car and smooth out his costume.

"I'm not sad," I explain. "I didn't realize how much I missed this until right now."

"You can always move back," Mom points out like she always does.

"I know." Usually, when Mom says stuff like this, I counter it with all the reasons why I wouldn't want to. But today, I don't. Because I could move back here, and the more I look around at the effort the town puts into Halloween for the sake of the children living here, the more I want to come back. "It's a nice place to raise kids."

Mom stops dead in her tracks. "Are you and Archer thinking about moving here?"

"I am," I say slowly. "And maybe Archer in a few years."

"A few years?"

I nod. "He got accepted into that fellowship he wanted, but it's in Boston."

Mom opens her mouth only to close it again. "And he's going?" she finally sputters.

"Yeah. And he should. He's been working towards this since he was eighteen, after all."

"You'd think he'd be ready to be done with school," Wes says, avoiding eye contact with me.

"Yeah," I agree. "It's not a permanent position or anything. Just two years of the program and then he'll be a certified trauma surgeon. I think. I'm not sure how that all works." I let out a breath. We stop at the first storefront and

Jackson gets in line to get candy. Mom sees someone she knows, which isn't hard to do in Eastwood, and goes over to talk to her. My mind is whirling, and my due date hangs above me like a ticking time bomb. I can move after Emma is born, I know, but I'd like to figure this out before then if possible.

I always thought I'd come back here, that my kids would grow up with their cousins and Mom and Dad would babysit on Friday nights so I could go out on a date night with my husband. Then I got my current job and realized how proud it made me to hold the position I do as a young adult woman and I didn't want to give up my career and be a stay-at-home mom in a small town.

It's funny how things change, and while working at one of the fastest growing software companies used to be my only driving force in life, being the best mother I can be is so much more important.

Jackson jumps around with excitement when he sees another kid dressed as a Jedi, and they do a little pretend fight scene. Jackson 'wins' and says he has to go and save more planets.

"He knows nothing about Star Wars," Wes laughs.

"No kidding." I slow my pace, getting another pain in my side. I feel it more when I'm stressed, and right now I'm pretty damned stressed. Wes slows with me, making sure I'm okay.

"Can I ask you something personal about Daisy?" I ask and start walking again.

"Sure."

"When did you know you two weren't right for each other?"

He considers my question. "Probably a few months after our wedding."

"Why did you stay together then?"

"I didn't want to admit it to myself or to anyone else. And I think part of me felt like it was a challenge I had to win. Relationships are hard, and I don't quit things."

"Do you wish you did?"

"Quit? Yes and no. I wouldn't change anything that would make Jackson not be here, but I think of the wasted time Daisy and I spent together. This might come as a shock, but we weren't exactly happy. Why are you asking?"

"Just curious."

"Are you wondering if you and Archer aren't right for each other?"

I shake my head. "No. Well, kind of. I think we want different things in life and it concerns me. He's really focused on his career, which isn't a bad thing at all. I used to think I was, until she came along." I pat my belly. "Family's always been important, and now that I'm going to have my own, it matters more than anything."

"When will you see him next?"

"Tomorrow. He got the weekend off and is meeting me here."

"Have a talk with him about all this. One of the biggest things Daisy and I did wrong was not talk about the nitty-gritty stuff. I avoided saying half the things I should have said because I didn't want to end our marriage. But it'd been over for months before Daisy left. If you and Archer aren't compatible, it's best you figure it out now." He gives me a sympathetic smile.

I nod, feeling both relief and anxiety. "Thanks, Wes."

He puts his arm around me. "Of course, Quinn. You know I'm always here for you."

"I know." That's another reason I'd love for Emma to

grow up here. Not only is it much safer than Chicago, but she'd be surrounded by people who love and support her.

I ACCIDENTALLY LEFT MY PHONE AT HOME WHILE WE WERE trick or treating. Not that it's a big deal or anything, but I did miss two calls from Archer followed by a text that says he got called into work and will be there all night.

Frowning, I hope he got at least a few hours of sleep. I text him back and take a shower, then sit in the living room with Mom and Dad for a while before going to bed. Rufus jumps up next to me and walks in a circle three times before laying down in the middle of the bed. I roll over, putting my arm around him. He lets out a groan and starts panting.

"Fine," I say with a huff, getting out of bed to turn the fan on. I check my phone, just in case, though it's been next to me the whole time and I'd know if Archer contacted me. I think about what Wes said, about how the need to clearly communicate what I want in a relationship is so important.

I want to be with Archer. I'm in love with him, and I want to raise our daughter together. But more than anything, I want us to be happy. Missing him and feeling pretty damn disappointed we won't see each other tomorrow, I look through our vacation photos until I fall asleep.

I wake up to someone sitting on the edge of the bed. I'm still tired, a little groggy, and not ready to get up yet.

"What are you doing?" I ask, eyes not focused enough to tell if it's Owen or Logan yet. They're identical twins, but I'm able to tell them apart.

"You awake?"

My brother leans in, and I don't have to see to know it's

Owen. "You smell like a distillery," I say and push him away. Brushing my hair out of my face, I sit up, eyeing the clock. "Why are you drunk at seven in the morning?"

"Why aren't you?" Owen shoots back.

"I'm pregnant."

"Oh, right. Why'd you go and do that?"

I flop back and pull the covers over my head. "Archer was too irresistible."

Owen stretches out and lays down, pulling my pillow out from under my head. "That's what the ladies say about me."

I yank my pillow back and give him a shove, and he falls off the bed. "Did that baby give you super strength or something?" he slurs.

"Yes. Better not piss me off even more, or I'll set you on fire with my mind." Yawning, I throw the blankets back and get up to pee. When I get back, Owen is at the foot of the bed with Rufus. I grab my brush from my bag and run it through my hair. The stairs creak, and Logan makes his way into my room.

"There he is."

I raise an eyebrow. "You lost him again?"

"Not technically. I knew he was here."

"Why is he here? And you? It's so early."

"We had a bachelor party at the bar last night. With strippers and everything." He wiggles his eyebrows.

"So that's why Owen is drunk."

"Partly," Logan says, lowering his voice. "Charlie was there. With her boyfriend."

Charlotte—Charlie—Redford was Owen's only long-term girlfriend. Things seemed to go really well between them, and then Owen did something stupid, like he usually does, that made her break up with him. He claims it only bothers him because she got away, but I still think he's in love with her.

"Whose bachelor party did you host?"

Logan shrugs. "Some guy named Bill. It was a crazy night."

"Looks like it. Though you still never answered my question on why the hell are you here?"

"We were supposed to go four-wheeling with Jeff and his brother, but this loser is too drunk to operate any vehicle. I dropped him off here so Mom could spend some quality bonding time with her third-favorite child."

"You mean so Mom can clean up his puke."

"Basically. I don't want to do it later." He pokes at Owen, and, realizing he's asleep, takes his shoes off. "Sorry he woke you up. I told him to see if you were up because I brought donuts and coffee."

"Smart to bring a bribe. Is Mom even up yet?"

"She's out walking the dogs."

I fold down the blankets and cover Owen up. "I'm sleeping here again tonight. If he barfs in the bed, I'll be pissed."

"I won't barf," Owen mumbles.

"Go back to sleep," I tell him and follow Logan down the stairs. I take my donuts outside, sitting on the patio with Logan while we eat. It's a chilly fall morning, warning us that winter is right around the corner. Hell, the weather could turn midday and we could wake up to snow in the morning. That's the weather in the Midwest for you.

After Logan leaves, I shower, get dressed, and find something to eat again. I sit in the living room, turning on the TV and call Archer, getting his voicemail. He's either in surgery or sleeping.

I think.

"Are there any donuts left?" Owen asks, slowly coming down the stairs.

"I'm surprised you remember going to get donuts."

"I always remember donuts." He brings the box from the kitchen and sits on the couch next to me, taking the remote.

"I'm watching this," I tell him.

"This show is shit."

I grab the remote from his hands. "You woke me up. Now you have to watch musicals with me."

"Fine," he grumbles and bites into a donut. "What's new with you?"

"Nothing yet. Still trying to figure things out."

"Stop trying and just go with it."

I give him a skeptical look. "Is that what you do?"

"It's worked out for me so far. Overthinking never leads to anything good."

"You're right on that. Overthinking leads to second-guessing."

"Exactly," he says with his mouth full.

I put my feet up on the coffee table, yawning again. "Thanks, O."

"Of course, Q. I'm full of brotherly advice."

I roll my eyes. "Too bad it's not all good advice."

"Hey." Owen elbows me. "Better me than Weany-Deany."

I laugh. "I haven't heard you call him that in years."

"He deserves the nickname after the way he freaked out about you and Archer."

"True. He's coming around now."

Owen shakes his head. "He's fucking ridiculous. Can you get me water?"

"Really?"

"Really."

"Fine," I say and take the last chocolate donut on my way to the kitchen. I fill two glasses with water and go back to the living room, watching the rest of the movie and talking to Owen. Then he goes upstairs to crash in one of the guest rooms, and I go out to lunch with Mom and Dad.

I still haven't heard from Archer, and I'm getting worried. I call his cell again and this time it goes straight to voicemail. Half an hour goes by, and the worry gets worse

I want to tell him I don't want him to go to Boston. I need to say my piece and I know Weston is right. I need to be honest and have the best communication as I can. That's why there'll be no regrets. I'll be careful not to tell him what to do but will express my own feelings on the topic. But mostly, I need to make sure Archer is okay.

I have Sam's number, and I pull it up. Archer wanted me to have it in case I needed to get ahold of him while visiting in Indy. After Bobby threw the door open at me, Archer's been a little overprotective while I stayed with him.

Sam answers after two rings. "Hello?"

"Hey, Sam. It's Quinn."

"Oh, hey. Is everything okay?"

"I think so but wanted to check on Archer. I can't get ahold of him and I know he's been working a lot. Is he around?"

A few seconds of silence tick by. "He didn't tell you?"

"Tell me what?"

"He's in Boston."

29

I sink into the driver's seat, squeezing my eyes shut for a second before starting the car. I just got home from Boston, and I have a headache. Both from lack of sleep and from everything going on. But after talking with my mother, I knew what I had to do. You make sacrifices for your children, and in the end, they're worth it.

I have two missed calls from Quinn, and it's been killing me not to call her back. I wanted to wait until I was in the car though, so she wouldn't hear the sounds of the airport. Leaving the parking garage, I call her, and she answers after the first ring.

"Hey, babe," I say. "Sorry I missed your calls. I was in back-to-back surgeries."

"You're at work?" she asks, voice flat.

"Yeah. But I'm out now."

"Sure."

"Are you still in Eastwood?"

"Yep. That was my plan. Stay here this weekend."

"I can meet you there."

"Are you sure that's what you want to do?" she snaps.

"Yeah. Quinn..." I exhale heavily. "We need to talk, okay?"

"We do."

"I'll be there in a few hours. Are you at your parents' house?"

"Where else would I be?" she asks, voice tight.

"See you soon. I love you," I tell her, but she doesn't say it back. She just hangs up. Swallowing hard, I put my phone in the cupholder and think about everything that's happened in the last twenty-four hours. I know I made the right choice.

Will Quinn think I did too?

I hope and pray I don't run into traffic, but I make it just a few miles from the airport and come to a standstill. It's Saturday afternoon and along with regular traffic, there's an accident closing down several lanes. I tap the steering wheel, feeling more and more anxious as time ticks by.

Everything I'm doing is to benefit our family in the long run, and I still have faith it'll all work out. I think of the life I had at home before Bobby started using. Our father worked hard to provide for us, and we had a damn good life. Which makes my anger at Bobby even stronger. We had a good thing going and he threw it all away.

I don't know how I feel about him moving to Eastwood and spreading his shit in the quiet, safe town Quinn still calls home. My mother has a point about taking Bobby away from the group of friends who are nothing more than enablers, but is moving away enough?

Traffic starts moving again, and my heart speeds up knowing I'm getting closer and closer to Quinn.

Quinn's Porsche is the driveway, and the dogs start barking as soon as my Jeep bumps into view. I put it in park and rush out, going in through the garage the way Quinn always does. The dogs are in the backyard, barking at the door, and I find Quinn out there with them.

"Hey," I say, stepping onto the patio. She's on the glider, with a blanket draped around her shoulders. Her eyes are a little red, looking like she was either crying or is really tired. Given the fact that she's been here all day, I'm leaning more toward crying, which worries me.

"Hi," she says, giving me a feeble smile. "How was work?"

"Busy." I sit on the glider next to her. I put my arm around her, heart swelling in my chest. Fuck, I missed her. Quinn rests her head on my shoulder. A cold wind blows, rattling the remaining dried corn in the field. "Want to go inside? It's cold out here."

"Sure." She wipes at her eyes, holding the blanket tightly around herself and follows me. The house is quiet.

"Where is everyone?" I ask.

"They're getting a drink at Getaway. Even Jackson. Nothing alcoholic, of course. And the bar isn't even open yet."

"Did they know I was coming?"

"Yeah. They wanted to give us space."

"That was nice of them." I sit on the living room couch. Quinn takes a spot next to me, keeping the blanket wrapped around her shoulders.

"It was." She looks away. "And speaking of space...are you going to tell me you need space?"

"No, not at all."

"Then why did you go to Boston without telling me?"

Shit. "How did you know?"

"I was worried about you and called Sam. Why did you lie?"

My brows pinch together. "I wanted to do it as a surprise."

"Do what?"

"Turn down the fellowship. Since I'd already accepted, I wanted to formally rescind my spot without burning bridges."

Quinn sucks in a breath. "You turned it down?"

"Yeah."

The blanket falls off her shoulders. "Why? I thought you wanted to be a trauma surgeon."

"There's something else I want more. You."

"But I could have come with you."

"I know. You wouldn't like living there basically on your own, and it's not what I want either."

"Tell me very clearly what you do want."

"This." I sweep my hand out at the living room. "A house in the country surrounded by family. Nothing is more important to me than you and Emma. I want to raise her together."

"Are you sure?"

"Positive." I reach into my pocket and pull out the ring. "Positive enough to give this to you."

Quinn's eyes widen and her lips part. "Just give it to me? Not ask anything along with it?"

I laugh. "I had a whole speech planned out and everything. I love you, Quinn. I've been in love with you for years." I extend the ring to her and she takes it, slowly examining the workmanship.

"It's beautiful."

"The two diamonds on either side of the center stone

were your grandma's. She gave them to me at the gender reveal party."

Tears fall from Quinn's eyes.

"You can put it on, you know," I say with a smile.

Quinn sniffles and looks up, meeting my eyes. "No," she says softly and puts the ring back in my hand.

"No?" Archer echoes, face paling.

"I want to hear the speech." I close Archer's fingers around the ring. "Ask me like you had it planned."

Archer looks down at the ring. "Are you...are you going to say yes?"

"Yes!" I say, and tears fall from my eyes. "I love you so much, Archer."

"I love you too," he says, wrapping his arms around me. He pulls me onto his lap, and when we kiss, everything fades away. Breathless, I break away, cupping Archer's face with my hands.

"How tired are you?"

"Pretty damn tired."

I gently kiss him. "Do you want to get a good night's sleep and make sure this is what you want?" I ask with a smile.

"It's what I've always wanted." He shifts his weight, holding me close. "I brought the ring to Hawaii with me."

"You've had this since then?"

"Not that particular one. Your grandma's ring. I bought this one yesterday."

"That was fast," I say, taking the ring from his hand. It's gorgeous, with a large oval center stone in between the two diamonds from my grandma's ring. The entire thing is encrusted in tiny diamonds that glitter and sparkle in the light.

"The setting was already made. They just had to put in the big stones."

"Big stones," I repeat with a smile. "Ask me now. I want to wear it."

Archer raises his eyebrows, laughing. "No. I want to do this right when you're not expecting it."

"I'm literally holding the ring."

Archer takes it from me and puts it back in his pocket. "I'll ask you later."

"Did you just take back your proposal?"

"You said no."

Shaking my head, I lean in to kiss him again. "You're lucky I love you."

He hugs me tight, then looks out at the yard. "I think one of the dogs got into something."

"Really? This is why I like cats." I get up and hurry to the door. I see Rufus and Chrissy roughhousing in the grass, Boots sitting on a lounge chair, and Carlos digging something in the corner. "I don't—"

I cut off when I turn around, seeing Archer down on one knee. "You weren't expecting that, were you?"

"No, not at all." I can't help the smile that takes over my face.

"What started as a teenage crush has turned into something more," he says, looking into my eyes. "You went from the hottest girl in the world to the most amazing woman in the world. I like waking up with you, even though you sleep with a million blankets and I wake up all sweaty."

I laugh and bring my hand into my chest, feeling so much for him right now.

"And if I start every day hot and sweaty but next to you, I'll be the luckiest man in the world."

I knew this was coming yet I'm still getting emotional. Archer opens the ring box.

"Will you marry me?"

"Yes!"

Archer stands and wraps me in his arms. "Good. I was a little worried there you changed your mind."

Laughing, I bring my hands to his chest, looking into his eyes. "I would have if the speech was a letdown. I had high expectations, you know. You nailed it. Not too long with just the right amount of sap. Can I try on the ring now?"

He takes it back out of the box and slides it on my finger. It's a little big, but not so much I can't wear it. We kiss again, and the garage door opens. Wiping my eyes, I turn to see who it is.

"Did you do it already?" Dean asks.

"Yeah," Archer replies, still holding me tight in his arms. "I couldn't wait any longer."

"Wait," I start, looking from Dean to Archer and Dean again. "You knew?"

"I did," Dean tells me. Kara steps in behind him, smiling. "I was going to record the thing. We know how you like pictures and videos and stuff." Dean kicks off his shoes and comes into the living room. "So I'm guessing you said yes."

"He had to do some begging, but I finally took pity and said yes."

"I did have to bribe her with diamonds," Archer says.

"Congrats, guys!" Kara says, holding up a camera. "We missed the action, but do you still want a photo?"

"Yeah," Archer says, turning his body into mine. "What was that one pose you suggested to them?"

"Put your hand on my waist," I tell him, and hold up my left hand. This time, it's anything but awkward.

I PULL THE BLANKETS UP AROUND US AND LEAN BACK ON THE pillows, looking at my hand. We're still at my parents' house, and after going out for a celebratory dinner with my family, Archer and I went to bed.

"Do you like it?" Archer asks, hooking his arm around me. He's exhausted, with dark circles under his eyes, and needs to go to sleep.

"I love it. It's beautiful. And having my Nana's diamonds in it makes it even more special."

"It also made it possible for me to get you a bigger center stone," he jokes.

"It's massive."

"Yep. I know," Archer says, nodding. "Oh, you were talking about the ring?"

"Hah, and yes to the ring, but that other thing is massive too."

"I wanted to get you something fitting for a doctor's wife," he jokes.

"Right. I can quit working and become your trophy wife now. You'll be my sugar daddy."

"You still have more money than me," he laughs. "Give me a few years."

I nestle my head against him, and everything feels perfect. And it is, in a sense, but there's still so much up in the air. Remembering Weston's words about the need for important communication, I lift my head off his chest and look into his eyes.

"What are you going to do about work now that you turned down the fellowship?"

"I'm going to give Dr. Crawford a call and apply to Northwestern as well as every other hospital within driving distance from your apartment." He takes in a slow, deep breath and runs his hands through my hair. "You need to know that even though I'm not taking the fellowship, I'll still be busy with work, especially within the first year or two. I'll be on call a lot, and will work weekends and holidays and there's nothing I can do about that."

"I know. I'll miss you, but we'll make do. Emma and I can come visit you at work or something if that happens."

"I've thought about this a lot," he says. "Pretty much the whole way I was in the car driving from the airport. Which was a long time since traffic was terrible."

"Thinking about what a lot?"

"How there's a good chance I'll be working over Thanksgiving or Christmas next year."

"Oh, right."

"And if we were in Chicago and it was one of my on-call nights, I couldn't leave to come back here to spend the holiday with your family."

"That's okay. I'll stay in Chicago with you. You'll be my husband by then."

"I know," he says softly. "But then I think of you sitting alone in the apartment on Christmas while I'm stuck at the hospital and it upsets me."

"You're a surgeon, Arch. I knew that from the start. It comes with the territory and I'm fine with that."

"What if there was a solution?"

Not seeing where he's going with this, I sit up and give him a quizzical look. "That'd be great. What is it?"

"We move here."

"Here? As in, Eastwood here?"

"Yeah. That way you'll be close to your family so when I'm doing an overnight shift at the hospital or attending to patients on Christmas morning, you and Emma won't be alone."

I blink, heart rapidly beating in my chest. I hadn't thought of that because I know Archer won't like it at a small county hospital.

"You'll hate it at the Eastwood hospital."

"I will for like a year or two."

I raise an eyebrow. "What'll change after a year?"

"The new hospital." He smiles, entire face lighting up. "Dean told me about the plans to tear down the current hospital and build a new one, replacing the smaller hospitals in the surrounding towns. It'll serve the entire county. The outpatient offices will be in the same area, and there's a chance of partnering with one of the nearby colleges for teaching opportunities."

"How does Dean know about it?"

"Your dad's company is doing some of the construction. The plans went through not long after I turned down the job, but I'm not above going back and begging for another interview."

"Wow," I say, taking it all in. I'm overcome with emotion again from Archer being so willing to do whatever it takes for our family. "What do you want to do? Don't think about me this time."

He laughs. "You're the deciding factor in everything, babe. You and Emma. Before, I wanted to keep going with schooling until they kicked me out, but that was because I didn't have anything else. Being busy kept me distracted from how much I wanted you, because I have for years. And now that I have you...I want us to be a family. I like Eastwood. It feels like home to me now too."

"You haven't answered the question." I rake my fingers through his hair and his eyelids become heavy. "What will make you the happiest? Don't overthink it. Just answer."

"I want to get married, build a house, and raise Emma in Eastwood. I'll probably knock you up again not long after you have our first kid, so being by family is a priority." He tips his head down to mine. "My parents even want to move here. They think it'll be good for Bobby to get a fresh start away from his junkie friends."

"Oh. I hope it is. Though there are a fair share of meth labs scattered in barns in the more rural parts of the county." I turn off the bedside light and lay down, rubbing Archer's back with my right hand. My left wrist has been aching again, and I'm trying not to move it so it'll rest and get better. The brace will clash with my new ring.

I kiss Archer's lips and smile. "Then I guess we better move here too."

31

ARCHER

"Everything was perfect at the latest scan," I say, taking the ultrasound photos from Quinn. We're at her parents' house again, two weeks after getting engaged. It's Thursday afternoon and a bit early for dinner, but Quinn has to drive back to the city tonight for work in the morning. I was able to get back in for an interview at the local hospital, and after talking with the head surgeon again, I think things went as well as they can after you turn down a job because you didn't think it'd be challenging enough.

"The OB thinks she's going to be big," Quinn says, cutting into her chicken.

"You are looking like a beached whale already," Owen tells her with a wink.

"I think you look radiant," Logan counters. "Simply beautiful."

"Flattery isn't going to make you be the godfather, dumbass," Owen spits, rolling his eyes at his twin.

"We already know it's going to be me," Dean counters, twisting the cap off a hard lemonade. Owen and Logan have been giving him shit all evening for drinking those over beer. "Archer is my best friend."

"How was the interview?" Mr. Dawson asks, talking over the guys bickering.

"I think it went well," I tell him. "I'm hoping for a letter of recommendation from a doctor at Northwestern."

"I'll blackmail him into it," Quinn says with a smile. "I'll refuse to let his son shadow me at work if he doesn't write you one."

Logan raises an eyebrow. "That's not blackmail."

"It's along the same line," Mrs. Dawson muses. "But I don't think that's a good idea."

Mr. Dawson nods. "We got the plans for the offices approved today. I'll have to show you."

"I don't want to get ahead of myself," I reply, though I am curious to see the plans. Mr. Dawson's already pulling out his phone and opening the email with the sketches. I imagine my name on the sign in front of the building.

"I have a good feeling about it." Quinn rests her hand on my thigh. "And I'm always right."

"Usually right," I say with a smile.

"So, have you two thought about when you want to get married?" Kara asks, trying to sound casual. Quinn and I both know she's worried we're going to get married before Emma is born, which means having our wedding before hers and Dean's.

I had wanted to at first, but Quinn wants to wait and not be pregnant at our wedding. And with everything else we have going on, planning a wedding is the last thing we want to do right now.

"I've always wanted a June wedding," Quinn answers and Kara visibly relaxes before tensing again.

"This June?"

"Next," I tell her, looking at Quinn. "Emma will be a year old and can maybe walk down the aisle as the flower girl."

"And I'll have time to lose the baby weight," Quinn adds with a laugh.

Mrs. Dawson gets excited. "Do you have any idea what type of wedding you'd like? Outdoor weddings are beautiful in June around here."

"Mom," Quinn says slowly. She doesn't want to upstage Kara and Dean or take the attention away from their wedding any more than she already is, even though it's through no fault of her own. But that's Quinn for you, always thinking of others.

Fuck, I'm so lucky.

"We're not in a rush or anything, okay?" Quinn smiles, trying to tell her mom to chill the fuck out as nicely as she can. "Right now, we're focused on work and having a baby."

"Right." Mrs. Dawson unfolds her napkin and puts it on her lap. We say grace and then start eating. We make it maybe thirty seconds before Mrs. Dawson starts talking about future plans again.

"Assuming you do get the job here, what's the next step?"

"Look for somewhere temporary to live until Quinn can join me."

Mr. Dawson turns to Quinn. "You won't be out here by the end of the year?"

Quinn flicks her eyes to me. "We're not sure," I answer.

"Not sure?" Mrs. Dawson echoes.

"Assuming we get the green light on starting this company," Quinn explains. "It'll be a while before I can operate from a remote location. And I'll still work through a full two-week notice before leaving my current job. I'll be here before Emma, that's for sure."

We're in love, getting married, and starting our family.

But proposing didn't make all our other issues go away, and we still have shit to sort through until we'll finally be together. She's going back to Chicago and I'm going back to Indy for the time being, which fucking sucks.

But we'll get through it together.

"I was hoping," Quinn starts, putting her hand on her stomach. She does that whenever Emma moves, and I don't think she realizes it. It's become a habit and it's adorable. "When I'm here for Thanksgiving, Dad, you could show me some lots for sale." She looks at me, green eyes sparkling. "We want to build."

Mr. Dawson beams. "I can certainly do that."

"Are you coming for Thanksgiving?" Dean asks me.

"No. I work that weekend. But my residency contract is up before Christmas. It'll be the first time since med school I haven't worked on Christmas."

"We'll make sure to have the best Christmas ever then." Quinn smiles at me, then picks up her water to take a drink. She was a little disappointed to hear about Thanksgiving and was more than willing to come down to Indy and eat a to-go Thanksgiving feast in the hospital cafeteria with me. Just offering was enough for me, and it took a lot of convincing to get her to go to her parents' instead—and save me a plate or two of leftovers.

"We can break ground once the frost-laws are lifted in the spring," Mr. Dawson says. "But it'll still take several months until the house is built."

"I know," Quinn tells him. "We'll probably rent something downtown until then.

"Live here!" Mrs. Dawson exclaims.

Logan lets out a snort of laughter. "They finally move in together and live here," he says sarcastically.

"What's wrong with here?" Mrs. Dawson shakes her head. "I'll be around to help with the baby."

The dogs start barking and scuttle to the garage door. Jackson runs in ahead of Wes, lunging into my arms. I pick him up, setting him on my lap, and he picks food off my plate to eat.

"Sorry we're late," Weston says, stepping over the dogs. He came from work and is still wearing his police uniform. "I was talking to Sheriff Reynolds."

"Everything okay with him?" Mr. Dawson asks as Wes pulls up a chair.

"Yeah. He thinks I should run for Sheriff once his term is up though." Wes shakes his head like the idea is crazy.

"You should!" everyone agrees at the same time.

Wes shakes his head. "I'll think about it." He picks up his fork and knife, cutting into the chicken on his plate. "How'd the interview go today, Archer?"

"Good," I say, and set Jackson in his spot next to me. Looking around the table, I know we made the right choice. Things still aren't ideal, with Quinn having to stay in Chicago for another few months, but perfect doesn't have to be ideal.

"You're such a bitch for leaving," Marissa says, standing next to my desk. "I'm going to miss you."

"I'm here for two more weeks," I remind her. "And Eastwood is two hours away. Less if traffic moves quickly."

"Which happens so often."

"I know. But I'll be in the city at least once a month."

"You better tell me every time you're here."

"I will," I say and look up from my desk. I put in my two weeks' notice today. I'd been dreading doing it and actually put it off for a full week before talking to my boss. I'm sad to leave, and part of me will miss this place. But it's mid-January and I'm so ready to go home and be with Archer.

We have a small apartment downtown and have been finalizing plans for our house to be built this spring. Feeling like I'm becoming my mother, I've been pinning and saving posts on Pinterest like crazy. Archer made a list of things he wanted and has left the rest up to me. I'm having too much fun.

"Anxious to go see your man?" Marissa asks, sitting across from my desk.

"Yes. It's almost worse having him be so close. People do commute from Eastwood to Chicago, and it's so tempting to stay there."

"Why don't you?"

"I'll have to get up at like five a.m.," I reply with a laugh. "And it's so cold to be taking the train and driving."

"You are such a diva."

"My coat doesn't fit." I put both hands on my large belly. "I have two months left. I'm not going to be able to move once March rolls around."

"Speaking of March, is Kara still being a twat about the wedding photos?"

"Ugh, yes." I save my work and shut down the computer. "Things seemed better after we said we didn't want to even talk about wedding planning until after Emma is born, and she even allowed Dean to move their shower date so we could take December, but now she's a bridezilla again. If I get like this before my wedding, please slap me."

"I would have slapped you even if you didn't ask." She shakes her head. "My sister got like that with her wedding. Two years later he cheated on her and now they're divorced."

"I don't get it. It's so much money too." I heft myself out of my office chair and change from my Toms to snow boots. I've given up on stylish footwear for the rest of my pregnancy. "Archer suggested a destination wedding."

"Oh, those are nice!"

"He thought Hawaii since we went there, but I'm kinda leaning toward Disney World."

"Please have it there! I need an excuse to go."

I laugh. "We'll start seriously planning after Emma. Though if we do want Disney, I'll probably have to book it soon. I assume they fill up fast."

"I'm sure they do."

She stands and puts her coat on. I do the same and struggle to get the zipper to go up past my stomach. Not wanting to rip it, I give up and follow her out. She hugs me goodbye and I go home so I can feed the cats.

"Two more weeks and you'll be coming with me," I tell them, running my hand over Neville's sleek fur. I debated bringing them for the weekend but don't want to stress them out too much by traveling back and forth.

I change into leggings and an oversized sweater and lug two very full suitcases down to my car. I've been bringing stuff little by little each trip, and movers are coming at the end of next week to pack up the heavy stuff.

We've been in the transitional phase since Archer started the new job in Eastwood, slowly filling our little apartment with all my stuff. We'll be cramped for sure, but it's temporary. What doesn't fit in the apartment is going in my parents' basement until the new house is built.

I text Archer when I leave so he knows when to expect me home. It's been snowing off and on all day, making us both a little nervous about me making the drive home. Part of me hopes I get snowed in Sunday night and have to take an extra day off this weekend before driving back up to Chicago.

He's at work now and is supposed to be off tonight and all of tomorrow. Currently, the hospital is slower paced than what he's used to, which is both good and bad for him. I know he's looking forward to the next few years when the new hospital is up and running. He'll have a bigger team and probably his own residents 'to boss around' as he likes to joke.

Traffic is slow thanks to the snow and several accidents, and I have to stop to pee before I make it into Eastwood. Archer calls to check on me, saying he's getting ready to scrub into surgery to do an emergency appendectomy.

Fifteen minutes after we hang up, I pull into the parking lot of our apartment complex. It's the only one in Eastwood and has been here since the 1970s and looks very much like the original.

Our door opens to the outside instead of a hall, and there are no attendant or security measures like my swanky place in the city. Neither are really needed here in Eastwood, but bad shit tends to happen when you get complacent.

I'm dragging one of the suitcases up to the door, debating on taking this one back to the car and keeping it at my parents' house since it's full of summer clothes when I notice the footprints. They're not fresh, but they're not old enough to be Archer's either.

And they go around to the side of the house.

I let go of my suitcase and pull out my keys, quickly unlocking the door. Snow crunches under someone's feet and I open the door just in time to step in.

"Quinn?" someone calls, and I catch a glimpse of Bobby walking around.

"Oh, uh, hi."

Archer's parents bought a cute little house in downtown Eastwood, with a 'man cave' over the garage that they've converted into a house for Bobby. They haven't been here that long, and we think Bobby's been clean this whole time. Archer doesn't seem that optimistic, but he's been talking to his brother more than he has in years.

"Is Archer home?"

"No, he's at work." Bobby isn't wearing a coat and has his arms wrapped tightly around himself. "Come in and warm up."

"Thanks," he says with a nod and follows me in, stopping when he sees the suitcase. "Is this yours?"

"Yeah."

"I'll get it. You shouldn't be carrying heavy stuff, right?"

"It's not too heavy but thanks." I'm probably stronger than Bobby, but the gesture is nice. We go in and, after taking off my boots and coat, I invite Bobby into the kitchen, which lacks a table at the moment. We'll use mine, though even with the leaf taken out, it'll be a tight fit. There's no point in buying new furniture before we move though.

"Want some coffee or tea or anything?"

"Coffee'd be great. Thanks."

I turn on the coffee pot and microwave a cup of water to make myself some tea.

"I had a British friend," Bobby says, eyeing the microwave. "He'd throw a shit fit if I made him tea that way."

Leaning against the counter, I laugh. "I've heard they think microwaving water is gross. I'm too lazy to use the kettle." I get out a tea bag and a jar of honey. "Do you and Archer have plans to hang out later?"

"Nah. I was walking around and got bored. Thought we could talk."

"That's nice. I'm glad you two are getting along. I know Archer likes it too."

Bobby diverts his eyes and nods. It's strange being around him, and I feel bad that I don't trust him. But he's family and if he and Archer can have some sort of relationship, it would be great.

We take our tea and coffee into the living room, and I turn on the TV to keep the awkwardness at a minimum. I debate texting Sheila and inviting her over for dinner or something. I don't want to have dinner with Archer's family tonight, and I don't want Bobby to think I don't trust him. I'm trying too, and I understand more why Archer feels the way he does.

Bobby finishes his coffee and gets up to use the bathroom. I slowly sip my tea, not really liking it but drinking it because it's supposed to be good for pregnancy. An entire commercial break plays through on the TV, and Bobby still hasn't come back. Getting up with the pretense of heating up my tea, I look down the hall.

The bathroom door is open, and I can see Bobby's shadow moving around in our bedroom. Dammit. I close my eyes and let out a sigh. Setting my mug down, I sneak down the hall, keeping one hand on my belly. My heart starts to speed up, and I stop right outside the door, looking in at Bobby.

My first thought is that he's looking for prescription pads, which is probably why he came bursting into Archer's apartment back in Indy. Instead, he's sitting on the foot of the bed looking through an old photo album.

"Bobby?" I ask, stopping by the doorframe.

"Sorry." He closes the album and looks up, eyes glistening a bit. "I saw it on my way out. I haven't looked at these in years."

"Bring it out in the living room. I'll look at it with you."

Nodding, he stands, tucking the book under his arm. He gets a second cup of coffee and sits on the couch next to me, going through the photos of him and Archer when they were children.

"Things were simple then," Bobby sighs.

"They can be again."

"Nah, I've fucked up too many times. Arch wants nothing to do with me."

I press a smile, knowing it's true. "He wants to give you a chance," I tell him. "It's never too late."

"Is it just me or is this really awkward?" Quinn leans in, resting her plate of appetizers on her belly.

"It's awkward. I feel like we should leave."

Her aunt Belinda comes over, arms extended. Quinn's eyes widen, and she nods, putting on a fake smile. We're at Dean and Kara's wedding shower, and Quinn and Dean's relatives are more excited about Emma's upcoming birth and the house Quinn and I are building together than the wedding.

Kara has been giving Quinn the stink-eye all afternoon, and Quinn and I retreated to the back of the venue, trying to escape the limelight. Quinn hands me her plate and gets up to hug her aunt. She winces when she stands, making me even more glad she's done with her job in Chicago. Emma is due in a month and the round ligament pain has gotten worse, as well as Braxton Hicks contractions. She's been a trooper though, hardly complaining at all. I've been working a lot of nights and weekends, paying my dues as the new guy on the team, and she's been dealing with a lot of this alone.

"Uncle Greg sent me over to look at this ring. He said it's impressive," her aunt coos, taking Quinn's hand. "He wasn't kidding!"

It's over the top, I'll admit, but I'll be able to pay it off in a year...or two. She lets go of Quinn's hand and rubs her belly. I can see Quinn grit her teeth. She hates when people touch her stomach.

"And you're still in the wedding party?" her aunt goes on.

"Uh," Quinn starts, eyes darting to mine for help. Kara tried to play it off as being concerned for Quinn's well-being, but even Dean finally admitted she's being petty. Kara doesn't want the attention on Quinn, and since Quinn's bridesmaid dress doesn't fit well anymore, Kara thinks she'll stand out 'in a bad way' in pictures. As of right now, Quinn has been officially kicked out of the wedding party, and it's been a mess since she got the boot.

Mrs. Dawson is upset. Quinn's feelings are hurt even though she's trying hard not to show it. I wasn't sure if I should refuse to be a groomsman with Quinn getting kicked out. In the end, Quinn assured me she's fine with me being in it. It's Kara acting crazy, not Dean. And things were strained with Dean long enough there's no point in making it a problem again.

I know he's torn between standing by his wife-to-be or his sister. I'd be torn too, though I can't imagine Quinn turning into such a bitch over a wedding. We decided on a destination wedding, and while we didn't want to do any actual planning just yet, we did have to book our date before the venue filled up.

"Maybe. We'll be cutting it pretty close to when this little girl makes her debut."

"You haven't dropped yet," her aunt goes on, running her

hands along Quinn's waist. "My guess is you'll be a day or two past your due date."

"Hey, if I am, then at least we'll make it through the wedding."

Her aunt laughs and talks to Quinn for a bit more before leaving. Quinn sits next to me again, letting out a sigh of relief. She tries to get comfy, propping her feet up on a chair across from her and rests her head on my shoulder.

"And now I have to pee."

Chuckling, I set her plate down and get up, holding out a hand to help her to her feet. I walk with her to the bathroom and wait for her in the hall right outside. Quinn takes my hand when she's done, and I pull her in for a quick kiss.

"Did I tell you I loved you yet today?" I ask, lips brushing against hers.

"Only once."

I wiggle my eyebrows. "One time isn't enough."

She smiles and slides her hands along my waist. "I know."

"Gross, guys," Dean says, coming down the hall.

Quinn kisses me again just to mess with Dean. "You're still not used to us being together?"

"No, I think it's cool. But I'll never be used to seeing anyone shove their tongue down my sister's throat."

"That's not all he shoves his tongue down."

"I fucking hate you," Dean says with a grin, shaking his head.

"Is Kara okay?" Quinn asks, turning the conversation serious. "I'm sorry everyone keeps asking about the baby. Jackson was the last new baby and people are excited."

Dean waves his hand in the air. "She's being dramatic, but can you blame her?"

Yeah, I can. But I don't say anything. Quinn winces and leans on me.

"You okay, babe?" I slip my arm under hers for support.

"Yeah." She rubs her stomach. "I've had enough practice contractions that real labor should be a breeze."

"Let's hope," I say with a laugh. We go back to the party and hit the buffet one more time. Quinn makes it halfway through her plate when she starts to feel even more uncomfortable.

We're both happy for a reason to leave early, and I help her to her feet and held her hand on the way out. We get stopped by another Dawson relative, who's talking to Quinn's mother and Kara.

"Look at you!" she exclaims, coming in for a hug. I think she's one of Quinn's cousins, but I can't remember her name. "You look good for being eight months pregnant. I looked like a hot mess from five months out."

Quinn laughs. "I feel like a hot mess. I can't believe I have a month left to go. I'm huge."

"You're tiny. You remember how big I was after my third. I looked like a Mack truck."

Quinn shakes her head. "You looked great, and you do now."

"Thanks for lying," her cousin says. "Ohhh look at that rock! Damn, girl!" She looks at me. "You did good."

I smile. "Thanks. I knew it would take something special to get her to say yes to me."

"Isn't being pregnant before your wedding reason enough?" Kara says, trying to be funny but the insult is there.

Quinn's cousin makes a face, looking uncomfortable. "Hey, I was pregnant when I walked down the aisle. No one knew it yet, but I was."

"It's modern times," Mrs. Dawson says. "All I care about is getting another grandbaby. Married or not, I'm looking forward to holding that little girl. Though I am excited to help with wedding planning. They're getting married at The Grand Floridian in Florida!"

Kara purses her lips, looking annoyed. She turns away, finding someone else to talk to. Quinn looks even more uncomfortable, and I want to take her home, rub her feet, and hopefully lay down and take a nap along with her.

"Thanks, Mom," Quinn says quietly.

"Are you two headed out?" Mrs. Dawson asks, realizing we were walking toward the door.

"Yeah," Quinn tells her, hand on her stomach again. "I'm having bad Braxton Hicks and need to lay down with my feet up."

"Should you go to the hospital and get checked out?"

"She's not in real labor," I say, needing to be the one to convince Mrs. Dawson that Quinn's okay. She believes me over Quinn since I'm a doctor. Years of med school and residency paid off just for this. "But she should rest and drink water."

"Okay, take care you two. Call me if anything changes."

Quinn hugs her mother. "I will. Love you, Mom."

"Love you too, hun. And you too, Archer."

Big fluffy flakes of snow fall around us when we step onto the sidewalk. I hold tightly onto Quinn, making sure she doesn't slip, and get in the car. She sinks into the passenger seat, and I start up the engine, giving it a minute to warm up before leaving. We're close to home and are inside our little cramped apartment in five minutes. We change into pajamas and settle on the couch. Neville snuggles with Quinn, and Bellatrix rubs against me until I pick her up and pet her.

"Wes is thinking about dropping out again," Quinn says, reading a text from her phone. She shakes her head. "He's going to give us all whiplash with this."

"He needs to run for sheriff," I agree. "He'll be great for the job."

"I know!" Quinn agrees. "I think he's hesitant about being away from Jackson more than he already is."

"I understand that."

Quinn responds to whoever she's texting and puts her phone on the coffee table. I lean over and kiss her, then run my hands through her hair until she falls asleep.

I look in the mirror, making sure my hair is okay. It's the morning of Dean and Kara's wedding, and I'm not feeling the greatest. I'd say I'm nervous, but I don't think that's the case. I got invited back into the wedding party at the last minute, and I really do think Kara feels bad about going psychotic over the details of her wedding.

I wasn't the only one who felt her wrath, and after her sorority sister threatened to drop out, Kara changed her ways. Still, things are tense between us, and Dean was given shit by Kara for hanging out with Archer. It bothered me, pissed me off even, and then I hit week thirty-nine and stopped caring about pretty much everything except getting this baby out of me.

She's still in there, chilling with no signs of making her debut into the world. She finally dropped a week ago and hasn't progressed since then.

"You look beautiful, babe," Archer says, coming into the room. We're at the venue, and I just got dressed and ready. He takes me in his arms, not able to hold me close since my giant stomach is in the way.

"Thanks," I tell him. "You're a hottie in a suit."

"I'm looking forward to *not* being in a suit." He wiggles his eyebrows and I make a face. For as overactive as my sex drive was in early pregnancy, I haven't wanted anything else inside me for the last week or two.

"You and me both," I say. "Though I'm not in a suit. This dress is tight, and my shoes are making my back hurt."

"I have a few minutes," he tells me. "Sit and let me rub it."

"Oh my God, thank you." I go to the only chair in this little dressing room and lean on the vanity, resting my head on my arms. Archer tries to work out the knots, and a weird, tight feeling comes over my abdomen. It's not really painful, but it's definitely weird. We get a few minutes together before we have to go and do pictures. Kara and Dean aren't seeing each other before the ceremony, but we're doing bridesmaid photos now to help move things along between the ceremony and reception.

I'm feeling better after having my back rubbed, but start to feel that weird tightening again...and again...and again as time goes on. When we're done with pictures, the tightening hurts. I pull out my phone and start timing it, sitting on the floor in the back of the dressing room while the guys get their photos done.

I feel it three more times, every twenty minutes or so. Oh no. The ceremony starts in forty-five minutes. I can last that long...I think.

Half an hour and two contractions later, I'm not sure.

We're called out, and I struggle to hold my flowers and keep a straight face as I fall in line with the other bridesmaids. Going from the dressing room to the ceremony location is difficult, and I fall behind, having to stop and wait for the contraction to pass. I'm not in labor. I can't be. Not now, not on Dean and Kara's fucking wedding day.

Saying I have to use the bathroom, I hobble away and grip the windowsill, waiting for another contraction to pass.

"Are you okay, Quinn?" Logan asks, coming out of the bathroom.

Gritting my teeth, I turn to him and force a smile. "I'm fine."

"Why do you look like you're about to burst into tears?"

"Weddings make me emotional." I let out a breath as the pain leaves.

"Sure, they do." His eyes narrow ever so slightly, not believing a word I'm saying. Owen comes over, flask in hand, and says the ceremony won't start on time because of some sort of technical difficulty with the lighting.

"You okay, sis?" he asks me, unscrewing the lid of his flask. "You look a little sweaty."

"Yeah," I shoot back right away. "It's hot in here." I find a bench at the end of the hall and slumped down on it, both hands on my stomach. Owen and Logan whisper-talk, laughing about whatever it is they're talking about, and I try to relax and convince myself this is just Braxton Hicks. "Can you get me some water?" I ask my brothers, not caring who answers. Logan goes off to get me something to drink, and Owen sits next to me.

"Are you sure you're all right?" Owen asks, tipping his head.

"Yeah, I'm fi—" I cut off when another contraction hits. I bend forward, clutching my stomach. Holy mother of God! That pain is intense. It's more than just my uterus contracting. It's as if my whole body is trying to turn inside out.

"Are you in fucking labor?" Owen jumps up, dropping

his flask. It clatters to the ground, but luckily the lid is screwed back on.

"No," I say through gritted teeth. "I...I can't be. Not today."

Owen isn't convinced and doesn't know what to do. "Why are you acting like someone is stabbing you in the stomach then?"

I squeeze my eyes closed, waiting for the pain to pass. Fuck. That was more like fifteen minutes instead of twenty since the last one. "Because that's what it feels like," I finally say.

"You're in labor."

"Nope. I told you, I'm fine." I get to my feet, doing my best not to grunt in pain, and pace to the window. "See? Totally fine."

Logan comes back with water, and I drink half the water bottle, hoping it'll make these Braxton Hicks contractions stop. Because that's what they are.

I. Cannot. Be. In. Labor.

Kara finally let me back into the wedding party. She stopped caring if Dean and Archer hung out. We're moving in the right direction and popping out a baby on the altar as she stands there looking beautiful in all white will only make things worse.

I take a few minutes to let the water hit me, not really knowing if that has any science behind it or if it just makes me feel better, and then get up to use the bathroom. Owen was right about being a little sweaty, and after going pee, I fix my makeup, smooth my hair, and go back into the hall. I'm walking back to the bridesmaids when another contraction hits.

Logan grabs onto me before I fall and leads me back to the bench.

"Are you still going to say you're not in labor?" Owen asks.

"I'm not," I groan, pain increasing as I talk. I don't know how much more pain I can handle. The contraction hits its peak and then slowly fades away.

"Really?" Logan asks, getting his phone out. "Because this looks like labor to me. Have you had any of the other signs?" He pulls up a list on his phone. "Backache, nausea, vomiting, diarrhea, bloody mucus—giving birth is fucking disgusting."

"Get Archer," I pant, still shaking the pain from the last contraction. My back is killing me. I had stomach issues all night. I'm in labor.

Owen nods and hurries down the hall, returning a minute later with Archer. He kneels down in front of me, putting his hands on my stomach.

"Are you okay, babe?"

"I'm fine," I grunt out, focusing on my breathing. "I have to be fine."

"If you're in labor, you're in labor. There's nothing you can do about that."

The wedding planner steps out and calls us to line up. We're ready to go.

"They've been happening every fifteen or twenty minutes," I say. "I can make it."

"The ceremony is a little over twenty minutes long."

"Perfect." I grip Archer's hand and have him pull me to my feet. His eyes are wide, and he looks at me in disbelief.

"Quinn, you're in labor."

"Nah." I wave my hand in the air. "I'm fine. See?"

"You were up most the night in the bathroom. You felt sick this morning. Those are common labor signs, and now having regular contractions...Emma could be here in a matter of hours."

"Good thing we have a twenty-minute ceremony."

"Maybe you should sit this out," Logan says, terrified the baby is going to just fall out.

"Kara would throw a fit if I dropped out at the last minute." I hold my flowers up in front of me. "I'm fine. I just need to make it down the aisle, stand at the altar for a few minutes and then writhe in agony as Dean and Kara say their vows."

No one looks convinced.

"Quinn," Archer starts but is interrupted by the wedding planner.

"Let's do this." I force a smile and get in line with the rest of the bridesmaids. Archer and I aren't walking together. As the best man, he's up front and I'm the last bridesmaid to go out. Feeling like a ticking time bomb, I watch the clock, praying I can make it down the aisle.

By some miracle I do, and another contraction hits me as soon as we're seated. I grip my flowers so tight a few stems break. I look up, seeing Archer watching me from the other side of the chapel. He's strained and looks about ready to jump and come to me.

I give him a feeble thumbs up, and try to relax the best I can once the pain goes away. We're halfway through the ceremony. My abdomen tightens, but it's not as bad as before. Maybe the contractions are fading? Taking slow, steady breaths, I get through the rest of the ceremony with no issues. And then I move onto my feet with the rest of the bridesmaids to walk down the aisle and feel the pain start to come on. I slow, one hand on my stomach, and internalize the pain the best I can. Feeling like I'm going to puke, I'm stuck, rooted in the spot and paralyzed by pain.

All eyes are on Kara, and I'm pretty sure only a few notice me as I hobble down the aisle trying to catch up with the rest of the party. As soon as we're outside, Archer finds me, taking me in his arms.

"You're in labor, Quinn."

"Yeah," I agree, breath leaving me. I want out of these heels and out of this fucking dress. "I am."

"You got here just in time," the nurse says as she inserts an IV into my arm. "There's a window for an epidural and you've almost missed it."

I look up at Archer, silently yelling. The anesthesiologist has been paged but hasn't come in yet, and if I miss my chance for pain meds, I'm going to be pissed. We stayed through pictures at the wedding, made it to the cocktail hour where I was able to force down some appetizers. Then the contractions started happening every five minutes.

No one wanted me to stick around. Archer drove me here while my parents stayed for the reception, and my mom has texted for updates constantly. Wedding day or not, this is what we wanted: just Archer in the delivery room with me.

Once the nurse is done, Archer brings a chair to the bedside, taking my hand. He helps me through another contraction. Each one seems to hurt worse than the last and I'm not entirely sure my body can handle this.

After what seems like an hour later, I get my epidural and can relax. Archer makes me comfortable and sits on the couch near my hospital bed. I spend the next few hours dozing on and off. I'm half asleep when my mom calls, and

Archer answers and gives her an update. I'm eight centimeters dilated and will be giving birth soon.

His words send a jolt through me and I wake up.

I'm going to have a baby soon. Emma will finally be here.

"Quinn?" Archer hangs up and rushes over. "What's wrong? Are you feeling pain?"

I shake my head, trying to move my legs. Archer sees and moves to the foot of the bed, moving my feet and fixing the blankets for me. "She's almost here and I'm scared and excited."

"Me too," he says, brushing my hair back. His eyes go to the computer next to me, watching the lines move up and down. "That was a big contraction. I think she'll be here really soon."

I smile, putting my hand on my stomach for the last time. "Ready, baby?" I ask. Yawning, my eyes flutter shut, and I lay back, resting until the nurse comes back in.

"You're crowning," she tells us and Archer smiles. He's right there, holding my hand. The nurse leaves to get the doctor, and I know this is it, after half a day of labor, our baby girl will be here.

Several minutes later, my OB and two other nurses come in. Archer holds my hand as I push as hard as I can, over and over until I feel like I physically can't anymore because my body is about to give up. Sweat rolls down my back and Archer holds my hand tighter.

"You can do this, babe," he says, stopping to run a cool washcloth over my face.

Nodding, I inhale and push again. I give it all I've got, pushing until my head hurts. And then I hear it: a tiny little cry that brings tears to my eyes—and Archer's.

The doctor quickly checks her over and places her on my chest, covering her with a blanket.

"Oh my God," I sob, looking down at the crying bundle on my chest.

Archer leans over, smoothing back my hair. His eyes are full of so much love. We gush over Emma, letting the cord pulse before Archer cuts it, and then it's back to the baby again.

"She's perfect," Archer whispers, smiling down at his daughter. He tucks the blanket around her and kisses the top of her head. I have to remind him to take a picture, and we have the nurse take some of the three of us before she takes Emma to get her height and weight.

"Archer," I say suddenly and his eyes widen, thinking something is wrong. "It's after midnight."

The biggest smile comes over his face and he bends to give me a kiss. "You'll never be able to top this birthday present."

When the nurse sets Emma back down on my chest and she nuzzles against me, I start crying. Happy tears only, of course, because right here and right now, I have everything I want.

35

QUINN

"I really think you should do it," I tell Wes, pulling down my shirt so Emma can nurse. "This town needs you."

Wes gives me a look. "You can only pull that Batman crap on Dean. This town is safe."

"And it needs to stay safe. Being sheriff is a great way to make sure it stays that way."

He considers it but shakes his head. "It's more than just agreeing to run. I need campaign money and someone to watch Jackson during the election and then again when I start working as sheriff. And that's assuming I even win."

"I can watch him," I offer.

"I appreciate the offer, sis, but you have a one-month-old and are building a new house and working. You're busy."

Transitioning into parenthood was an adjustment. It's still an adjustment. Archer took a few days off before going back to work, and I still haven't fallen into a routine with Emma. But we're happy and we're together, and that's all that matters.

"Jackson's no trouble at all."

"He'll go to school two days a week starting this fall."

"Oh, right. That's okay. Emma loves car rides!"

"I can't make you do that. Jackson is good for you now because he doesn't stay with you often. I promise you he's a little shit and will get jealous of the baby. You two have a good relationship now. Let's keep it that way."

Frowning, I know his words are true. "What about Mom? She loves watching him."

"The new hospital project has her really busy."

"What about a nanny?" I suggest softly. The last time I brought it up, Wes seemed a little offended.

"I've thought about it, but anyone who's good is either still in high school and can't take Jackson to school or is a lot more than we can afford."

"Let me do this for you," I offer. "We can call it your Christmas present if it makes you feel any better."

"That's a big thing to offer." West sits back on the couch. He's on duty and stopped by to say hi and see his niece. "I can't accept."

"You can. Come on, Wes, it's not like Archer and I don't have the money. We'd love to do this for you—if that's what you want. But know we both think you'd make a great sheriff in this county and it's always good to have an in with someone high up in the law."

Weston laughs and lets out a breath. "I don't know."

"Don't think, just answer, okay?"

"Okay."

"Do you want to run for sheriff?"

"Yes."

"Is the only reason you're not running because you're worried about Jackson?"

"Yes."

"See," I say, readjusting Emma. No one prepared me for the extreme pain of breastfeeding. "Let us do this for you."

He runs a hand through his dark hair and looks up at me, smiling. "Fine."

"Yay! This will be great! I know lots of people in Chicago who can recommend a good nanny."

"Still...a nanny? Sounds too fancy for me."

"Call her a babysitter then if it makes you feel any better."

He chuckles. "It kind of does. Let me talk to Nancy about running for real this time and I'll get back to you. Then if—and only if—there's no way I can campaign and not risk being late for the preschool pickup line, I'll let you know about the nanny."

I beam. "You won't regret it. It'll be a huge help to you! What could possibly go wrong?"

SIDE HUSTLE, a single-dad/nanny romance featuring Weston Dawson is coming Fall 2018.

ABOUT THE AUTHOR

Emily Goodwin is the New York Times and USA Today Bestselling author of over a dozen of romantic titles. Emily writes the kind of books she likes to read, and is a sucker for a swoon-worthy bad boy and happily ever afters.

She lives in the midwest with her husband and two daughters. When she's not writing, you can find her riding her horses, hiking, reading, or drinking wine with friends.

Emily is represented by Julie Gwinn of the Seymour Agency.

Stalk me:
www.emilygoodwinbooks.com
emily@emilygoodwinbooks.com

ALSO BY EMILY GOODWIN

First Comes Love

Then Come Marriage

Outside the Lines

Never Say Never

One Call Away

Free Fall

Stay

All I Need

Hot Mess (Luke & Lexi Book 1)

Twice Burned (Luke & Lexi Book 2)

Bad Things (Cole & Ana Book 1)

Battle Scars (Cole & Ana Book 2)

Cheat Codes (The Dawson Family Series Book 1)

Made in the USA
Monee, IL
29 March 2021

64196866R00184